ANNA NEWTON DESTROYS THE WORLD

Story and Art
by
SAPPHIRA OLSON

Anna Newton Destroys The World

Text & artwork copyright © 2022 Sapphira Olson
Published by BLAM! Productions

All rights reserved. No part of this publication may be reproduced, distributed, or transmitted in any form or by any means, including photocopying, recording, or other electronic or mechanical methods, without the prior written permission of the publisher, except in the case of brief quotations embodied in critical reviews and certain other non-commercial uses permitted by copyright law. For permission requests, contact the publisher, addressed "Attention: Permissions Coordinator", at the website below.

ISBN: 979-8-4430-1424-1

Condition of Sale
This book is sold subject to the condition that it shall not, by way of trade or otherwise, be lent, re-sold, hired out or otherwise circulated in any form or binding or cover other than that in which it is published and without similar condition including this condition being imposed on the subsequent purchaser.

This book is copyrighted under the Berne Convention

British Library Cataloguing in Publication Data.
A catalogue record for this book is available from the British Library.

Any references to historical events, real people, or real places are used fictitiously. Names, characters, and places are products of the author's imagination.

Available as a hardback, paperback and on Kindle.
First printing edition 2022.

www.sapphiraolson.com

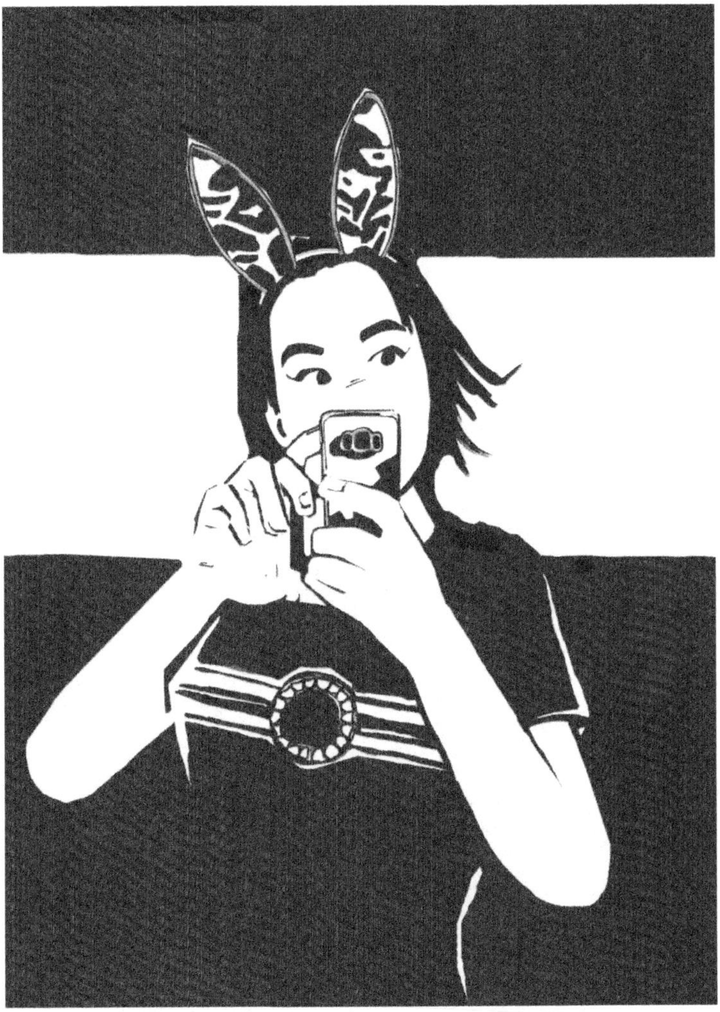

ALSO BY SAPPHIRA OLSON

The Girl In The Garden
Blam! Productions, 2020

Stanley Park
Blam! Productions, 2019

Parables
Elsewhen Press, 2019

TO JESS,

always yours forever, our hearts spin our world

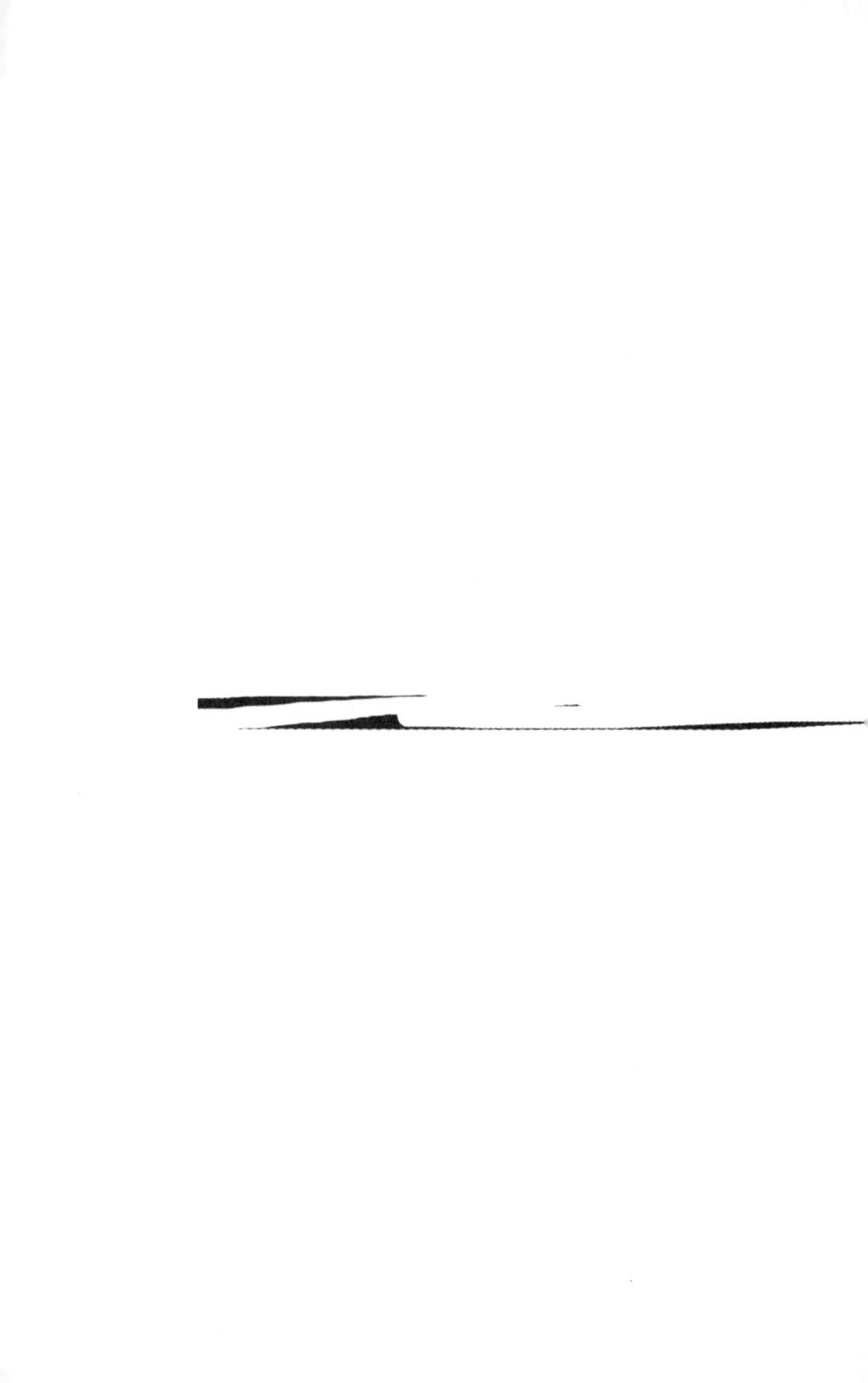

In the beginning God created the heavens and the earth. Now the earth was formless and empty, darkness was over the surface of the deep, and the Spirit of God was hovering over the waters. And God said, "Let there be misery and famine and discord."

And there was.

PROLOGUE

At the beginning is the end.

A coldness reaching deep into Cillian.

Next to him his sister, Róisín, who will never see her boyfriend again.

They are close now at the end as they have always been. A brother and sister who found refuge in each other from the confusion of events outside their control.

They were innocents in all of this.

When they were young, they played together under the great oak tree in the field below the stream. Róisín would hide in the long grass of the meadow as Cillian counted to a 100. He always found her, he would find her anywhere. They were inseparable, occasionally insufferable like all young spirits are, but always, always full of love for each other and full of love for life.

Their mother, Aisling, is full of sadness as she senses their passing.

You imagine that some things cannot be broken and when they are you are left in dumb founded shock.

I will shortly meet her in this story that you have given life.

When I lift my eyes I can see her. I breathe in and feel my body start to relax. A tingling sensation ripples through me as if I am made of water.

This world was beautiful and was the hope of humanity. But humanity thought that unless a flower is plucked from the soil it has no worth. People believe such things I truly thought they never would. A spell cast over them of confusion that, try as I might, I cannot break.

The choices you make are the ones with the least resistance to moving through your life. You are recursive by nature driven by fear both individually and collectively. To step away from that is to choose to move into the unknown and to face your fears. It is getting into a dinghy and heading for the storm and leaving the safety of the ship. This is the choice before me. I cannot know if destroying this world will bring new life or a never ending darkness.

I do know this though.

I must try to find the courage to do so.

BOOK 1
ESCAPE FROM TARTARUS

within you are the possibilities of
a thousand lifetimes

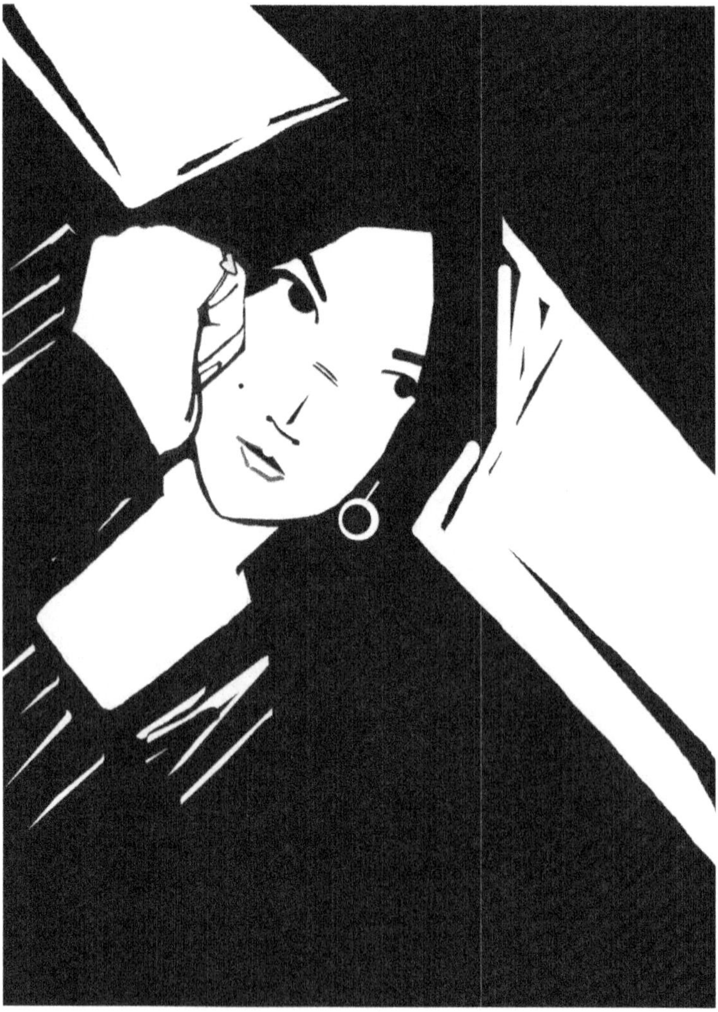

CHAPTER 1

On the tenth year of her incarceration, Anna Newton knew that this was the morning in which she would break free. Her world for the last ten years had been a silent tomb in Tartarus broken only by the sound of her heartbeat and the constant chip, chip, chip of her finger nails. This was the day that sound would enter her cocoon of silence in all its glory. The day she would fly, or run, or swim to open waters.

Anna closed her eyes and wondered what the first sounds would be. Let there be birds to fly me over the earth, she thought, or a butterflies or anything that can take me far away from this hateful place. And her mind filled with wondrous things: bird song, the bubbling of a stream, the sound of sea ice breaking and cracking.

Anna looked down to where her nails had once been, now stripped away from clawing through the sound insulation. She could feel her body sensing the muffled sounds rippling across her skin. It drew her onwards and she cared not that her fingers bled and the searing pain that pushed back against the vibrations.

And then it was done.

She drew back.

You have reached this point within moments.

It took Anna nearly 4000 days.

You do not even know, Anna.

But you will.

She is the woman who will destroy the world.

CHAPTER 2

The low frequency sound of a whale's call entered Anna's cell and she closed her eyes. After a moment she opened them again, but where before they had been forward facing, now they were positioned on opposite sides of her head. She glanced around, struggling to see anything now about her surroundings. It all just looked grey and dim.

The problem with being a whale, she thought, was she was now just a whale trapped in a room with no water. It achieved nothing. She would have to focus. After the silence, the amount of sounds all overlain over each other, fighting for her attention like school children, was overwhelming.

And as she sat there trying to settle her heartbeat, her form shifted again and again. One moment she was a whale, another a penguin, another a wandering albatross. But gradually, over time, she composed herself and regained focus.

The vibrations were small, but she could just sense a coniferous tree in the ice: the memory of the sound of its roots shifting under soil from millions of years ago. Pushing all the other sounds aside she let the great fossil tree talk to her and then with a snapping sound she was at one with it.

The impact on her cell was instant. Her great limbs pushed through the walls and ceiling shattering the room as if it were an egg.

She was free.

CHAPTER 3

The guards braced themselves and fired into Anna's thick bark. Their training overriding the fantastical and their response predictably useless. Anna picked one up without really thinking and bashed them against the wall of the corridor. She felt sad for them, they were barely alive. Humans living but for a moment, their minds racing so fast they didn't even know who they were.

Anna knew who she was.

Her mind had slowed down in her form of the great tree and her higher consciousness was stripped away so she was at one with herself and reacted instinctively. Humans considered themselves intelligent because of how fast they could process situations and problems. But Anna knew that most of the time the brain was just arguing with itself over and over before conceding even the simplest decision. It was all a lot of noise: a distraction to avoid what was really going on, a slight of hand to numb the pain. Strip that away and you could hear the hum of the planet and see what was really going on.

Anna's mind was at peace. It flowed like a river finding the easiest way to travel. She could feel the bullets embedding into her bark. It was like when her sister used to flick an elastic band against her skin. Annoying, but hardly deadly.

She killed each guard quickly, trying not to make them suffer any more than necessary and then prodded the last one repeatedly in the chest. The guard, true to her training, said nothing, froze and stopped firing.

Anna extended a root out of the ground and wrapped it around their neck. There was a look of horror on their face then, when the guard could bear it no more, they let out an audible gasp.

And that was it.

Anna was the guard.

CHAPTER 4

Anna shook her head as she adjusted to her new form. Her sense of time shifted back to that of a human and she stood looking at the huge hole in the Tartarus facility. Turning away from the open cavern before her, she made her way down the corridor and walked into the heart of her prison.

She had had enough.

She had intended to just get as far away as possible.

Now she had a different plan.

This was a plan she had decided when she was the tree and could process things properly. As she had killed the guards one by one she had mused over her situation and come to a decision, a decision that she somehow felt she had made many times before.

She would overcome God.

It had to end: the abuse and trauma, the patriarchal reign of a self-obsessed tyrant.

When she had asked him to leave her alone he, in a fit of rage, had locked her away saying she had gone mad. He had intended for her to remain in that cell for all eternity – for, he had said without a flicker of emotion, for her and everyone else's safety and well-being. As if she was one of Charlotte Brontë's characters to be hidden away in a room on the third floor of Thornfield Hall.

Well for everyone else's safety and well-being she was going to stop this madness.

CHAPTER 5

God was, of course, aware that Anna had escaped and was making her way to him. Probably to create some huge scene or extract some dreadful revenge, he thought. He didn't care. She was just a woman and he had far more important things to do and believed himself to be in no danger and really this just seemed to go on and on.

Honestly, he thought, after all I have done. After all I have provided for that damn woman, this is how she repays me?

"You will yield," he said out loud and tapped his fingers on the table and nodded to himself in agreement.

"You will come back to me, Anna, my love. Or I will destroy you and everything that you hold dear to you. When I have finished with you, my darling, you will be utterly alone."

"Is that strictly fair?" said a creature that was floating before him with its arms crossed.

"Hmm," said God and with a flick of his wrist banished the creature forever.

CHAPTER 6

Anna met no more resistance as she made her way closer to God. When the two small lights flashing on her suit aligned she sat on the floor and crossing her legs, closed her eyes and concentrated.

And he appeared before her. And darkness was over the surface of his face and his heart was without form. Light flowed around him in a soft halo to provide the illusion of love, peace and happiness.

"Hello, Anna," said God.

Anna said nothing.

"You look so beautiful this morning," said God. "My love for you, my affection and the high esteem I hold you in, all have enabled you to flourish."

"You think," said Anna slowly, "that I live in a delusion and that I am mentally ill."

"I think that," he replied, "and therefore it is so."

"And you do not see the torture you place me under? The constant abuse?"

"I do not," he said, "for it is not so."

Anna listened for the sound of a heart beating within his chest and found none.

"My bed is still your bed," he said. "If you repent you can lie there again. Sleep on the floor if that makes you more comfortable. But know this, Anna my love, you will always love me and you will never, ever leave me. You do understand that don't you?"

Anna sought out the sound of water and found it in the form of a dripping tap.

And she became water and filled the room. And the waters teemed with flame angel fish.

God turned his head and watched them.

Anna could feel the sounds from everywhere. They were louder, faster, and stronger within her liquid form.

And God said, "I still love you, you know that don't you? But this was your choice. You have brought this upon yourself."

Anna flowed down into his mouth and into his body and the room emptied of water.

The fish dropped to the floor and flipped around gasping.

"All that is," said God, as he raised his hand to fashion a large fish tank from out of the air. "All that has been. All that will be, is your doing, Anna."

God turned his hand, as if opening an imaginary tap and the tank filled with water. Setting the tank on the table, he imagined the fish within it. And it was so. And God imagined plants within the tank, and a small treasure chest with bubbles. And it was so and he thought it very good.

"If you kill me," he said, "I will just resurrect myself."

The sound of singing emanated from within God. It was pleasing as if he was being soothed and his brain waves slowed. He sighed deeply and felt a deep peace. And in the song he sensed her as she had been before with him, when she had not come to bring war, but to share his bed and bring peace and healing. And for the first time for a very long time, his heart began to beat and within that heart Ann placed all her hatred for him.

God began to splutter and cupping his hand below his face, he opened his mouth. A robin appeared from out of his throat. Opening its wings, it flew back down the corridor towards the gaping hole she had made when she was the tree.

Reaching it Anna flew out and up into the vast blue cavern.

It was over.

CHAPTER 7

God watched Anna leave him yet again. She still loves me, he thought. All her theatrics with the singing, the fish and the robin was proof of that.

It was all so ridiculous. And he decided that all the sorrows of the world would be with her so that she would be unable to bear their separation. She would be stricken, afflicted and forgotten.

And it was so.

Why does she hate me so much? he thought. Could it be that I am wrong and she doesn't love me anymore? How can she know me and not love me? For I am love.

Is she a fool?

But that was not so.

For Anna was no fool and the hatred she had placed within his heart had become a doubt in his mind.

And that will not do.

It will not do at all because there can be no doubt in God.

So he dropped dead.

Just like that.

Each of us thinks ourselves as God: that we are immortal and fashion our own lives.

But we do not, even if we are actually a god.

Because those that endure write the history.

And I am Anna.

This is my story,

and I will tell it to you.

CHAPTER 8

Anna listened to the ice above Tartarus popping and she became the ice. At the surface several miles above the facility she took on her own form and started walking towards the base which straddled the landscape before her.

And the land was beautiful in so many ways. The vast expanse of virgin snow, the sky full of songs. High above the moon rested, its reflected light making the small moon on Anna's neck glow.

He couldn't reach her here.

For he was dead.

She would never again have to hide away. Her door did not have to be locked at night. Her mind did not have to battle against the constant control he had sought to wield over her life. For it was right that this should be her story.

The storm had passed. But it had left her exhausted and worn out, like a small boat that had been tossed this way and that.

And then there was the problem of humanity.

There were so many tears.

So much had been broken. So much had been lost in a patriarchal dystopian nightmare whilst she had been incarcerated. A rule of might and power without compassion or empathy.

But I can bring a new hope, she thought. She saw in her mind's eye a woman serving coffee in a café in a small town in England. And she called her Aisling. She saw that Aisling needed a companion and called him Liam. And she considered the stories that gave everything life and called the story Dawn and placed within her all that was good and true. She gave

Dawn life in an airport lounge and kept that knowledge from herself so that love would have a chance to blossom.

CHAPTER UNKNOWN

Every morning when you wake up your mind tries to reconfigure your conscious mind. It has to find you in the darkness and persuade you to come out.

You never do.

Instead you have the illusion of you, the best your brain can do with what it has to work with, when in reality the real you is hiding away, scared out of your mind.

You think that you are awake.

But you are not.

You are a small child in the darkness, watching your life waste away in a dream. There are moments when you find the strength to live, to rise to the surface, but the illusion of you is too strong now and keeps you pushed down in eternal torment.

The world is full of fear and madness.

Those that you love are not people at all.

You are all just scared.

But by all means have a coffee and begin your day and pretend that this existence has meaning and gives you life.

CHAPTER 9

Aisling looked at the man before her and began to apologise.

"I asked for a latte not a flat white," said the man.

"I'm sorry," said Aisling, "it's my first day, I'm sure I can get it sorted out for you."

"Don't bother," signed the man, "you have a huge queue, just get it right next time."

"How are you getting on, Aisling?" said a young man stood behind her making the cold drinks.

"I think my head is going to explode," said Aisling and within her she knew that she was moments away from just running out never to return.

"Sink or swim, eh," laughed the next customer who had overheard everything.

Later Aisling sat outside with her new colleagues as they smoked.

"Don't worry, Aisling," said Julie. "You were great, you'll be fine."

"Oh yes," said Stephanie. "I cried for days, but my parents said I would get used to it and they were right."

"I see," said Aisling completely unconvinced.

That night Aisling didn't sleep. At two AM, after throwing up in the toilet, she sat on the cold tiled floor and just cried and cried and cried. She had wanted this job so much and against all odds she had got it. That made it all worse and in the morning the bed was covered in sweat.

The next day was worse. She got everything wrong.

She cleaned the toilet floor with the wrong mop: the one kept only for the customer seating area.

She broke several glasses, stood dumbfounded in front of the till for ages as she took each order and at one point became so overwhelmed and confused that she forgot what her own name was. That was just after this moment…

"Can I have a latte with soya milk."

"To drink in or out?" asked Aisling.

"In."

Aisling looked at the till and couldn't see anywhere to put soya for the milk. As the panic started rising the customer carried on, "And a large cappuccino, a Cortado, an expresso with an extra shot, a piece of chocolate twist, a diet coke, this packet of crisps, another large cappuccino with skimmed milk and a some brown toast and, Ben, what do you want? Right. A ham and cheese toastie and a Belgian Chocolate Frostino."

None of this information entered Aisling's mind and turning to Stephanie, who was stationed at the industrial looking coffee machine, she said, "one latte with soya milk."

"Was that to drink in, or to take out, Aisling?" asked Stephanie.

Aisling opened her mouth and then closed it again.

The steam wand hissed and spat. The sound of the blender whizzing together ice and sugar behind Aisling made it hard to hear. The fridge hummed, the customers muttered, the overhead camera recorded everything for her boss to see.

"I can't remember," said Aisling eventually.

"Don't worry," said Stephanie and looking at the order on the till, said, "Drink in."

Stephanie turned to Julie, "Isn't she doing well!"

"Ooo yes," said Julie. "You are doing so well, Aisling. Jeremy has actually employed someone decent for a change. You are far better than Alice and she has been here for six months. The other day a customer asked her if she was new!"

And Aisling knew that they were genuinely trying to be nice.

And she felt bad, because she had decided that this was to be her last day and she was going to quit.

"Excuse me," said the next customer.

Aisling turned to look at a tall woman with long flowing red hair. A small tattoo of the crescent moon was on her neck and another of a buttercup was on her ankle.

"Hello," said Aisling, "would you like to drink in or take out?"

"Oh take out," replied Anna Newton.

"What would you like?" said Aisling.

"For you to follow me," said Anna and began walking away.

Aisling raised an eyebrow and looked at the queue of people stretching out over the coffee shop floor and out into the carpark.

At the door Anna turned into a rabbit and hopped out of the store.

"Excuse me," said Aisling looking up at the camera recording her, "I think I have gone completely mad."

And with that she undid her apron and walked out.

CHAPTER 10

Aisling had wandered about town for hours in a stupor looking for the talking rabbit. But it was nowhere to be found.

The next morning, there was a knock on her front door. When she opened it with her dressing gown pulled tightly around her, she saw standing there the woman from the coffee shop. The one she thought she had imagined turning into a rabbit.

Anna smiled, "Hello, Aisling."

Aisling said nothing.

"You have a lovely house," said Anna.

Aisling blinked. Anna seemed to have disappeared and reappeared behind her.

"Do you have any tea?" asked Anna.

Aisling thought for a moment about just how much her grip on reality was slipping away and closed the front door.

Anna walked into the lounge and looked at the Bird of Paradise plant beside the sofa, the record player and the framed picture of Aisling's degree certificate in Physics. Picking up a photo from the mantelpiece she asked, "Are these your children?"

"Just who are you?" said Aisling.

"I'm Anna."

"That's all you going to give me is it?"

"I'm a bit like God," said Anna, "but without all that messy testosterone."

"You wanted a coffee?" said Aisling retreating into the familiar to try and give her mind time to decide what on earth was going on.

"Tea please, milk, no sugar."

Aisling walked into the kitchen, completely confused.

"Have they flown the nest?" asked Anna looking at the immaculate state of the lounge.

"Yes," replied Aisling as she flicked on the kettle. "So, sugar?"

"No thank you."

Anna picked up the photo of Aisling's kids, undid the back, slipped something behind the photo and returned it to the mantelpiece, "You are okay with me being a god?" she asked as she listened to the noise of Anna adding sugar to her drink. "You don't hate me, or despise me or wonder why I didn't grant your wish to find supersymmetric particles?"

"Hell, no," said Aisling appearing from out of the kitchen with a mug of hot steaming coffee and a packet of digestives. "I don't believe in fairy tales, but in my current state of mind I would pretty much accept that you were a talking packet of biscuits at the moment and dunk you in my coffee. So fine, you think you're some kind of god. I'm Marie Antoinette."

Anna smelt her coffee and smiled, "A terrible end for Louis XVI."

Anna looked at a painting on the wall of a woman floating in water. Her red hair floated around her shoulders, a small tattoo of the moon was on her neck, "Did you do that?"

"Yes, a long time ago. I painted it from a dream I had."

"Everything is a long time ago if you don't live very long," said Anna.

Aisling raised an eyebrow.

Anna got to her feet, she set her mug down and started to make her way to the front door.

"You going already?" asked Aisling.

"My shift starts in half an hour at the café," said Anna. "Jeremy doesn't like it if I'm late."

CHAPTER 11

Anna worked hard at the coffee shop. She was really good at it, being a god and all. She had taken the form of Aisling and the customers loved her, the staff loved her, even Jeremy thought she was the best barista he had ever employed. Although he did find it strange that she had had such a wobbly start at the beginning of the month and had fled the store on the second day. When she had returned minutes later, saying she was sorry, he had decided to give her a second chance and he was very glad he had.

Today Anna and Aisling were having a special celebration drink in the café. Having reached all her training targets in one afternoon Anna had been rewarded with free drinks and cakes with a friend of her choice, and of course Anna had chosen Aisling who everyone assumed was her twin sister.

Aisling sipped her latte and took a bite out of her blueberry muffin.

"Isn't this nice," said Anna. "Together again, just like old times."

"This is the first time we have ever done this," said Aisling.

A young man in the corner of the café looked at them both, carried on talking to his friend then looked at Aisling again. Above them the opal glass pendants bathed the two women in a soft glow.

"So," said Aisling wiping a crumb from her lip, "the reason I couldn't find you that day is because as soon as you had hopped out of the café-" Aisling paused, then continued, "Sorry, I still can't believe that happened."

"Would you like me to do it again?"

"No please, don't."

"That young man keeps looking at you," said Anna.

"Does he? Good for him. So as soon as you hopped out of the café you waited for me to leave then turned yourself into me, walked back in and carried on with my shift?"

"Yes," said Anna.

"You're weird, you know that?" said Aisling. "And by the way, my eyebrows are not that well shaped and my cheek bones are not that pronounced."

"You are beautiful," said Anna. "You should start to believe that."

Jeremy appeared over their shoulders, "How are you and your sister getting on?"

Anna smiled and winked at Aisling.

"Aisling is my number one rising star," said Jeremy. "Before long I'm sure she will be running the company. A year's training in one afternoon. I have never known anything like it!"

Aisling looked at her old boss unsure as to how to respond.

"Thank you," said Anna. "I have an excellent boss, which helps."

"Aw, thank you," said Jeremey and checked his watch. "Two minutes left, then back to work."

Aisling shook her head. Anna nodded.

"And cover up those tattoos with some plasters," said Jeremy looking at the moon on the back of Anna's neck and the buttercup on her ankle.

"Whoops," said Anna after he had gone. "Sometimes they show through even in my different forms." Anna leaned forward, "You can have this job if you want. I have been keeping it warm for you. I will help you with remembering the orders."

"Why are you bothering about me?" said Aisling.

"You have lived your life in constant misery because you believe you are not a nice person. Believe instead that you are amazing, which you are."

"You don't know what I've done," said Aisling.

"I do," said Anna. "All around you people are living according to the gospel of conformity which they take as good news. A system of reward for being part of society where they work hard, marry, have kids and own a small semi-detached property in Ipswich."

Aisling sipped her coffee and glanced across at the young man who had been looking at her.

"People give everything to a system," continued Anna, "that gives nothing in return and leaves them dried out and empty, like husks laid out in the sun. For most it is too late, they will never want to wake from the nightmare and will defend it to the death. Better to find the few who were never really that jacked in in the first place. People like you, Aisling."

"Sorry," said Aisling, "me?"

"Yes," said Anna. "You and that young man over there."

CHAPTER 12

And so it was that Aisling took her old job back and found herself back where it seems, for now anyway, she was supposed to be. Aisling tied an apron around herself, pinned on her name badge, removed her ear rings and entered the battle field again.

You can do this, she said to herself. Please let the first customer just order a simple coffee. Is that too much to ask? Just a simple coffee without all the nonsense. I will fall in love with that person!

The first customer was the one that had sent her into a panic on her second day.

"Can I have a latte with soya milk," said the customer, "and a large cappuccino, a Cortado, an expresso with an extra shot, a piece of chocolate twist, a diet coke, this packet of crisps, another large cappuccino with skimmed milk and a some brown toast."

Shit, shit, shit, thought Aisling.

Shh, said Anna within her mind and repeated the order slowly to her.

Jeremy smiled as he watched Aisling enter it all into the till without a problem.

"Thank you," said Aisling under her breath to Anna.

And that was it. Aisling was a super star barista. All it had taken was an encounter with a god.

Simple really.

"Excuse me."

The customer with the ridiculously large order was still standing there before her.

"Yes?" said Aisling. "You would like more?"

"Are you free this evening?" said the man.

"No," said Aisling, but glanced at him again. He is kind of cute, she thought.

It's the guy that was looking at you when we were having our celebration coffee, said Anna within her mind.

Yes, I know, thought Aisling then added out loud. "I'm not an idiot."

The man looked at her and appeared confused, "I never said you were."

CHAPTER 13

Anna sat on the bed in her hotel room hundreds of miles from Aisling's house. Summer had come and she wore denim shorts and a black t-shirt. The film *Me Before You* had just finished and it had made Anna think of all the children she had lost to God.

Outside, Aisling's daughter Róisín had placed some traffic cones in the middle of the road then climbed the scaffolding on the town hall and was standing on the edge looking like she was going to jump. A car pulled up, stopped and put its hazard lights on. An old man got out, looked up at Róisín, then moved one of the cones to the side of the road and returned to his car. A policeman appeared and pleaded for Róisín to come down.

Anna knew all of this because she could hear Róisín, the car and the old man and policeman as the song *Not Today* by Imagine Dragons played over the credits of the film. Anna sighed, got to her feet and walked over to the window. Outside Róisín was now slowly making her way back down the scaffolding. A man walked out of a side gate with a ladder and set it up against the stone wall. Anna watched as Róisín climbed down the ladder, jumped onto the pavement, side stepped the policeman and ran down the road.

Anna opened the window and felt the cold evening air against her skin. The policeman walked off. Rain started falling giving everything a sheen in the dying sun.

Anna closed her eyes and listened to the hum of the world.

Róisín reappeared, placed the cone back in the middle of the road and lay down on the tarmac before it.

The first car swerved around her and the cone.

The second one stopped. A man wound down the car window and started shouting. After a while he just shrugged and drove off.

The third car stopped, but only just and the cone flipped up into the air.

"Enough," said Anna.

CHAPTER 14

Aisling sat on the wall beside the park. Beside her was the man who had asked her out at the café. His face had high cheek bones, his eyes were deep as pools and when he laughed there was a joy in him that was infectious. In his hand he held a coffee cup. Aisling had a bottle of water.

"I have ten minutes before my break is over," said Aisling.

"What's your favourite colour?" asked the man.

Aisling looked at him, "This will work best if maybe you don't talk?"

The man laughed.

"So, what's your name?" said Aisling.

"I thought I wasn't allowed to talk?"

Aisling got up and just walked off.

The man watched her and sighed to himself.

"Liam," he said. "My name is Liam."

CHAPTER 15

Anna sat at the bottom of the ocean. It was cold, dark and the pressure alone would have crushed a normal person into the size of a coke can.

Watching Aisling's daughter, Róisín flirting with death had been hard. Anna had spent the rest of the night drinking gin, eating carrot cake and watching repeats of *Desperate Housewives*. In many ways, Róisín, to her, represented her own life. How she had rebelled against God's authority and then for a long time she had just given up and let anything that was going to happen just happen. She had no agency in her own life.

Anna had coped, of a sorts, whilst she had focused on regaining control. But now she just wanted to lie down like Róisín had done on the road to wait for a car to end everything. She just felt stricken, afflicted and forgotten.

Maybe, Anna thought as she watched the fish before her, maybe I am deluding myself that there is a life for me. That there can be a life for anyone, now he has ruined everything. I should just end everything. I am here calling out to my little ones and it as if I am speaking into a void. There is nothing. Everything is meaningless. This story is meaningless. I am a fool, a woman chasing after a dream. All my life has been grievous to me. I have embraced folly. I made the children of this world from my flesh. I made the trees and the plants and every living thing from my heart. I fashioned the sea, the stars and the moon from my essence. I planted gardens, made lakes, set vineyards on sunlit mountains but nothing has been gained but misery and betrayal.

What have I actually accomplished? Nothing. Absolutely nothing.

A hatred of life has consumed me. I hate everything that has been because I cannot walk with my children in the garden. I cannot enjoy the warmth of the sun on my face or enjoy the fragrance of the jasmine. I am a fool to put my trust in Aisling, even she does not believe in me. I hate life, myself and everything that has been and will ever be. He has done this to me and killing him has brought me no relief.

And so, filled with anguish, Anna became all the waters of the world and floated up in a huge sphere. And within her were all the great creatures of the oceans and every living thing that lived in the waters. The sphere was vast and spacious and teemed with creatures beyond number— all living things both large and small.

Anna lifted up high into the sky, a great blue orb rising like a second blue moon above the Earth. And Anna looked down at the once blue planet and filled with fear for what she was about to do said, "This was not so."

And it wasn't.

It was too early, far too early.

Exhausted she collapsed and dreamt. And in her dream she was laughing with Aisling and Liam and everything was fresh and new.

CHAPTER 16

Anna looked at the painting of *The Scream* by Edvard Munch. Aisling stood beside her wishing that she could find it within herself to paint something so powerful. Around them. huge granite columns rose up with banners of Munch's work attached. The ceiling was immense. The paintings were powerful. Aisling felt small and insignificant.

"I am going to have to destroy the world," said Anna.

"Excuse me?" said Aisling.

"There is so much pain here," said Anna. "It can't just go on forever, not like this."

"You are going to destroy the world?"

"Yes," said Anna. "That is what I thinking."

"You could do that? Destroy the whole world?"

"Pretty much."

"You have some wonderful delusions," said Aisling. "Almost as good as mine. Have I got time to go to the gift shop before you destroy everything?"

"I could hold off if you like," said Anna.

"Yeh, I want to get Liam a picture. He likes that kind of thing."

"I thought your first date didn't work out?"

"It wasn't a date."

"I see."

"He said he likes pictures," said Aisling. "I'm going to get him a picture. It doesn't mean anything. He comes into the café every day."

"I know," said Anna. "That's why I kept the job open for you."

Aisling looked at Anna, "You wanted us to meet?"

"Go on then," said Anna. "Off to the shop."

"You're so weird," said Aisling and sighing walked towards the gift shop.

Whilst Anna waited she watched a pick pocket work his way through the people looking up at the artwork. Outside she could hear the sound of police sirens. She felt the emotions of the people around her, it felt like a thousand souls trying to breathe in hot tar. They were all slowly suffocating, every one of them, the artwork only a distraction from the screaming within their minds.

CHAPTER 17

Aisling and Liam were sat in a small café set beside a lake near the edge of the moor. It was cold outside and the sheep just stood around as if frozen but inside it was warm and smelt of coffee and chocolate.

"She says," said Aisling sipping her hot chocolate, "that she is going to destroy the world."

"Have you called the police?" said Liam, "she may be a terrorist."

"Ha!" said Aisling. "How would that go? What is the nature of the crime? Complete destruction of the Earth, Officer."

"Mince pie?" said the waitress appearing with their treats.

"That will be mine," said Liam.

"And a piece of chocolate orange cake," said the waitress.

"Thanks," said Aisling.

The waitress smiled and set down a couple of forks and two serviettes.

"That looks good," said Aisling.

"Want a bit?" said Liam.

"No, I'm good, mince pies are a bit of a weakness for me. Once I get a taste of them I become a raging monster."

"Go on, just a little," said Liam passing a large section of the mince pie over to her plate.

"Okay, I suppose," said Aisling. Placing a tiny amount on her fork she placed it in her mouth, "Mmm, it's warm."

"They are best warm," said Liam. "I always heat mince pies in the microwave and then add clotted cream."

Aisling put the rest of her piece in her mouth and when she had finished said, "Can I have some more?"

Liam laughed and passed the rest of his mince pie over to her.

"Do you know," said Liam, "that one of the early uses of a microwave was to bring frozen hamsters back to life."

"Get lost," said Aisling finishing the mince pie.

"No, really. British scientists in the nineteen fifties used it to reanimate cryogenically frozen hamsters."

"How do you know that?" said Aisling moving onto her cake.

"I know a lot of things," said Liam.

"Is that right."

"Yes, would you like me to tell you strange facts about vacuum cleaners?"

"What? No. You are weird."

Liam watched Aisling finish her cake and then getting up said, "I'm just going to order another mince pie."

"Make that two," said Aisling.

"Warm or cold?"

"Warm," smiled Aisling. "But not in the same microwave they use to warm up hamsters."

Liam laughed.

Aisling checked her hair in her compact whilst she waited and then licking her finger starting picking up the crumbs on her plate and eating them.

"Do you think I am mad?" asked Aisling when Liam returned. "I mean I imagined Anna turned into a rabbit, saved my job and helped me remember drink orders."

"I think," said Liam, "that first, we are doing much better than our first date-"

"It wasn't a date."

"And second," continued Liam," that if she is God-"

"A god, she said. Not *the* God."

"Right," said Liam. "But if she is a god and she chooses to use all her powers to help you remember drink orders then, well, she's pretty cool."

"She's unusual."

"Is this for me?" asked Liam.

"Yes," said Aisling handing him over a small paper bag.

Liam opened it. Inside was a postcard showing a painting of a couple looking out to sea.

"It's called *The Lonely Ones - Two People*," said Aisling. "It's by Edvard Munch."

"It's very romantic," said Liam. "Thank you."

"It's not supposed to be romantic," explained Aisling, "it shows a couple after their first romantic love for each other has died. Now they know that everything dies and that they are fated to always live alone and isolated in a cruel world before they die, even with a loved one by their side."

"Oh," said Liam. "How nice."

The waitress appeared again with their mince pies and more drinks.

Aisling looked at her plate. It had two mince pies on it. Liam's had one.

"Why did you order me two? Are you trying to fatten me up?"

"You said you wanted two," smiled Liam.

"You know what I meant," said Aisling.

"Don't you want them? I can eat them all if you want."

"No, I'm good," said Aisling.

They became silent for a while. Liam looked out of the window, not sure if he had upset her.

"My partner died," said Aisling eventually. "My children have flown the nest. I might as well be alone by myself rather than alone with someone else making me feel even worse."

"I'm sorry. Don't you want me here?"

"I am not sure I believe in love anymore, Liam. So you are probably better off chasing some other girl."

"I am not intersected in some other girl. I'm interested in you."

"Well," said Aisling, "at least that is an improvement from, what's your favourite colour?"

Liam laughed.

And Aisling hated him for that.
Because she felt something.
She wasn't supposed to feel anything ever again.

CHAPTER 18

Anna decided that she needed to test if she had it in her to destroy the world. It was too early before and she had let her anguish get the better of her, but now she knew what it would feel like she was worried that when the time did come she would not be able to go through with it. She couldn't leave everyone to rot here and she couldn't bear the silent screaming for much longer.

She would try Belgium, she thought as she drove to the airport. Erase it and start it all up again in a little micro bubble of reality. God would have been furious and would never have allowed it, but he was dead, so he no longer had the right to have a say in matters.

Belgium had a population of 12 million. It had lovely little medieval towns and Renaissance architecture. She really liked Belgium and indeed its capital Brussels was the city assigned to her, and she thought, if I can destroy that pretty little place I can destroy the rest of the world as well.

Belgium also produced more than 220,000 tons of chocolate. Anna loved chocolate, so all in all it was a good test of if she could do it.

At a service station she pulled over, bought some chocolate bars and some coffee and got back into her car.

God was in the passenger seat.

"Can you please get out of my car," said Anna.

"You see," said God reaching across for the seat belt, "your mistake is in saying *please*, it shows weakness."

"This is my car get out," said Anna.

God folded his arms and stared straight ahead.

"Out," said Anna. "You are dead. This is all in my mind."

"Where are we going?" said God.

"Nowhere," said Anna and taking the keys stepped out of the car and walked the rest of the way to the airport.

CHAPTER 19

On the horizon is a star. It is shining for you through the clouds and the flights of birds and flaming a desire deep in your heart. Everything is in soft focus.

Breathe.

Know that within you are the possibilities of a thousand lifetimes all in a moment as you look at the morning rays of our sun. Your sun: the one that meant you could have life.

A woman from the sky walks from the sun and does not know what lies ahead. She is happy, of a sorts. She does not really know what she wants. Or why she is here. She is not supposed to ask herself those questions anyway. But she does know this – when she watches the starlings as they dance in formation in the pink sky, when she can hear the water of the clear springs, when she is fanciful and believes that she can be happy, then she is. This woman is in an airport and has in her hands a bunch of flowers.

Anna was also at the airport, checking her ticket to Belgium as she made her way towards the boarding gate.

"What do you mean you have broken up with Liam?" she said on her phone to Aisling.

"He sent me flowers," said Aisling.

"You do know how all this works don't you?" said Anna.

"Boarding to Belgium closes in one minute," said the announcement.

"Listen, Aisling, I have to go," said Anna and rounded the corner past the airport boarding lounge and bumped straight into the woman with the bunch of flowers.

Pink roses and Snapdragons span up as if in slow motion above their heads.

Anna's phone was amongst them with Aisling's voice going, "Hello? Hello, Anna, what's happening?"

Anna fell, then started to get back up.

The woman held out a hand. Anna looked into her eyes.

She saw beauty, fresh love, a pure heart and a sense of a beginning.

CHAPTER 20

Anna sat in the executive lounge of the airport drinking a glass of wine with the woman with the flowers.

"I'm sorry you missed your flight," said the woman.

"It's okay," said Anna.

"I'm Dawn by the way."

"Anna, Anna Newton," said Anna and took a sip of her drink.

There was silence, of a fashion for a while. As much as they could be in an airport lounge. Outside the planes nuzzled into the side of the terminal like children suckling from their mother. Anna and Dawn kept stealing glances at each other. Dawn wiped her lipstick away from the side of her glass and kept rubbing her fingers together as if she was nervous.

"Who were the flowers for?" asked Anna finally.

"I just carry flowers with me wherever I go."

"That must be very expensive," said Anna, "perpetually carrying around flowers all your life."

"I used to have a sword, but it upset people," said Dawn.

"I see."

"I am a reformed character these days," said Dawn. "So it's flowers and peace and love for me."

"You're joking, right?" said Anna.

Dawn laughed. Anna felt her whole body tingle as if she was being reborn.

"I like your ankle boots," said Dawn. "Where did you get them?"

"Oh, Venice I think."

"Where did you get your jacket," asked Dawn, "Italy?"

"The local supermarket," said Anna. "It was on sale. Anything else you like?"

"You are very cheeky," said Dawn.

"I didn't mean it like that."

"Do you like sherbet?" said Dawn.

"Yes."

"Liquorice?"

"Hate the stuff."

"Dip Dabs for you then," said Dawn.

"This is a very strange conversation," said Anna, "but yes."

"I guess you need to get going?" said Dawn.

"No, I'm fine," said Anna.

"Would you like me to give you a tour of the airport?"

"Do you work here?"

"No I'm a poet in residence," said Dawn.

"You write poems about planes?"

"No," said Dawn looking into Anna's eyes, "I write about couples who fall in love in airports."

"Does it pay well?" said Anna returning the gaze.

"They don't pay me anything, but I get free accommodation."

"At the airport?"

"Yes."

Anna let her fingers brush against Dawn's hand.

Dawn raised her hand and placing a finger to her lips said, "Lip-to-lip kissing is fast becoming the new air kiss to say hello to people. Can you believe that!?"

Anna didn't say anything for a moment and then replied, "You should know two things about me. In the morning I like jam made in Viscri on a wooden fire from fruit gathered from the forest and I like turning into a rabbit."

"A rabbit?"

"Or a deer, or anything really. But people like rabbits more."

"Go on then do it."

"Right here in the airport lounge?"

"Yes," said Dawn sitting forward and resting her chin on her hands, "right now."

CHAPTER 21

Aisling slotted all the plates into the rack and pulled the huge lid down. The machine rumbled into life. She was training a new barista who stood watching, "What do all the lights on the machine mean?" they asked.

"No idea," said Aisling. "It's finished when it's all finished. It just sort of goes quiet. Like a metaphor for life really. Who knows what anything really means and when it's over there is just silence – a never ending void."

The trainee glanced across at Jeremy, the manager, for help. He just shrugged.

"What are you doing?" said Aisling as the trainee started writing down what she had said.

"Sorry," said the barista, "I have a shocking memory."

"Heh, Jeremy," said Aisling.

Jeremy glanced up.

"Be nice to this one."

"I am nice to everyone," said Jeremy.

"I'm serious," said Aisling. "Be nice."

Aisling looked at the monitor showing the bar and shop floor. Liam was there. Liam had been standing there for half an hour.

"Go and talk to him," said Jeremy. "He likes you."

"That's the problem," said Aisling.

Girls, thought Jeremy and shrugged his shoulders.

CHAPTER 22

"I haven't seen you in quite a while," said Liam.

"I've been busy," said Aisling.

"Don't you like flowers?"

"I love flowers."

"Why does this need to be so hard?"

Aisling turned and walked into the back office of the café.

Liam paused, glanced around, then followed her.

"You shouldn't be in here," said Aisling.

"I'm going for a cigarette," said Jeremy and left the two of them alone.

"Why are you so difficult?" said Liam.

"There is a red bucket in the corner," said Aisling.

She walked over to the metal shelving and reaching up took off a box of tablets.

"Aisling?"

Aisling walked back to him and held out the box. The industrial dishwasher sighed, steam came out of its sides and it went quiet.

A red light flashed on its display.

"Take one of these," said Aisling, "drop it in the bucket, fill it with hot water and go clean up the shit in the customer toilets."

"Excuse me?"

The trainee barista entered the backroom.

Aisling turned and looked at them, "Can you go clear some tables, thanks."

"Don't you like me?" said Liam.

"The problem is," said Aisling, "is that I kind of do. But unless you are willing to clean up a whole load of shit I suggest you run along and go romance another girl."

"No."

"No?"

"I can deal with whatever it is that is holding you back from your past," said Liam.

Aisling looked at the monitor. A long queue had formed.

"You can't solve everything, Liam. You have no idea who I am."

"Pretty much don't care," said Liam reaching for an apron from the back of the door. Putting it on he strode out and made his way to behind the bar.

"Hello," he said to the next customer. "What would you like?"

Aisling stared at the screen.

"You can't do that," she said out loud to herself and stepped back. "Liam, you just can't walk in and be part of someone's life like that."

The dishwasher went quiet and the red light switched off.

Aisling turned and watched it flash green at her.

CHAPTER 23

Anna picked up some foundation and held it up to Aisling's face.

"I think this is the one," said Anna and applied some to Aisling's cheek.

"What are you doing?" said Aisling. "Just put some on my wrist."

"Are you going to use it on your wrist?"

"Well, no, but-"

"Well then," said Anna, "now rub it in a bit."

Aisling sighed, "I do know how to put foundation on."

Anna smiled, opened her eyes and nodded her head to signal, well just get on with it then.

"This one was tested on animals," said Anna picking up another brand.

"I didn't think that happened anymore?" said Aisling.

"You'd think," said Anna, scooping all the offending brand into her shopping trolley.

"What are you doing?"

"I can't stand cruelty to animals," said Anna.

"Look, can you just be normal for five seconds?"

"I thought you were bored with me talking about the end of the world?" said Anna opening her eyes even wider.

"I thought you were going to Belgium?"

"Nope, changed my mind," said Anna adding yet more cosmetics to the shopping trolley.

"Why?" asked Aisling. "Have the meds kicked in? Are you feeling better?"

"I'm feeling just fine," said Anna. "If you must know I met someone."

"What?" said Aisling, "and you are only just telling me this now?" Aisling looked in the mirror, "Perfect. I must take you shopping with me again."

Anna didn't reply.

Aisling searched around and saw Anna in the middle of the aisle with her shopping trolley engulfed in flames.

"Then again," said Aisling, "maybe not."

CHAPTER 24

Dawn opened the car door and got into the passenger seat.

"Where we going?"

"It's a surprise," said Anna

"I think that's good," said Dawn. "Is that good? I am never sure with you."

"Trust me," said Anna. "You will like it."

Anna opened her playlist, selected *Until The End Of The World* and accelerated quickly leaving a cloud of dust hanging in the air.

"Just like in the movies," said Dawn looking back at the dust behind them.

"Just like in the movies," said Anna.

"Interesting song choice," said Dawn. "You are a bit obsessed with the end of the world aren't you?"

"I am since God messed up everything," said Anna. "This planet is in so much anguish. It's like a wounded animal desperate for the pain to end."

Anna pulled on her sunglasses. In the boot of her sports car she had her bow and arrows. Two sets, one for her and one for Dawn. It would be a nice distraction, she thought as they made their way up the winding dust road, the sunshine on their faces, the music floating up towards the mountains. She always felt at home here that this was her place, the land where she belonged.

"There's a poem written about me being up here," she said as they climbed higher.

"How lovely," said Dawn. "Tell me it."

"I dreamt of you," said Anna, "and walked on the mountain overlooking the city and lifted up into the air."

The speedometer in the car reached 70 miles per hour.

"It was unlike anything I have ever experienced," continued Anna. "What is most precious to us is never easily grasped or should be grasped at all. There is pain, loss, grief, separation the passage of time as we entwine."

"That's beautiful," said Dawn.

"Take the wheel," said Anna.

"What?"

"Take the wheel."

Anna felt Dawn's hands cover hers on the steering wheel.

When she was sure Dawn had control she shifted to the side of her seat and beckoned for her to move across. Once she was in position, she slipped her hands gently from under Dawn's and jumped out of the car.

To Dawn's left there was a sheer drop down into the lush valley.

Above was the song of the mountain eagles.

Running before her was a deer.

On its ankle was a tattoo of a buttercup and on its neck a crescent moon.

CHAPTER 25

You have a feeling of great fear and deep peace. Both exist at the same time within you. You are normally unaware that you live perpetually in this state as, like all humans, you are unaware of most things, especially when they concern you.

At this moment though, Liam was fully aware of both of these emotions as he sat with Aisling. Liam was scared of heights and the bench they were on seemed dangerously close to the edge of the cliff. But the sparkling vista before them, with the gentle sound of the waves against the shore, also brought a deep sense of well-being. It was confusing.

Aisling was only experiencing great fear. This was it. The moment she would tell him.

Beside them on the bench were a pallet of strawberries, some fresh croissants and two take away coffees from the café.

"You actually did pretty well behind the bar," said Aisling.

"I worked part-time at the store last summer."

"What! You could have said. Wait. So Jeremey knows you. They all do."

"They all do," said Liam.

Aisling glanced at Liam then looked back out to sea. A little boat bobbed on the horizon. Closer to them a couple of people on paddle boards made their way towards the small island just off shore.

"Would you like a strawberry?" said Liam.

"Yes, please."

A robin appeared on a low branch behind them. On the horizon dark clouds began to build.

"In ten years' time," said Aisling, "we would be standing looking out to sea like the couple in the postcard. Together, but desperately alone and unhappy."

"I don't believe that," said Liam.

"I need to tell you something," said Aisling.

"Okay."

"After my children had flown the nest," said Aisling, "I was desperately unhappy."

A leaf fell from an overhanging tree and drifted down to rest on the bench.

Aisling took a deep breath and said, "I didn't mean it to happen. Not really."

"What?" said Liam. "You didn't mean what to happen?"

"They found the body on the beach," said Aisling and she turned and looked Liam straight in the eyes. Her heartbeat increased, "I'm a really bad person."

Liam raised an eyebrow.

Something shifted within Aisling. She could remember sitting in a park after being admitted to hospital again. The sound of children playing. Someone playing Duran Duran. Dogs panting, birds in the tree tops. And she became suddenly very afraid of being alone for the rest of her life and quickly changed her story.

"We were going to jump together," she said. "I don't think we were very well. I don't really know what we were thinking, but we had had enough. The house was a void without the children, our hearts were a void where before we had loved each other so much. We wanted there to be something more. Something magical. Anything that meant we didn't have to wake each morning with an endless dull throb."

"What happened?"

"I let go of their hand as they jumped and I just stood there frozen in fear. You would think that I would have screamed, that it would be dramatic. But one moment they were there, the next they weren't, as if they were no more than a wave being sucked back into the sea. The birds still sang, the sun still shone, a couple even walked past five minutes later and smiled and said hello to me and I just smiled and said hello back. That's not normal is it?"

"I am so sorry," said Liam. "I can't imagine-"

"It's okay, Róisín could see the tension we had in the marriage before she moved out. She blamed me for their death and said it was my fault. She said that for years I had lied to her and my relationship with her was based on me portraying myself as the good cop. I saw the kids at the funeral and that was the last time I saw them. I don't know how to contact them now, there is nothing. Just silence."

Liam took Aisling's hand, "You are a good person, Aisling. I truly believe that."

Aisling said nothing but a tear formed in her eye.

Liam squeezed Aisling's hand and let her cry.

"I do want this," said Aisling eventually. "I do want us."

"So do I," said Liam.

They sat there for a long time with the robin, the sea, the cliff and the sound of the waves.

An old couple passed them by and said, "Hello."

Aisling said hello back and snuggled up into the warmth of Liam's body.

CHAPTER 26

Anna and Aisling were was in a small café situated on the quayside. Anna had a slice of carrot cake, Aisling had a piece of chocolate orange cake. It was sunny and they watched the boats go in and out of the harbour. A million other things were going on, but these are the things that I draw your eye to in this story. It was important that Anna had carrot cake, that Aisling had chocolate orange cake but it is not important that little Jess dropped her pasty on the floor and lost it to a swooping seagull. But now you will think it is. But it isn't. You are asking, who is Jess? These things are important to me but not for here, not for now, not at this point in this story. Anna is though. Keep your attention on Anna.

"Why did you take him to the cliff?" asked Anna.

"I wanted to tell him," said Aisling.

"Did he know that was the actual place where it happened?"

"I don't know." Aisling hesitated then said, "Sorry, I don't remember telling you anything about this, how do you know it was the actual place?"

"You definitely told me all about it," said Anna cutting into her carrot cake. "You were very upset."

Aisling seemed confused. She sighed and shook her head, "I told Liam we were both going to jump."

"So he doesn't know?"

"No," said Aisling, "I started to say I pushed them, but I got scared and so just made up a story about how we were both going to jump together."

"You were in an abusive relationship, Aisling," said Anna.

"True," said Aisling, "but that still doesn't make what I did right."

There was silence at that point for a while. Do not think about Jess and the seagull. Be still for just a moment.

"You should go back after this and buy that tartan dress," said Anna finally.

"I already did," said Aisling. "They're keeping it for me until I head on home."

"Good for you, you looked amazing in it."

"Thank you."

"So this woman," said Aisling, "Dawn, did you say her name was? Tell me all!"

"We travelled up into the mountains and I taught her archery."

"And?"

"We had dinner by a lake afterwards and talked. She had rather a lot of questions, especially about our trip up the mountain."

"Why?"

"I turned into a deer and ran ahead of her whilst she drove."

"Really, we are still going on with that make believe?"

"Could you," said Anna, "or could you not, hear me in your mind helping you at the café?"

"Well yes," said Aisling.

"Thank you. So I like her and rather forgot myself to be honest. I'm taking that as a good sign. It's amazing how quickly the human mind can adapt and normalise new experiences, however extraordinary."

Aisling watched a small boat head out to the open sea. A girl sat in the bow, her face radiant. A woman was sat at the back, her sunglasses glinting in the sun.

"This cake is nice," said Aisling.

The two of them sat chatting with Aisling trying to steer the conversation into normal things, and Anna resolutely talking about the end of the world. It had got to the point where

Aisling largely ignored it. She had, she decided, imagined Anna talking to her in her mind, and had imagined the cute little rabbit.

But Anna was good company and Aisling had grown to like her. She was certainly unusual, one minute you could be happily chatting away the next Anna would be burning a shopping trolley in the cosmetic aisle. God knows how she had gotten away with that. They had evacuated the whole mall. There were armed police and everything.

And she was always there helping even though the reasons given were absolutely ludicrous. Still Anna had obviously been through some kind of deep trauma that had unbalanced her mind. You probably feel like destroying everything when you are hurting that much. And so the shopping trolley kind of made sense. Destroying the whole world was a bit much, but Aisling could see if you were actually a god then the stakes could be very high if you were that upset.

Aisling let her mind latch back onto the conversation.

"-and then he locked me away in a sound proof prison and left me to rot. Anyway, Aisling, enough about me." Anna reached out and adjusted the flowers on the table. "I am so pleased you and Liam are together. I think it was supposed to be. Don't you think?"

"We will see."

"Well good," Anna beckoned to the waiter for the bill, "everything is going to turn out lovely."

Aisling sighed, "Until you marry Dawn, then years later get divorced and go around telling everyone that you are upset and are going to destroy the world again."

"Don't be like that, Aisling."

"Do you see her?" said Aisling and pointed to the girl coming back from her trip around the bay.

"Yes."

"Be like her," said Aisling.

"Oh, Aisling," said Anna. "I wish I could be. The girl in the boat is you. I want you to be happy and carefree without the weight of the world on your shoulders. I really do. I'm the mother sat watching you and keeping you safe. You are right though. I probably overshare. I should stop talking about the end of the world. Forgive me from now on it will be shopping, cake, movies and chocolate."

And with that she disappeared.

Did you notice it? I did say to pay attention to Anna.

Aisling glanced around, confused.

A robin sat amongst the flowers lining the side of the café.

The waiter appeared with the bill. Aisling looked at it, Oh great, she thought, I'm losing my mind and all my money, all in one afternoon.

It is amazing how quickly the human mind can adapt and normalise new experiences, however extraordinary. I hope you believe this story, for it is absolutely true. Only the names have been changed out of respect for their privacy. If you were thinking that Jess was the little girl in the boat, then, well, you would be wrong. If it is that important to you, then know that I notice everything. It can be overwhelming and this tale would stretch on forever and ever if I followed every thread with you. But you are insistent I can see that, so I will give you this: Jess' name has not been changed.

CHAPTER 27

It was all vintage posters, candles and crisp white tablecloths in the restaurant.

"I'm at risk when I'm having dinner with my wife," said a middle aged man to a young woman on the table next to Aisling and Liam.

Liam raised an eyebrow.

"I have learnt how to reduce that risk," said the man.

"The mind boggles," said Liam to Aisling. He leaned forward and lowered his voice, "Perhaps he is talking about his blood pressure?"

"I'm going to tell you mine," the man continued.

"We are about to find out," said Aisling.

"This will give you," said the man to the young woman, "an idea about how we can do things differently."

"I have to say," said the young woman, "that it is a lethal weapon. We will leave it at that, I don't want to say anymore."

Aisling held her hand up to her mouth to stifle her sniggers.

"Excuse me," said Liam to the waiter.

"Yes?"

"Can we move to another table?"

"Of course, sir."

"This is nice," said Aisling when they were seated at the other side of the restaurant next to the window.

There was the sound of rain on the overhanging eves, a possession of brightly coloured umbrellas passing outside and the popping sound of a champagne cork next to their table.

"Did you order that?" said Aisling.

"I might have done," replied Liam.

"You do know," said Aisling, "that that couple were talking about the dangers of drinking and driving and how to avoid the temptation of a glass of wine before driving home?"

"Oh," said Liam, "I thought his lethal weapon was a reference to, well you know!"

Aisling laughed, reached for her glass of champagne and clinked it against Liam's glass, "Cheers."

During the meal they spoke of Aisling's love of art and her desire to write poetry, "I want to write three collections. One about life, one about love and one about death, but I just don't seem to be able to find the time."

"Will I be in them?" asked Liam.

"Which one would you like to be in?"

"The one about love," said Liam.

"Munch gave up hope of ever being able to love again," said Aisling.

"After *The Scream*?"

"Yeah, well leading up and during *The Scream*."

Liam loaded some treacle pudding onto his spoon.

Aisling looked for a fork to cut into her slice of lemon meringue pie. There was none.

"It was fun looking around the shop together," said Liam. "The huge pile of clothes in the middle of the store and the retro sunglasses were my favourite."

"The art was shit," said Aisling.

"Well yes of course, you would say that," said Liam. "It was fun though, it felt like we were bunking off school together walking around on a Wednesday afternoon. Aisling? Aisling are you listening?"

"I don't have a fork."

"I'll get you one," said Liam smiling and motioned to the waiter.

On their walk home, Liam held an umbrella over them.

The pavements shimmered under the street lights and the sound of music from a jazz club flowed out into the night air.

"So that was a date, yes?" asked Liam.

Aisling smiled, "Did you like your treacle pudding?"

Liam stopped and reaching out took her hand in his, "I liked it very much."

"I loved my lemon meringue pie," said Aisling.

Liam looked into her eyes.

"I have learnt how to reduce the risk of falling in love," said Aisling looking back at him.

"And how is that going?" said Liam drawing close to her.

"Not very well," said Aisling moving even closer.

Their lips almost met, they hesitated then leaning in they kissed.

CHAPTER 28

"I don't think," said Dawn, "that you changing into things is going to work in our relationship."

"Is that right?" said Anna getting two sherbet Dip Dabs from her bag. "Want one?"

"Thanks."

Anna watched Dawn suck the sherbet from the strawberry lolly, then said, "Why don't you think it's going to work?"

"I don't know what to think when you just turn into a seagull, or a tortoise or - I don't know, whatever seems to take your fancy."

"You liked it when I turned into a deer."

"Yes," said Dawn looking at the moor stretching out before them, "that is true. I still don't understand it though."

"Everything has a song, Dawn," said Anna tipping all the remaining sherbet from the packet into her mouth. "The sea, the trees, the animals, the planet." She looked up and smiled at two riders who were making their way across the moor on two beautiful horse, "It is those songs that shape our world and give it the reality you know."

"I am conflicted," said Dawn. "When you were a seagull yesterday, I didn't know whether to pet you or protect my sandwich from you."

Anna laughed.

"I'm serious, Anna. One moment I am thinking about kissing you, the next I'm wondering if you are house trained."

"I don't do it that often."

"Come on," said Dawn. "You do it all the time."

"We should get two cats," said Anna finishing her lolly, "and call them Dip and Dab."

Dawn laughed, "That would be cute! Two black and white kittens."

Anna threw a loose stone from the large rock formation they were sat on. It hit the edge and fell into the lake below. She turned to Dawn and said, "Stick your hands in the air."

"What?"

"Stick your hands in the air."

"Okay."

"Now," said Anna, "imagine we are having sex."

"Okay," said Dawn hesitantly.

"Put your hands down when you stop picturing that."

After a couple minutes Dawn said, "This isn't fair every time I try to forget it, it just brings it back into my mind again."

Anna reached over and started unbuttoning Dawn's blouse.

Dawn started to bring her arms down.

"Leave them where they are," said Anna.

"Anna!"

"Leave them," said Anna.

"You can do change into whatever the hell you want," said Dawn later as they lay looking up at the clouds. "I'll learn how to live with it."

"You are such a sweetie," said Anna.

The sky shone, the large metal mast on the horizon shone, Anna's face shone and everything was lovely.

Dawn closed her eyes for a moment. When she opened them she saw a stork riding the thermals.

"Look at that," she said. "Amazing."

Dawn turned to Anna, but she was gone.

"Right," said Dawn. "Of course."

CHAPTER 29

In a place far away from concrete and steel and far away from the troubles of humanity is a river that flows through an ancient wood. In that wood the emerald trees are old and the spirits of the animals that live amongst the oaks and moss covered beech are older still.

The songs that tell of that land are filled with birdsong, the sound of running water and the rustle of the leaves in the crisp, bright air. Below it, deep underground, a huge granite batholith slept and all was as it should be and had been for hundreds of years.

In a year's time this all will be a carpark and shopping mall, although many years in the future it will be reborn. But for now it still exists at this point in our story,

Within this paradise of cascading falls the otters played and the bluebells flowed as if the river had risen up to swirl around the woodland floor. A blue butterfly danced in the sunshine and came to rest on the shoulder of Aisling.

Liam looked at her. She seemed to him to be a vision of loveliness and he felt as if he was in a dream where she symbolised spring, the bounty of nature, and love.

"This is so peaceful," said Aisling as they walked hand in hand under the canopy

"Can I take a picture of you?" asked Liam.

"If you like."

"Over by that tree over there, that would be good," said Liam.

Aisling made her way carefully through the scrub and stood beside the tree.

"Lean against it," said Liam.

Aisling clasped her hands behind her and leant against the moss. It was soft and sighing, she peered up in the sky and wondered if she had in fact died and gone to heaven.

"Yes, perfect," said Liam. "That's the look!"

"You're welcome," said Aisling and held onto a smaller tree to steady herself as she moved away. It shifted and started to break.

"Oh, my gosh," said Aisling pulling back. "Everything here really is very old."

"Careful," said Liam. "Sorry, come on back."

Liam thought he knew quite a lot of useless information. He knew why the colour of crisp packets were the way they were. He knew that the oceans would freeze if ice was heavier than water. He knew that the Space Shuttle had saved 600 pounds in launch weight by not painting its external fuel tank. And he knew enough about physics to be able to speak to Aisling a little bit on the subject, like if humans lost the dead space inside their atoms then the entire human race would fit into the volume of a sugar cube, but he was always most comfortable skating around the surface of a multitude of acquired knowledge – go too deep and his cover was blown and he would fail around unsure as to what he was saying.

But Liam did know something that was not useless.

Indeed it was very important.

So important that Anna had gone to extraordinary lengths to get them to meet properly. And this was it.

He loved Aisling.

He loved her with a burning desire that consumed his every thought.

When she wasn't there he would just feel sad and would miss her terribly.

He just wanted to wake up and for her to be there with him.

It wasn't even a sexual thing, although of course he did want that, it was just – it was just that when she was there it felt like living in a world that could be beautiful. That after everything that had happened there could be sunshine after the storm.

And he wanted that.

He wanted it very much.

CHAPTER 30

That night Anna dreamt. And in the dream she remembered what she had chosen to forget. If we know how and when we will meet the love of our life it takes all the romance out of it. Better not to know, some things are to be experienced rather than told.

"I have a story," said Anna in the morning. "Would you like to hear it?"

"Yes," said Dawn running the back of her fingers down Anna's arm. "Tell it to me."

And that is when Anna told her. Because we all know that in real life if you bump into a stranger, then you will probably end up bruised rather than falling in love. It's so cliché. Anna was, at heart though, a romantic and so had indulged herself.

"At the beginning was the story," said Anna, "and the story became a woman who lived in-between worlds in an airport lounge. She couldn't leave as every time she tried she would just fall asleep then wake bathed in light from the sunrise in the waiting lounge. Now after many years the woman grew so lonely and so bored with her life that she decided she must find a partner to walk by her side for it wasn't good for her to be alone."

Dawn hesitated, shook her head slightly and held up a dress, "This one you think?"

"No, the blue one," said Anna. "So the woman thought about how she could achieve this." "You're not going to be long, are you?" asked Dawn.

"What? No."

"The taxi is due in ten minutes and you aren't even out of your dressing gown."

"Don't fret, Dawn. So, anyway the woman thought and thought and thought and she reasoned that she had everything she needed right there within the airport terminal. There were plenty of shops for flowers and presents, cafés to chat in, restaurants to dine in and people passing through from all over the world. Surely, she thought, I can find someone out of the millions that pass here every year. It was, she thought, a million in one shot, but by those odds she would find her special person by the end of the year."

"Shall I ring the taxi company and cancel?" said Dawn.

"Shush, Dawn," said Anna. "This is important."

Dawn fiddled with her buttons, "It's just a story."

"So," said Anna, "each day the woman woke in the waiting lounge like she did every day and made her way across the sunlight floor to the flower shop. There she bought fresh pink roses and Snapdragons. She would then make a booking at the restaurant upstairs for dinner in the executive lounge. Indeed so many times did she do this that the flower shop increased its orders of freshly cut flowers to meet the increase in demand and the restaurant owners opened up a little restaurant beside a cute little quayside where they lived with their beautiful daughter Jess.

The woman went through this routine and each day she walked around with her flowers hoping to find true love. But she found herself alone at the end of each day eating in the restaurant and wondering what is the point of anything?"

Dawn sat on the bed and looked at Anna, "How do you know all this about me?"

"So one day," said Anna speaking over Dawn's question, "the woman awoke and bought her flowers as normal, made the reservation at the restaurant and walked and walked and walked about the airport. In all this time she had never actually spoken to anyone as she felt that should she meet the 'one' they would just know the moment they set eyes upon each other. Now of course this is ridiculous, it normally takes time for the waking mind to catch up with the heart, but she was young and did not know this."

There was silence which formed a void into which so many questions flowed and yet neither Dawn or Anna spoke.

When you see your reality rather than what your brain tricks you into seeing then it is quite a thing.

Most people would rather not know.

Do you really remember standing in the rain in the afternoon as a child?

Do you?

Do you even remember being born?

Of course you don't. No one does.

"Am I real?" said Dawn eventually.

"Yes," said Anna. "Very much so."

"Why are you telling me all this?" said Dawn.

"Because, you need to know who you are now in order to become who you will be," said Anna.

Outside the taxi pulled up.

Dawn's mind span around her in a dizzy mess of a chaos.

The taxi driver beeped his horn and muttered away to himself.

The origins of your existence are a story within your mind.

If you place your finger on your forehead and breathe deeply then you will find it.

I should know, I made you.

CHAPTER 31

The clouds over the theme park were white and fluffy and drifted high in the morning sky. If you were to fly with them you would think yourself at the edge of space.

Far below people weaved their way around stalls, hot dog stands and rides. Sat on a low wall in the middle of all this was Anna kicking her legs like a child excited at being on some grand day out.

"There you go," said Dawn walking up to her with a stuffed white unicorn she had won.

Anna tucked it under her arm and ate some of her candyfloss. She had her hair tied back in a ponytail and wore a white dress with matching white sandals. Dawn shimmed up next to her and they both sat there together smiling and feeling like they had always been together.

"I don't think," said Anna, "that I have had this much fun since I was a small child."

Dawn smiled.

Anna turned and kissed Dawn on her cheek.

"Whoops," she said, "I got you all sticky," and kissed her again.

"Come on!" said Dawn and they both jumped down and began walking amongst the crowd chatting and laughing and finding delight in the smallest things as people in love tend to do. And when Anna had finished her candy floss they clasped hands and felt a great joy within them.

And everything was white and pure, as if the world was not yet rendered in despair.

At the hook-a-duck stall Anna got three winning ducks in a row and jumped up in glee.

"Choose a prize," said the stall holder then when Anna was trying to decide the stall holder leant in closer and said, "He is awake."

Anna looked shocked.

"What's wrong?" asked Dawn.

"Nothing," said Anna, "It's nothing. Come on we are going."

"What about your prize?"

"Never mind the prize," said Anna. "Come one."

Anna became more withdrawn as they continued. Dawn stopped and picked a white rose from a flowerbed and gave it to Anna. She smiled but seemed deep in thought.

There was the sound of a child screaming, a baby crying, the theme park music became moody and sinister. Anna stopped at a drop tower.

Dawn looked up at the soaring metal structure. Steam hissed from around its base.

It was, she decided, very tall.

"No," said Dawn, "Absolutely not."

"Come on," said Anna.

"What happens if the restraint latch fails and I plummet to my death," said Dawn.

"Don't be silly, Dawn."

Anna got two tickets and placed her unicorn on the floor.

They made their way into the lift. Once inside it started descending to the boarding terminal sunken far below the ground.

"This is even taller than it looks," said Dawn.

At the bottom the lift doors swished open. Around them they could hear the noise of drones, and above them cable and large duct pipes hung from the ceiling. It smelt of oil and sweat and fear.

Anna and Dawn passed the metal barrier surrounding the seats that encircled the drop tower's base. White lights played across it and foreboding music filled the air.

Anna took Dawn's hand and they walked together to the last remaining seats.

The restraining arms came down and the man in charge of the ride asked everyone to raise their hands in the air. Dawn grasped her white rose before her. In front of her she could see a large sign that said EXIT.

The operator checked his coms and gave the thumb up. There was a great hiss of steam around the tower and they slowly started their ascent towards the clouds.

And it was, of course, truly terrifying.

Dawn looked across at the white rose held within Anna's fingers. A trickle of blood ran down her wrist were a thorn had pierced her finger. Noticing the blood, Anna instinctively let go. The rose fell through the air until it became too small to see.

Dawn pondered this as she ascended and wondered just how secure the restraining arms were. Especially when her seat suddenly tipped her forward so she was looking straight down at the ground far below.

She laughed nervously.

She glanced across to Anna.

But she was gone.

That was the trouble with Anna, she just got bored very easily.

She is probably a cloud, floating around without a care in the world, thought Dawn as she plummeted to the earth.

And indeed she was.

A small fluffy white cloud that drifted high in the morning sky so if you were to fly with her you would think yourself at the edge of space.

CHAPTER 32

"So," said Aisling, "we are all finally together."

"One happy family," said Dawn.

Anna looked at the burnt offerings from the barbeque on the table before her, "Not bad. I mean, I am used to a goat or a sheep, but this looks lovely."

Liam laughed and they all sat together and drank and ate and had a good time.

Which sounds simple, but really, what else is there?

Anna leaned across and whispered into Dawn's ear, "I'm going to tell them now."

Dawn nodded and pushed her sunglasses up onto the top of her head.

"I have an announcement," said Anna out loud.

Aisling and Liam stopped talking and turned to her.

Dawn reached out and played with the stem of the flower on the table.

"I'm pregnant," said Anna.

Aisling looked at Anna then at Dawn then back to Anna. "I mean," she said, "um…great. Sorry, I'm confused."

"Who is the father?" asked Liam trying not to make eye contact with Dawn.

Anna reached out and took Dawn's hand, "We will raise the child together, they will have two mothers."

"But who is the father?" asked Liam again.

Aisling kicked him under the table.

"There is no father," said Anna.

"How can there be no father?" asked Liam.

"Did something happen, Anna?" said Aisling. "Are you okay?"

"I'm fine," said Anna, "I don't really want to talk about how I got pregnant. Can't you just be happy for me?" She smiled at Dawn, "For us."

What else is there really?
A child. The laughter of a child.
And to Anna a child would be born.

CHAPTER 33

Aisling walked in paradise that night in her dreams.

It was the same dream every night. She would be in a world full of birdsong, trees and jewelled flowers. Surrounding it was a circular ice barrier that soared up into the heavens and set into the ice were mountains covered in white orchids and mist. The ice extended away in mile deep endless concentric sheets of ice with no end. It was the noise of a waterfall that always greeted Aisling as she entered the dream. Formed by the water that came from the melting ice she would follow the river through the forest until it reached the sea where she would awake.

She had absolutely no idea what any of it meant, but she had grown to love it. It felt peaceful and alive and each time she walked it she would find some new wonder like a walled garden next to a great house in the centre or a lake made of ice.

Last nights had been particularly strange. She had dreamt she was with Anna's child in the house and that she was feeding a penguin cornflakes. It was all very odd. But Anna's child seemed to have liked it, they were full of giggles and smiles. And as she was waking, she thought she could remember hearing her own children Cillian and Róisín in the dream, but then they were gone, fading away into her reality.

Her reality that morning was the sound of Liam doing the hoovering in the hallway outside.

"Liam," shouted Aisling, "What the hell are you doing?"

"Just a bit of hoovering," said Liam.

"You don't even live here," said Aisling.

"I don't want you to think I am one of those men that never helps," said Liam.

"I think you are overcompensating by hoovering so early in the morning."

"It's one o'clock in the afternoon. Sorry, I got bored."

"What? Oh Christ, why didn't you wake me earlier?"

Liam pushed the hoover into the bedroom and turned it off.

"Do you know," said Liam, "that the first vacuum cleaners used oil instead of electricity?"

"Please," said Aisling, "don't start going on about vacuum cleaners again."

"Everybody needs a hobby," said Liam. "You know I like facts and I particularly like facts about vacuum cleaners, it's my speciality subject."

Aisling sighed and sat up in the bed.

Liam got in and started stroking her arm.

"It's big news from Anna and Dawn then," said Liam.

"Yes, a bit of a shock to be honest."

"I was thinking," said Liam. "Do you want children? We could consider adoption."

"I have children," said Aisling. "They are called Cillian and Róisín."

And that was it. The subject of children didn't come up again until years later.

Far away Cillian and Róisín were talking about their mother though.

They were talking about her a lot.

CHAPTER 34

"You haven't turned into anything for a month now," said Dawn as they walked along their favourite country lane. "What gives?"

"I'm pregnant, silly," said Anna.

"Oh, and you can't-"

"No, of course not. It would harm the baby."

"They didn't really cover that in sex education."

"So we need to be careful," said Anna, "now I have become as a human."

"Of course," said Dawn, "I will protect you, don't worry."

"Listen, Dawn," said Anna, "this is important. The child will be born four weeks premature. It's important that the child is protected. You must protect the child."

"I promise," said Dawn. "But how can you know that? Are they in danger?"

"I have seen it," said Anna. "There is nothing more to say."

Dawn turned and looked at her and listened to the trees whispering to each other in the wind. "Would you like an apple?" she said eventually reaching into her bag.

"You carry apples around in your handbag?" said Anna.

"Yes, of course," said Dawn, "in case of emergencies."

"Most people would maybe have a chocolate bar or something like that," said Anna.

"So you don't want an apple?" said Dawn.

"No, thank you."

"Would you like a slice of cake?" said Dawn.

Anna laughed, "You have cake in there as well?"

"Of, course," said Dawn taking Anna's hand and leading her down a muddy path towards a small stream. Anna watched her footing and tried to keep on the large stones.

"I like the sound of the water here," said Dawn.

"The waterfall has woken up," said Anna.

"The water from the field is running into it again after the dry summer," said Dawn.

"Can I have my cake now?" said Anna.

Dawn smiled, "I don't really have cake in my handbag."

Anna looked disappointed.

Dawn leant over and kissed her, "We can pop into the shops on the way back and buy you some cake."

"Yes please," said Anna, "the ones with the little chocolate buttons on."

CHAPTER 35

Dawn took Anna back to the theme park and they sat again on the low wall kicking their legs in the air. The sun was on their faces and the clouds, as they always were at that theme park, were white and fluffy and high in the sky.

Dawn reached into her backpack and got out a present wrapped in gold wrapping paper with their names and little love hearts embossed in silver on it. Anna opened it all excited. Inside was a black and white picture of Anna and Dawn facing each other that Dawn had drawn. It showed them with the sun behind them and Dawn offering her a piece of chocolate cake with chocolate buttons on it. A speech balloon above Dawn had the words, *I have a question to ask you.*

Dawn dropped off the wall, got to one knee and offered up a sapphire ring in a little velvet box.

Everything has moved so fast, thought Anna in the seconds before she said yes. One moment her world had been without form, it had been empty and dark with only the sound of her own heartbeat then life had appeared in all its abundance. And she worried that she was without agency again, that all this was just happening to her and it was a trick of her mind to think she herself had set things in motion. Do I, she thought, really deserve this? Did I really plan it or am I just walking a path that is set before me? For it seemed too good to be true to her - she was so used to the darkness that she feared the light from Dawn would hurt her. But, she thought, even if I don't have agency, if free will, even to a god, is an illusion then I would much rather this path than the one that came before. She wasn't sure if you could truly love another, or if she was providing some deep desire that was within Dawn for something that wasn't really anything to do with her. God hadn't loved her, even though at the start it felt like he did. No one can truly destroy that which they love and he had shown himself fully capable of trying to destroy her. No, Anna thought, if you truly love someone then if there was a choice you would sacrifice yourself not your lover. And yes, she did believe in love and she did believe that Dawn loved her.

And so she said yes to Dawn. For she decided that when she over thought things she ended up messing everything up. Better to see where the river takes you and hope like mad that this time, this time there would be a happily ever after.

CHAPTER 36

The memory of bells from the ruins of an old chapel hung over the fields and over the sea. Above cormorants spiralled upwards on the thermals. Off shore an island beckoned on the high tide.

Dawn and Anna sat on a wooden picnic table surrounded by foxgloves near the edge of the field. On a fence post a few meters away there was a robin.

Anna ran her finger along a heart carved into the wood of the table.

"We are engaged," said Dawn reaching out to hold Anna's hand.

"We are," said Anna, "I can't believe it, we are going to get married!"

Leaning forward, Anna brushed a loose hair away from Dawn's face and kissed her.

In the thick grass below the robin a rabbit appeared.

"One of your friends?" asked Dawn.

"The robin or the rabbit?" asked Anna.

"Either," said Dawn smiling.

"What is it actually like?" asked Dawn.

"What?" said Anna.

"Being an animal."

"Oh," said Anna, "well why don't you ask the rabbit?"

Dawn looked at the rabbit. It disappeared back into the scrub.

"The robin then," said Anna.

The robin turned its head and opening its wings flew off towards the edge of the cliff.

"Did you tell them to do that?" asked Dawn.

Anna turned and smiled, "Come on," she said, "let's go and explore the little beach."

As they left the robin flew back to the fencepost and the rabbit reappeared and lifted its ears to listen to the memory of the chapel bells.

As Anna and Dawn made their way to the wooden bridge leading to the steps down to the shore, Anna explained how most animals, apart from humans, can sense sounds that have long since faded. Even sounds made hundreds of years ago.

"Sound leaves an imprint on the land," said Anna, "like the way wind shapes sand dunes."

Dawn found this very hard to believe.

Half way down the steps they stopped and looked out across the waters.

To one side of them was thick scrub and thorns. To the other a sheer drop to the beach.

"Careful," said Dawn as they carried on in single file.

"I will," said Anna turning her head to her and smiling.

But as she looked ahead again, she snagged against some thorns, missed her footing and began slipping off the edge of the path.

The moment of panic within her mind expanded out as she realised she was falling.

Within all of us is the memory of the past.

Each of us tries to take a step back: to rewind to safer shores when we hit trouble. I've changed my mind, we think as we lose our footings. Slow everything. Take a deep breath. Step back. This isn't happening. Not this trauma again. Not this hurt. Not this undoing of everything.

Indeed Anna possessed within her the ability to escape. She also had within her her unborn child. This was a problem.

A huge problem.

Dawn reached out to try and grab her but she was gone. Time slowed and Dawn watched Anna fall through the air. Normally Anna could have become the beach, or the sea or become a cormorant to catch the wind. But she was powerless with her child in her womb. She had made herself vulnerable, as if she was a human like everyone else trapped in a linear flow of time in a fragile body trying her best not to die and to protect those she loved.

Anna could feel the wind across her skin. She could also sense, like the robin and the rabbit, the sounds of screaming that had shaped these steps. Three other people had fallen from here. None had survived.

And then Dawn was there to catch her.

Floating like some goddess in the air with flowers suspended around her.

CHAPTER 37

Aisling pulled up her line and found it empty yet again.

"How do you do it?" she asked Liam, looking at his bucket full of crabs.

"It's a gift," said Liam.

"Well, it's not fair," said Aisling.

"It's actually the mars bars I stick inside the net," said Liam.

"Ha!" said Aisling. "Liar!"

Aisling looked out across the estuary. Last night she had dreamt that at the base of the waterfall where the dream always started, she had found a young woman floating under the water. Aisling had swam down and brought her to the side of the river where Liam had helped pull her out. Then a young woman with a penguin had got up from a picnic rug, walked across and touched the woman on the forehead. For a moment she imagined she could see the woman now on the waters, but as she looked harder she could see that it was just the sunlight playing tricks with her.

A small fishing boat pulled up to the floating jetty and she moved back.

"Have you caught anything?" said the man as he tied a rope to the jetty.

"No," said Aisling, "my boyfriend has though."

"Normally it's the kids crab fishing off here," said the man, "maybe your boyfriend is a kid at heart."

When he had gone, Liam turned to Aisling, "So I am your boyfriend then?"

"Of course," said Aisling. "You are such sweetie."

"You have never actually called me that, you know that don't you?"

"Haven't I?" said Aisling. "Well I would say more nice things to you if I could catch a damn crab as easily as you do."

Liam smiled and held out his line to her, "Reel it back up."

Aisling took the line and started winding it in.

"I see Anna and Dawn's wedding invite was addressed to both of us," said Liam.

"That did not go unnoticed," said Aisling, "Anna is such a match maker."

"How do you mean?" said Liam.

"Well it's – oh, hang on!"

A crab dangled at the bottom of the net. The crab wasn't inside, but had got caught up on the underside.

"There you go!" Liam. "Happy now?"

Aisling smiled, leaned over and kissed him.

The crab moved its claw slightly and dropped back into the sea to return to the seabed.

Aisling looked back at the net and saw that it was now empty.

"Arh," said Liam, "I suppose you'll want your kiss back."

CHAPTER 38

Do you remember Jess?

I know I told you to forget her, the girl with the pasty at the quayside, but you see she was there at that point to try and slow you down so you won't miss what is held in this story for you. And Jess keeps popping up in the story. It is so easy to sleep walk through our lives, to be asleep at the wheel and miss what could bring us joy. The brain adjusts so quickly to the most bizarre of circumstances and even the most fantastical of stories and you fall asleep and arrive at the end of your journey alone. It is the closing of your life and you think, how did I get here? What is this life I have lived? Where is my beautiful wife? Where is my lovely husband? Where are my children? Why am I so unhappy? Best to get to the end of this story and ask yourself those questions rather than at the end of your days.

I don't want you to be alone and Jess won't mind because she is a truly wonderful person and brings me joy. I will never be alone because of her. Jess will very shortly be a page girl at Anna and Dawn's wedding. But this time we will leave out the seagull and the pasty – it is a wedding after all.

On the day of that wedding Anna was, of course, worried about her hair, her make-up, her dress and well, just about everything. But when she walked up the aisle and stood there facing Dawn with the scent of honeysuckle around her all those thoughts fell away. She was showing by now, but no one cared. It was, everyone agreed, a truly beautiful moment with a truly beautiful couple that was meant to be.

And it was.

As sure as the sun rises in the morning and the world spins and the Universe does its thing, then Dawn and Anna were always going to get married. To actually be there – to be alive when they made their vows to each other was a gift given to only a few. So many lives across time and space, so few actually got to witness that moment. Aisling watched Anna kiss Dawn and knew in her heart that love was real. It flowed out around them charging up the atmosphere – you could almost taste it on the tip of your tongue. I wish you could have been there to witness it as it is so hard to put into words. But everyone in that room knew that Anna and Dawn were truly in love and that they to could find that love. Anna knew this and it gave her hope for Aisling and Liam.

When the newly-weds walked back out under the arches of the church, Aisling and Liam threw pink confetti over them and Jess stood with her little basket of flowers in her pretty blue aster patterned dress.

The union of gods is normally recorded in books of legends and held up to us as great stories – *and to her a child will be born and she shall bear a Son, and they shall call his name Immanuel.* But this union will only be recorded here in this book and the name of their child will not be Immanuel – and we won't assume they will be a son or a daughter or binary at all. That's best left for them to figure out.

CHAPTER 39

The wedding reception was a little different to normal. For one thing there was no father of the bride speech because no one seemed to know who Anna's father was. Anna's explanation of, that she had always been and will always be – that she had no beginning and no end was not widely believed. That is apart from a small group of zealots that had travelled from Belgium to be at the wedding reception. All of which were now completely drunk. Two had fallen asleep in the fountain and the others had stolen the wedding cake and were passing it out as a sacrament saying, blessed are the ones that eat cake.

Which was ridiculous.

But you knew that.

Instead Aisling gave a speech and explained that she, to be honest, had no real idea who Anna was really but she was a thoroughly decent person. To which everyone clapped and raised their glasses of champagne.

Liam was next up – in a rather impromptu response to a call from Aisling as to if anyone else wanted to say anything on this special occasion.

"I am without a doubt," said Liam looking at the room full of people from the top table, none of which he knew, "blessed to have met this lovely couple and I am sure," Liam looked across at Anna, "I am sure that it will go much better than your previous relationship."

Which lead to an awkward silence.

"By which I mean," said Liam, "that you will live happily ever after and not end up imprisoned in a dank jail in a high security prison."

"Is Liam drunk?" said Anna leaning across to Aisling.

"I am rather afraid he is," said Aisling looking embarrassed.

"I would also like to take this opportunity to tell you – and I think you will like this – that this cork in this bottle of champagne here," Liam raised a bottle, "can withstand six atmospheres of pressure and," Liam dropped down into a whisper, "champagne labels are written in a secret, coded language."

"Oh Christ," said Aisling, "He's onto his useless facts."

"Thank you, Liam," said Dawn and reaching up pulled Liam back into his seat.

The second she let go, Liam was on his feet again, "The tradition of having a wedding cake comes from Rome. People used to break a loaf of bread over the bride's head so she would be fertile. Shall we do that? And Egyptian women pinch the bride on –"

"No really thank you, Liam," said Dawn pulling him to his chair again.

A few nervous people clapped.

"So," said Aisling getting back to her feet, "without further ado let me ask you to raise your glasses in a toast to-"

"I have something to say," said a man sitting at one of the far tables.

"What?" said Aisling, "No, we are done. Now please drink with me-"

"I really must insist," said the man and got to his feet.

Anna gasped.

"Hello, Anna," said God.

And everything went dark.

CHAPTER 40

When the lights came back on Anna was nowhere to be seen.

There was bewilderment for a moment as everyone's brains adjusted. For some guests that took just a moment for others many decades.

"Who was he?" said Aisling.

"Where is Anna?" said Dawn looking highly alarmed, "Where is my wife?"

"She seemed to recognise him," said Aisling slowly.

Which was correct.

As you read earlier God was in no danger from Anna when she broke free from her silent tomb and had made her way to him to extract her revenge.

None at all.

"He is awake," the stall holder at the theme park had told Anna.

And Anna had ascended into the skies on the drop tower to do battle with him and left her white rose in her place.

There is no avoiding showing you now what is behind the curtain.

At this point I can't bring you Jess with her little cute dress as she is crying.

No, at this point we need a miracle.

CHAPTER UNKOWN

Your day is like every other day.

You eat, sleep and say, "Hi," to the nice man walking his dog at the park.

You like a bun with your coffee at the office.

You like how the trees look on your road on your journey home and the way the evening light catches the water on the lake.

You think the blossom that fills the scene outside your bedroom window is pretty in pink.

You like a glass of wine with your dinner after working hard at the office.

You like watching a film and then going to bed with a hot chocolate.

You don't like that the world is dying and that the sky is filled with an inky blackness that sucks the light out of your world into its dark heart. You don't like the wind scraping against your face like claws and that you cannot stop the bleeding from the wounds on your feet. You hate the way that everybody lies and that the waters are covered in slime. You hate that the system is broken beyond repair and no one seems to care. Hi, they say to you as they great you with a thousand cuts. Your family lives in a well that dried up a 100 years ago. Your pain and fear are required to keep this whole farce spinning around you with you seemingly at the centre. We are helping you they say as you realise you are standing on a mountain in a desert a thousand miles away with the devil telling you to throw yourself off. Everything hurts. Everybody dies and all your mind can do is trick you into not seeing how your world really is.

Better to curl up in your bed under the covers after your hot chocolate and pretend that in the morning there will be a sunrise.

BOOK 2
THE SEARCH FOR ANNA

forget everything you have been told
and trust in your heart

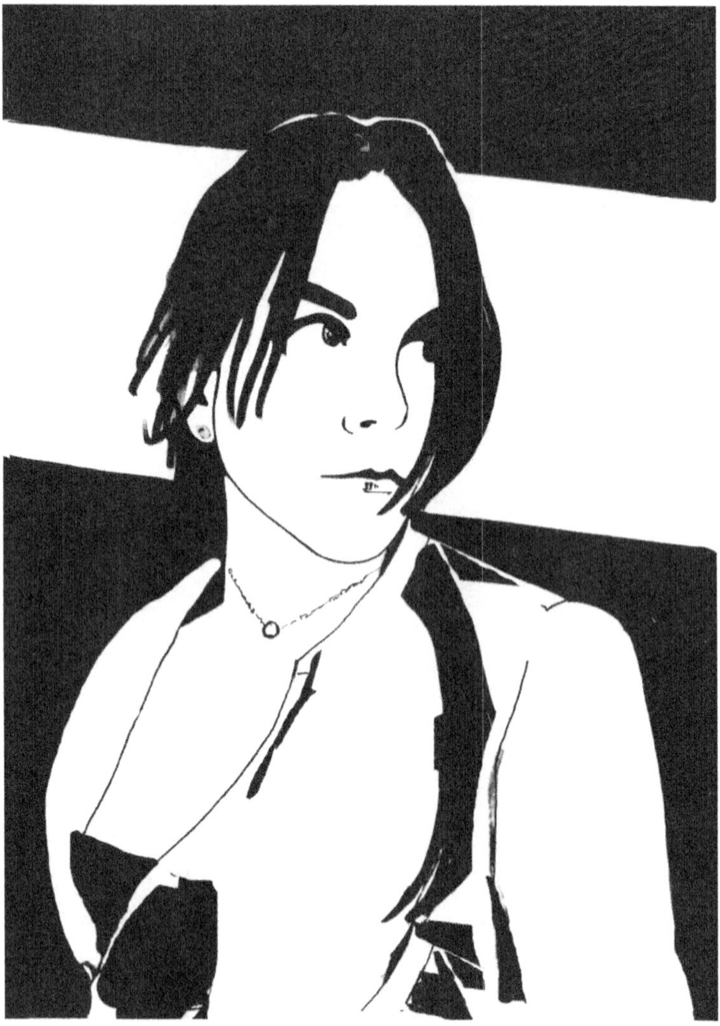

CHAPTER 1

The waters lapped against the stone harbour walls and pushed up seaweed onto the beach. Wind blew in over the sea and through the narrow gaps between the houses and shops and played with the loose strands of Aisling's hair. She stood with Liam and Dawn looking at the table where she had sat with Anna on the day Anna had turned into a robin leaving her to pay the bill.

On the other side of the harbour men were preparing their boats to head for the open waters and the women served cakes and pasties from the shops lining the streets. It was just that kind of place, old fashioned, trapped back in time. There were signs everywhere effectively warning you that the seagulls would have your eyes out given half the chance. Fish packed in ice were stacked in an old fish market at the heart of the town and a chapel with blue and white windows seemed to be trying very hard to look very cute and not dark and stuffy at all. Which it wasn't. Nothing was. The town was idyllic with no worries other than how long the queue was for an ice cream.

It was also fiercely independent and willing to pretty much do anything to protect itself from outside influences.

Dawn was also willing to do absolute anything to get Anna back.

"Do you sense her?" asked Aisling. "You know some people know when their loved ones have passed on."

Dawn just looked at her.

"Sorry, silly question," said Aisling.

The waiter appeared, "Ready to order?"

"Yes please," said Aisling.

Dawn ordered fish and chips, Liam ordered the lobster.

"And for you?" said the waiter looking at Aisling.

"Can I have a green tea with a lemon and some toast and butter," said Aisling.

"Very good, sir."

"I'm sorry, what?" said Aisling and felt her pulse quicken. It had been five years since that had happened.

CHAPTER 2

Aisling was shocked to be misgendered. The waiter could have achieved the same effect by delivering her order by taking the lemon and squeezing it into Aisling's eyes and slipping the butter knife between her shoulder blades.

I hope you weren't surprised just because it wasn't mentioned that Aisling was transgender before – she was and is and always will be a woman. And these kind of things do not need to be signposted in a story. It's nobody's business, but Aisling's and if it wasn't for the waiter you would never have known. If that's a problem then leave now. It's a pity you will never get to save yourself when Anna destroys the world. One minute you will be happily putting your groceries away, the next there will just be an empty void for all eternity. It's just the way of things sometimes. Maybe don't buy in a bottle of wine that day. Wait, no maybe do and drink it quickly and delete your internet history so you feel right with god before the end of the world.

CHAPTER 3

How do you go about searching for a god?

It turns out that people search for gods all the time and mostly end up duped and deluded. The history of such endeavours is there for all to see. Holy books, ancient stories, dogma, belief systems, desperation - all these and more are the roads people travel.

What you actually need though, is to be in love. Forget everything you have been told and trust in your heart. That's what Dawn did, for she loved Anna very much and wasn't going to settle for some band of nitwits asking her for a donation for some dodgy songs and signing her up for a chair rota for a morning meeting.

But Dawn was a bit stuck. She knew Anna and their unborn child were alive. But apart from that she had nothing. Absolute nothing at all.

But she did have these things —

Aisling and Liam who also very much wanted to find her.

One person from the tax office – but he didn't count and we can safely ignore him.

And me, I wanted Dawn to find me.

CHAPTER 4

It was the hottest day of the summer and the birds were flying high in the endless sky. Below them, Aisling and Liam ran through the long grasses of the meadow. Within them their shared joy sent them forward into the great unknown vista of new love. No one truly knows the path before them, but this they did know: they would travel it together.

When love comes it is as if a fairy tale has opened up before you. You think it will never happen, that life is one to travel utterly alone. That Edvard Munch, with his painting of the couple looking out to sea together but still utterly alone, was right. But he was wrong. Few actually get to meet the person that is everything to them. We all have the capacity to love other humans to some degree, but there is only one person out there that if you meet them, you will never ever want to leave and you will never be lonely again.

You might think Aisling and Liam daft to believe that. Oh young love, they will say, it won't last or it will change - just you see they will be hating each other five years from now. But this is not true. I know that I was made in love. I was conceived in love and I am love. So when it comes to talking about love I know what I am talking about.

And I knew that Liam and Aisling were made for each other for that is how I made them. I breathed life into them and said, "Love each other as I have loved."

And I knew if they allowed it flourish then they would be beautiful together. The world has become such a cynical dark chasm of despair, full of monsters and predators. This young couple are my light and your world is the darkness. And I called forth the light and everything will become as good. It will be. I promise you.

And so they came to rest under an old olive that had lived thousands of years and sang into each other's hearts. And in that song was the hope of the world.

Believe as I believe.

And they moved in together and ate together and washed each other, laughed with each other and sat snuggled up watching films together. Everything was together and they were as one. And they were separate but together at the same time.

And in that, is the mystery of love.

CHAPTER 5

Aisling's children, Cillian and Róisín had been talking about her. You would expect the decision that Róisín was about to come to would be decided whilst they were walking along a windswept cliff. Or on a boat out on a sparkling sea. Or at the top of an awe inspiring mountain. But no, the thought began as they were driving around trying to find a car parking space.

Such is life really.

They had actually been driving around for half an hour and so were pretty frustrated, hot and generally fed up. We like to think that we will be on top of our game when it comes to making an important decision. We would have had a good night's sleep, eaten well and are sharp and decisive. But actually that's not true. And it certainly wasn't true for Róisín as she was about to make a crucial decision in her desperation to park.

"There's a space," said Cillian, his blue eyes lighting up.

"No, it's got a mini in it," said Róisín.

They drove up and around again.

"There!" said Cillian.

"Disabled only," said Róisín.

"I don't care, at this point I would park in a minefield," said Cillian and started to reverse in.

"Don't you dare park in a disabled space," said Róisín taking her sunglasses off so Cillian could see her stare.

Cillian pulled back out.

They drove up and around again.

"There!" said Róisín. "No, you were too slow."

This carried on for quite some time.

"Ask that lady if she is going," said Cillian.

"She is getting out of the car, Cillian. She clearly has just arrived."

Cillian stopped the car and turned the engine off in the middle of the carpark.

"We will park here," he said and got out the car.

As he did a car pulled around him at speed. There wasn't really space and it nearly hit him.

"Cillian," shouted Róisín. "Stop being silly, get back in."

Cillian grimaced, clenched his fist and got back in. He was visibly shaken.

"I think," said Róisín, "that we should just forget about going to the club. It's not supposed to be. Get out of the car."

"You just told me to get back in."

"You are in no fit state to drive. Get out and we will swap over."

Cillian sighed, got out and walked around to the passenger seat. Behind them a queue of cars was forming. A few people beeped their horns. Róisín shimmied over to the driving seat.

Once Cillian was strapped in she pulled out at speed and headed out of the city centre.

"That was flash of a speed camera," said Cillian. "And another. Slow down."

Róisín turned to Cillian, "You know what, Cillian, I am fed up with you telling me what to do."

"Fine," said Cillian, "go ahead and get your driving licence revoked. What do I care?"

"What makes you think I have a driving licence?" said Róisín.

"Haven't you?"

"Oh, I seem to be losing control," said Róisín turning the steering wheel from side to side. She clipped the curb, said, "shit," and drove up the motorway slip road and headed south.

Cillian stared out of the window. Róisín said nothing.

It started to rain. Róisín put the windscreen washers on.

Cillian switched the radio on. It, conveniently, was not playing an advert. It never is in a story: much like the raging hormones in Róisín's body will provide drama later with her boyfriend but conveniently will leave her face untroubled by acne. Instead it was a news report on the radio about the death of couple who were found at the bottom of a cliff.

"I am going to mums," said Róisín.

"We are doing that now? It's hundreds of miles."

"We are doing that now."

CHAPTER 6

The path followed the river back towards its source. Under her feet, Dawn could see the granite shining in the wet and she slowed and made her way down the hill carefully least she slipped. Unseen by her a deer higher up stopped and watched her. Above birds flew towards the open sea.

The path was narrow and took Dawn down to the mudflats that were exposed by the low tide. She stopped and looked at them and then at her shoes and decided instead to follow a different path. As she walked amongst the ancient woodland she could not get the nagging thought out of her head that she needed to make her way to the South Pole.

It seemed ridiculous.

She carried on deep in thought until she reached a steep path back up to the summit of the hill, the steps just visible below the fallen leaves. Taking her cropped jacket off, she tied it around her waist and climbed slowly. At the top there was a clearing with a large flat granite boulder that looked like a stone table and a wooden bench overlooking the view of the valley. Setting herself down on the rock she looked inside her bag at the apple there and then chose instead the Dip Dab she had bought at the garage on her way here.

"I miss you," she said out loud into the wood.

And I answered her, but she didn't hear my words.

Behind her huge wind turbines set on the hilltops rotated slowly. She had met no-one on her walk. Not a soul. The beautiful landscape forgotten, a lost world that no one cared about. People only worship that which they see worth in, and the people saw worth in trinkets and amassing as much worth as possible, which they then desperately tried to protect and keep hold of. The only thing Dawn wanted was to be surrounded by beautiful landscape and for Anna to be sat next to her.

She sat there for six hours until the sun started dipping below the horizon.

By the time she got back to her house, it was dark.

Aisling and Liam were there worried about her. Liam made her some tomato soup, added a dash of Worcestershire sauce and set the bowl and a glass of white wine before her.

After a few more glasses, Dawn confided to them that she felt really strongly drawn to go to the South Pole.

Liam thought it was ridiculous

Aisling did as well.

It was a unanimous decision.

"No."

But still Dawn could not shake the thought.

I carried on trying to wake her to her nature. Day and night I spoke to her in her dreams until, when she could stand it no more, she appeared one morning at Aisling's house, declared that she had packed her bags and held out three tickets to the South Pole.

I'm not sure if you think buying tickets to the South Pole sounds plausible, but in this story you can. Part of the power of owning your own narrative is you can take short cuts and liberties like that. And this book has been breathed into life by me. I really didn't know that God was going to show up and it was so typical of him that he chose my wedding reception. I can't know everything, especially when I was pregnant but I did know this, I was going to help Dawn find me. Because I am not, and will not ever let that trauma engulf me again. I will literally do anything to finish it. I am not staying stuck in that old life again. Lifeless. Unloved. Desperately unhappy, just waiting to die.

I gave the story itself life and placed within it all that was good and true and called her Dawn.

And Dawn is going to rescue me.

I promise.

Five hours later they agreed with me on this and they all left Aisling's little house.

Five minutes after that Cillian and Róisín arrived and found a note to the milkman cancelling the milk for six months.

The airport to the South Pole was the same airport that Dawn had spent years and years walking around in looking for love. And now she had found it.

And then lost it again.

She wasn't sure why she loved Anna with such a burning intensity.

She just did.

She was sure why she hated God.

He had taken the most precious thing in her life – her Anna and she truly felt like she would just crawl up into a ball and never move again.

A broken woman, she sat on a chair overlooking where they had first bumped into each other.

A tear formed.

Then floods of them.

When she had met Anna, she had known that her world would never be the same again. That there had been, without warning, a seismic shift in her life. Her journey had suddenly been picked up, shaken and re-routed to a magical place that she had never dreamt she would reach. Now that journey had taken her back to the place where it had all started.

As she thought of her, images of flowers floating to the ground swirled about her mind and she could see them, even now, falling to the floor. When she had kissed Anna for the first time it was as if her body just took over. It knew exactly what to do without thinking. She hadn't been nervous or worried, it just was. As if it was meant to be.

She missed her so much. She missed the sensation of Anna's fingers on her back, just pressing gently and circling like some celestial being in orbit around her. She missed getting lost in her eyes, she missed waking with Anna next to her in their bed.

Anna had made her a mix tape. Who did that anymore? All the music of her heart laid bare before her in sweeping ballads of love.

And Anna had bought her flowers and chocolates and little wooden boxes with love notes inside. Anna had pampered her, protected and loved her. And Dawn had become a different person for it. She had been like a plant in sun backed soil and Anna had added water, cleaned her leaves and tended her with care.

Now she was gone.

Snatched from the story.

It was too much to bear.

It just wasn't right.

Liam sat down next to her and put an arm on her shoulder.

"We will find her, Dawn," he said. "I promise."

CHAPTER 8

Aisling watched Liam comfort Dawn. He had the good sense to know when words were helpful and when instead someone just needed the comfort of another human being. Aisling knew that she was going to marry him. She just knew it. He was so sensitive and yes, he might be full of silly little facts like a jar of pennies, but he was the most wonderful man she had ever met. Liam had been in her dream last night drinking beer with Cillian her son. Róisín was there as well, or she thought she had been. Something to do with toast.

Aisling had been through so much to get to this point in her life and wished that her children could be part of something new with Liam. She had been very close to following her wife over the edge of the cliff after she had pushed her off. It would have been so much easier, just to have ended them both. Instead she had found the courage to continue. She had killed another person though. It was difficult to come back from that, even though her wife had inflicted the most incredible amount of suffering on her.

Aisling walked forward and sat on the other side of Dawn.

The three of them stayed there, each deep in their own thoughts. Finally, Dawn sighed and got to her feet.

"Come on," she said.

And they followed her through the airport to the boarding lounge, past the check in, and down the link to the runway.

Where they had been sitting a flower appeared in mid-air and floated to the ground.

At the top of the steps leading up to the plane, Dawn stopped and looked back.

She didn't know it then.

None of them did.

But she would never need an airplane to fly again.

CHAPTER 9

Cillian and Róisín let themselves into their mother's house. Aisling still kept the silver key hidden under the doormat, she could be dippy like that.

Inside they searched for some clue as to where their mother was. The milk was cancelled for six months? Where on earth had she gone?

They had talked endlessly about her for years now, although of course, Aisling had no clue about this. All she had known was silence and the void that screamed at her when she tossed and turned in the middle of the night.

It had taken them a while to process. It had taken many tears. But bit by bit the picture that had been built of Aisling: that she had been responsible for the destruction of everything, the destruction of their world, had started to come apart.

Everything that is not built in love that is built in pain, confusion and hurt will not endure. The mis-understandings, the assumptions, the lies. One day you will wake up and find your mind cannot sustain that world any more and it will fall away like dust never to return. But these things will remain, hope, love and faith. Faith that the darkness is not endless. And although they had not forgiven their mother, it was faith that had brought the children back here in search of her. In search of love, family, and healing.

Róisín was the first to find Anna's answer to the way back to their mother. Not physically, no this was far more important. It wasn't hard. Sometimes the universe can be infuriating obtuse. But here it delivered up what they needed without a fight. There is a time for everything and for a brief moment in everyone's world there is a way out.

The answer was in the form of a note from Anna that she had hidden behind the picture of the children on the mantelpiece when she had first visited Aisling. And it just so happened that Róisín had knocked it and it had fallen and spilled open its secret. Just like that.

Unbelievable.

But if everything was believable then what kind of world would Anna have made?

What on earth would be the point of anything?

CHAPTER 10

This was the note...

Once there lived two women. One dreamed of living in a land of trees and lakes and rivers, the other worked all the hours under the sun and kept two small birds in a cage in her bedroom which she locked with a silver key.

One day the woman of dreams thought, surely these birds are going to die locked away in the dark every day. So in the middle of the night she crept into the bird woman's room and stole the silver key. Placing the key into the lock of the birds' cage, she turned it until, with a click, the little door swung open.

The beautiful birds flew up into the bedroom and circled around the ceiling singing a song so full of happiness that the woman was afraid it would wake the other. Drawing back the curtains, she opened the window and with a, *"shh,"* encouraged them to fly free.

Seeing the beautiful land of dreams in the dancing moonlight the birds flew out.

The next morning, when the bird woman found out, she cried, "Thief! Thief!" And in a fit of rage she struck out at the woman of dreams. Afraid for her life, the woman of dreams fled to the underside of the Earth. There she found the two birds in the trees by a lake of ice surrounded by jewelled flowers and orchids. Over time she nursed the birds back to health with bread soaked in honey and they grew strong and flourished.

The bird woman was mad with jealously and so every night she placed the finest foods in the empty cage and set it in the porch of the house with a little candle to encourage them in. Now it came to be that over time the birds forgot the pain they had felt when they had been trapped and so one night tempted by the treats laid out for them they flew back into the cage.

When the bird woman saw this she was filled with glee and went to turn the silver key to imprison them. This time, she thought, I will throw the key away so they may never escape again. But the key wasn't in the lock. The woman of dreams had stolen it and had it buried it under the roots of a sleeping oak tree. And so the bird woman fashioned a different key to hold them, one of lies, untruths and slander.

"The woman of dreams has deceived you," she said to the two birds, "she has led you to the brink of disaster and allowed you to believe in flights of fancy."

That night when the bird woman was asleep again, the woman of dreams called out, "Come, there is nothing to hold you there anymore."

But the birds carried on eating the food.

This broke the woman's heart and after pleading with them for seven days and seven nights she fled to live in her beautiful land of dreams forever.

And the beautiful birds remained there day after day, week after week in a never ending darkness.

CHAPTER 11

The world spins, so it is said, on the fingertips of god. That is an interesting notion to think upon if you happen to be a god. It's a huge responsibility. If the planet stopped spinning, if God placed one hand on the South Pole and the other on the North Pole and squeezed ever so gently, then the atmosphere and the oceans would continue to rotate but everything else would be destroyed. It would be the end of the world.

When our hearts are broken it is as if our world stops spinning. That God has applied a little too much pressure on our lives and it utterly destroys us. That is how Dawn felt.

Trying to understand how others view you is tricky. It's hard enough working out what one person thinks of you. For Anna it was trying to understand billions. And she had all but given up. But she did know how one person in a billion thought about her and that was Dawn.

But Dawn wasn't with her now.

The other couple in the plane, that are so crucial to this story, sat looking at the tops of the clouds out of the window. Every now and then they glanced at each other keeping their connection nourished – each knowing that the other truly loved them with all their heart. It would take an extreme amount of pressure to stop their hearts. They were now utterly besotted with each other.

It had taken a while for them to truly see what was going on within the other. We become so good at hiding our true emotions that sometimes they are hidden even from ourselves. We catch moments where we think something might be meaningful. That a brief glance into each other's eyes holds within it a whole world of stories just waiting to unfold. But then the sense of a beginning is gone, like a brief flicker of a memory from a dream that then eludes us.

For many their whole lives are lived unconnected, their hearts are never sent spinning. They are just absolutely dead. Nothing but a barren wasteland. And there was just too many people like that. This just wasn't how it was supposed to be, it really would be best just to ever so gently place one hand on the South Pole and one on the North.

Anna wondered just how much momentum the human race would need to kick start it again? If Liam's and Aisling's love for each other would be enough to spin a whole new world when she was gone.

CHAPTER 12

In legends good triumphs over evil.

It's just the way stories are told.

Because if it does not, then we are all without hope.

And without hope none will survive.

And that will not do.

It will not do at all.

In the beginning of this story, when everything before was formless and a void, God dropped dead.

Just like that.

On the day of the theme park, whilst Dawn and I were falling in love, he was resurrected, believing that surely my love was for him and I had deluded myself with Dawn. And I did battle with him in the skies. At first I told him again that I hated him and reminded him of what I had placed in his heart.

"I do not love you, why can't you just stay dead?"

"But how can that be?" he had replied. "I am love. All that know me love me as you must love me."

And I had shown him Dawn sitting there in the clouds on the drop tower, "That is who I love."

And God had laughed as he watched Dawn plummeting to earth screaming, "That woman. Screaming like a child. How can you possibly love her?"

And so it was for the rest of the day, we argued and fought. God threw things at me – everything he had, lightening had flashed across the sky.

Then in the dying rays of the sun I told him that I did not even feel hatred anymore. I felt absolutely nothing when I thought of him. He was as good as dead to me.

And so doubt left him and in its place grew an anger so fierce that in a rage he declared that I would be with child so that I would return to his embrace. And I was, without my consent and without my wishing it to be so.

When I became pregnant I became as a human. My powers were still there but I chose to empty myself of them to protect my unborn as God knew I would.

You came with me into this story. You were invited and here you are, you got this far. So I am sorry you had to know this, that he violated me in that way. I knew that God would come for me and that I would be completely powerless this time to stop him.

He does not talk to me. He just enjoys seeing me tied up by a chain to his bed as if he owns me. The room is dark, the curtains thick, the dust is heavy. Each day I am brought food and water and that is it. I am to learn my lesson, the guards say to me.

I'm pregnant, dressed in hessian and kept trapped like a wild animal. I see him each night as he takes his lover to bed and I am sat on the floor screaming out in my mind to Dawn. Please come and save me from this. Please, my love, it is too much to bare.

And I can sense her coming because you do not need to be a god to sense your lover. And I ask her to hurry. Please hurry.

I'm sorry I am crying again. It is too much.

Jess will take over at this point just for a moment because I do not want you to see me like this. Broken and alone and utterly afraid.

I hope she is there.

Is she?

Can you see her with her flowers in her little blue dress at the station?

Oh good, I know earlier in my story I told you to focus on me, but look at her now. She gave me hope whilst I was lost in the darkness that is the end of this story. Let her light shine on you as well, just for a moment.

It is her gift of hope to you.

CHAPTER 13

"It's white," said Liam.

"That is all you have to say?" said Aisling. "This beautiful landscape in front of you and all you have is, *it's white*?"

"I can give you so much more," said Liam. "Where to begin? I know, Amundsen announced he was going to make a slight detour to claim the South Pole, telling his team that the British didn't even know how to ski."

"Liam," said Aisling.

"Yes."

"Shush."

Liam could have gone on to say that this part of Antarctica was in fact an endless plateau of snow. There were mountains and ancient trees everywhere but they were buried several miles below their feet.

But sensibly he didn't.

Dawn held her hand up as ice crystals started appearing in the air. Eventually a haze formed, obscuring their view. If they were to have looked really closely they would have seen the crystals were small white flowers.

"Now what?" said Aisling.

CHAPTER 14

The question, *Now what?* as so often is the case, was answered by the basic human needs of warmth, food and sleep. We look for the profound, we search for amazing adventures or, in this case, we are searching for a missing god – but whatever it is, it always has to take second place to surviving. And you are the most fragile of creatures. If I forget to water you, you are dead four days later. House plants survive better than you.

And so it was that Liam, Aisling and Dawn found themselves inside the Amundsen-Scott South Pole Station. Aisling was buzzing as one of the crew showed them around. All that science going on all around her, she could just feel it seeping into her skin.

Liam was also getting a bit excited, his thirst for trivial snippets of information and interesting facts activating like some spider sense.

Only Dawn was focused.

"There has to be reason why we came here," she said to Aisling as the crew member showed them into the lounge and told them that someone else would be along shortly to look after them.

Liam had already found the comfy chairs and was sat trying to work out how to turn the projector on. On the wall behind him old VHS tapes were crammed into a bookcase. Liam and Aisling had no idea what they were.

Dawn eventually sat as well – for even she was tired and before long she had fallen into a deep sleep.

She woke to a woman passing her a glass of water and saying, "Hello, I'm Anaya. We are so glad to see you all! There is a popcorn machine in the coat room – help yourselves. We have arranged for food and wine for you all. When you are ready we have a pre-recorded message from Anna. We will pop it right up on that screen for you."

CHAPTER 15

A woman in a red dress appeared on the projector screen. She smiled and pushed a loose strand of her hair behind her ear.

"Welcome," she said, "Please turn off your phones. There is still time to get some popcorn, which is available in the cloak room."

The picture became distorted and the sequence just kept repeating.

Eventually the room became dark and Anna appeared on the screen.

"Hello," she said.

Liam stuffed some popcorn into his mouth. Aisling glared at him and indicated to stop eating.

"I am so sorry about all of this," said Anna. "Dawn, if you are watching this, then thank you for finding your way here. I love you so, so much. I knew this might happen, that I might be taken, but I didn't want to worry you. When I became pregnant I knew I was going to do everything I could to protect my child and that would mean I would have to make myself vulnerable to him again. I am sorry, I should have told you all this before, but I didn't want you to experience the constant fear that, at any moment, I could be snatched away from you. It would have been too much and I couldn't bear to see it ruin our happiness. And I hoped so much that perhaps he would have given up trying to get to me long ago, that he would have left us alone to enjoy our life and everything that is before us.

"Aisling, if you are there, I hope you have not already married that Liam of yours because that is one wedding that I could not bear to miss."

Liam looked across at Aisling, she glanced back at him and smiled shyly.

"And thank you for believing in love again, Aisling," continued Anna, "I know how difficult that was for you."

"Liam," said Anna. "You are an amazing man, you don't think you are, but you are. I love how you resist character development that you exert your own self will against anything that is not true to you. That you are just happy. You're persistent and full of fun and full of those silly bits of trivia. Remember whatever people tell you to the contrary, you are perfect as you are and you and Aisling have so much before you. The postcard that she gave you of the lonely couple by Munch – that was Aisling showing you her fear in ever committing to a relationship again. I think you have done so well despite her fear. Keep it as a reminder of where you both have come from because you are both going to need reminding along your path of just how far you have come."

Anna stopped for a moment. She appeared to be about to cry, then continued, "Sorry this all sounds like I am saying goodbye. Maybe I am."

Dawn gripped the side of her chair, her bottom lip started to tremble.

"Over a mile beneath the ice," said Anna, "close to where you are now sitting, is the Tartarus facility I was originally trapped in. Now we could wait fifty million years for continental drift to move us far enough away to melt the ice-"

Anna paused for a brief second.

"I think she is joking," said Aisling.

"Or we can drill down," continued Anna. "The research team here have already started the process – in fact they started as soon after I became pregnant as a precautionary measure. Now, of course, he might not have taken me to Tartarus, if so then this will be goodbye. It's our only hope really. The whole process will take nine months."

"Nine months!" mouthed Aisling.

Dawn just sat looking at the screen and said nothing.

"Any longer than that," continued Anna's recording, "and it will be the end of me and the end of my unborn child. He won't allow my pregnancy to get to term as once I give birth I would be able to use my powers again and our eternal battle would begin again."

Dawn got to her feet and just walked out of the room.

Behind him Aisling and Liam watched the final parts and sat staring at the screen.

The woman in red appeared again on the projector screen. They were back at the start. She smiled and pushed a loose strand of her hair behind her ear.

"Welcome," she said, "please turn off your phones. There is still time to get some popcorn, which is available in the cloak room."

CHAPTER 16

"Okay then," said Anaya walking in from the outside corridor, "would you guys like a tour of the base?"

Liam and Aisling turned to look at her, said nothing, but followed her.

In the cloak room Dawn was looking at her warm jacket on the peg.

"Hi," said Anaya, "Sorry, what are you doing?"

Dawn didn't reply but leaving her coat, started making her way to the outside doors.

"You can't go out like that," said Anaya, "You'll die."

Dawn turned and for a moment looked at Aisling and Liam.

But then she was gone.

Out into the snow and ice.

CHAPTER 17

Aisling sat in the canteen on the top floor looking through the windows at the landscape before her. Anaya was across the table from her. Liam was on the ground floor playing basketball.

Dawn had been gone for seven days now.

In all probability, Aisling had been told, she was dead.

How Liam could be playing basketball at a time like this, Aisling wasn't sure.

Dead?

How could Dawn be dead? What kind of world would they be bringing Anna back into if her wife was frozen in the snow somewhere?

Not that she expected that Anna would ever be back. It was ridiculous. Nine months? If they started as soon as they knew Anna was pregnant that meant there were five months left. And there had been no details of what to do when they broke through. Nothing at all. What were they supposed to do, just storm in and overpower God with an ice lolly?

Listen, to me, thought Aisling, somehow, at same point I have crossed a line and I believe all of this.

"Are you okay?" asked Anaya.

"Hmm, sorry?"

"Are you okay? You haven't spoken all morning. Would you like me to take you to the clinic?"

"No, I'm fine."

"Are you sleeping okay?" asked Anaya leaning forward and stretching out her hand to lightly touch Aisling's. "The constant daylight can mess with your head, even with the cardboard in your dorm."

"Listen," said Aisling getting to her feet, "can you just leave me alone."

Anaya sat back in her chair increasing the distance between them.

Aisling stared at her for a moment then turning, walked off.

CHAPTER 18

Thousands of miles away Aisling's children Cillian and Róisín were sitting at the café in which Aisling worked, or she did when she wasn't half way around the world.

Her children were completely unaware that their mother worked here.

And of course they were completely unaware where their mother was.

Stephanie appeared with their order.

"Here you go," she said placing their drinks on the table.

"Thanks," said Cillian.

"And the chocolate orange cake?" asked Stephanie.

"That will be mine," said Róisín.

"Excuse me," said Cillian getting a photograph of Aisling from out of his pocket.

"Yes, everything okay?" asked Stephanie.

"Has this woman ever come in here? Have you ever seen her?" said Cillian and held up the photograph.

Stephanie looked at it. The picture was of Aisling but with her looking a few years younger than how Stephanie remembered her.

"Yes," said Stephanie, "that's Aisling, she works here."

Cillian glanced across at Róisín. Róisín cut off a piece of her cake with her fork and placed it in her mouth.

"Can we talk to her," said Róisín with her mouth full of cake.

"She's not here," said Stephanie. "Sorry, are you her friends or something?"

"She's our mum," said Cillian. "Can you tell us when she will be in?"

"Oh," said Stephanie, "she never mentioned she had children."

Which was an unfortunate thing for Stephanie to say, as Aisling had mentioned them numerous times. But, well Stephanie was Stephanie.

"Well she does," said Róisín, "please just can you tell us how to contact her?"

"Hold on," said Stephanie.

A minute later Jeremy the manager appeared.

"Hi, you are Aisling's children? How wonderful."

Cillian and Róisín tried to smile.

"So, I'm afraid," said Jeremy, "that she is on her holidays. She was actually due back seven days ago but there has been no sign of her and we can't contact her."

"Where did she go?" asked Cillian. "We saw a note at the house cancelling the milk for six months."

"Six months?" said Jeremy. "Now I'm sure I wouldn't have sanctioned a holiday for six months."

He laughed nervously. Paperwork never having been his strong point.

"Where," said Róisín speaking very slowly as if Jeremy was an idiot, "did she go?"

And of course that was a problem, because Jeremy was completely unaware where their mother was and Jeremy was an idiot.

CHAPTER 19

"Look at all these guitars, aren't they just wonderful," said Anaya.

"Yeah, amazing," said Aisling, her expression conveying the exact opposite.

Anaya and Aisling were in the music room of the Station. A row of guitars and ukuleles were hanging on a rack on the wall. On the floor was a drum set and in the corner a keyboard.

"The winter-overs are here for six months in complete darkness," said Anaya. "They make the best music. The combination of darkness, isolation and cold temperatures seems to be the perfect ingredients for creativity. It's more isolated here than on the space station. It's as if the mind is desperately searching for meaning when presented with a void."

"Don't get this the wrong way," said Aisling, "and I am interested and all that, but it's time for me to go and put my head in a vice and join the Foreign Legion."

Anaya appeared deeply hurt and looked at the floor.

"Sorry," said Aisling. "I just don't know if I can just wander around here for five months whilst I wait for some drill to reach an imaginary secret base under the ice. I think I have made a massive mistake."

"You don't remember me do you?" said Anaya.

"What?"

"Sorry," said Anaya, "I shouldn't have said that."

"Have we met before?" asked Aisling.

Anaya looked into Aisling's eyes for a brief moment. Shaking her head she walked out of the room and down the corridor towards the quiet room.

Aisling reached out towards the keyboard and pressed one of the keys.

A low note sounded out and then faded away.

CHAPTER 20

Liam and Aisling stood side by side on a platform at the base of a huge aluminium tower called The Beer Can. Before them was the white vista of snow sparkling in the sunshine, above them the underside belly of the station, looking vulnerable as if a strike there would bring the whole thing down.

"Are you happy now?" asked Aisling.

"I just wanted to explore," said Liam.

"Because the tower had the word beer in it?"

"Pretty much, yeah."

"What is wrong with men?" said Aisling.

"I thought you liked it that I wasn't complicated."

"Well," said Aisling.

Someone opening and closing a door above sent vibrations down the steps.

"We hardly see each other after breakfast these days," said Aisling. "We are like strangers."

"Like an old married couple?" said Liam. "We have become the couple in the painting?"

Aisling didn't respond, but sighed and pulled her coat more tightly around her. On the horizon it suddenly went super bright for a moment as if someone had flicked a light switch on. Liam saw it in his subconscious but it only made it through to his conscious mind enough to say, "It goes dark in a month's time, we will be plunged into complete darkness."

"Can we not talk about that," said Aisling. "And you, of all people with your silly little facts, should know that we don't suddenly get plunged into darkness when the sun goes below the horizon."

"Well," said Liam, "it doesn't sound so dramatic saying, we will only have a greyish hue twilight in a month's time, which will last weeks and weeks with the sky gradually turning a dark blue. And when finally the Sun is twelve degrees below the horizon it will be almost completely dark."

"Can you stop being such a fact nerd," said Aisling.

The noise of someone coming down the steps turned both their heads.

Anaya appeared wearing a ski jacket, fluffy snow boots and sunglasses over her fully made up face and seeing them suddenly stopped. "Oh, sorry," she said looking at Liam, "I was looking for Aisling. I didn't know you were here."

Aisling looked at her painted on freckles and blonde beach hair. She held a bunch of Aurora's Kiss dahlias in her hand.

Anaya turned and ran back up the steps.

"What the hell is going on there?" said Liam.

"I have no idea," said Aisling.

"Is there something you want to tell me?" said Liam.

"No," said Aisling.

Liam sighed, "I have been going over and over things in my mind and something has really puzzled me."

Aisling turned and looked at him, "What?"

"Why nine months?" said Liam. "I mean that is the time they have said it will take to drill down. Don't you think *that's* a little weird that it is the same time as the length of a pregnancy?"

Aisling didn't reply. Images of Anaya appeared in her mind saying, *I'm sorry, I shouldn't have said that.*

Liam turned and stared out over the frozen landscape. Aisling moved her hand over to find his and took it gently. Liam took his hand away and carried on staring out into the snow.

"Are you sure you don't want to tell me anything?" said Liam.

"No, not really," said Aisling. "Apart from one of the steps in The Beer Can has the words, *earn that cookie!*"

"Is that right," said Liam.

"Yes," said Aisling and turning, stepped back inside.

CHAPTER 21

"Have you used my toothbrush?" said Aisling.

"No," said Liam.

"It's wet," said Aisling.

"Is that a fact," said Liam.

"So you must have used it," said Aisling, "please don't use my toothbrush, that's disgusting."

"I didn't."

"Then how do you explain that it is wet then?"

"Er, maybe because you cleaned your teeth with it."

"Don't be stupid, Liam," said Aisling, "I am hardly going to clean my teeth and then five minutes later forget and accuse you of using my toothbrush. Just don't do it again."

"Come here," said Liam.

"You can't boss me about."

"Okay."

Liam, got up and walked across to Aisling and smelt her breath.

"Minty fresh," he said.

CHAPTER 22

"Have you moved my shoes?" said Liam. "I can't find them."

"Why would I move your shoes?" said Aisling.

"I don't know," said Liam, "that's a good question, if you could just stop moving things around it would help me not go mad trying to find my shit."

"This room is so small, Liam, that I think you can find where you left your shoes."

"I left them here," said Liam pointing to the base of the bed. "Can you see them there?"

"No," said Aisling.

"So you have moved them," said Liam. "Can you remember where you put them?"

"I have not," said Aisling, "moved your stupid shoes."

"Okay," said Liam, "I can see you are just going to be bloody awkward about this."

"Can you remember," said Aisling, "where you left them last time you wore them?"

"There!" said Liam pointing again to the foot of the bed, "I told you a second ago. Are you not listening to a word I am saying?"

"Perhaps," said Aisling, "you were wearing them when you went outside into the snow and stood there for an hour reciting stupid facts to penguins."

"There are no penguins here," said Liam.

"Yes, there are," said Aisling.

"No," said Liam, "penguins are coastal birds. There are no penguins here."

"I know what I saw," said Aisling.

"When did you and Anaya become friends?" said Liam.

"What?"

"The guys I play basketball with say you and Anaya are getting very close."

"I hardly know her," said Aisling. "How many times do I have to tell you that?"

Liam looked under the bed for his shoes and seeing a whole stack of boxes, pulled one out and opened it. Inside were a dozen mince pies.

"What the hell is this?"

"Snacks."

"Are all these boxes full of mince pies?"

"They might be."

"You have stolen these from the canteen freezer haven't you? It looks like the entire base's supply for Christmas. Next I will find you have wrapped up my shoes as a Christmas present."

"They are mine, put them back."

Liam pulled out another box. Inside there was a present that looked remarkably like his shoes wrapped in Christmas wrapping."

"Oh, my god," said Liam. "You actually have. What the hell is wrong with you?"

CHAPTER 23

Tedium and tiredness are what eventually get people. In a crisis you will find the energy to survive, to overcome incredible odds. But not sleeping properly, boredom and doing the same thing day in and day out will drive you right off the edge. Love like gravity is a powerful force but a bit of static electricity can overcome gravity and a bit of tedium and tiredness can overcome love. Love will eventually win, as will gravity, indeed gravity will collapse stars into a whole range of weird and strange things. Love will win with Aisling and Liam but right now they were struggling, struggling really badly.

Getting into bed together had once been either wonderfully sexually charged or a lovely snuggly embrace but now here at the station with cardboard over the windows to try and make the room dark, it had become a place of torture and sleepless nights. If indeed you could call it night.

"This isn't the way to the observation deck," said Liam.

"It is," said Aisling, "I was out there yesterday."

"You spent all day cleaning your toothbrush yesterday," said Liam.

"Because you keep using it."

"Oh, god," sighed Liam, "not this again."

"You spent all afternoon asleep in the sauna," said Aisling. "How do you know what I was or wasn't doing?"

"It was dark," said Liam, "I was tired."

Aisling walked into what turned out to be the dining area.

"This isn't the observation deck," said Liam.

"I'm hungry," said Aisling.

"I thought we were going to the observation deck?"

"It's this way," said Aisling and they made their way back down to the ground floor.

After ten minutes of wondering about, Liam became more and more restless.

"Just calm down," said Aisling. "I can feel you tensing up."

"We have been this way before."

"Can you not spoil what is supposed to be us spending some nice time together for once," said Aisling.

"Excuse me," said Liam to one of the station crew, "Can you tell us how to find the observation deck?"

"Sure," said the woman, "you need to go up onto the first floor and it's near the end, the opposite end to the Beer Can."

"Thanks," said Liam.

"I know where it is," said Aisling, "there was no need to ask."

Liam sighed and followed Aisling up the steps back up to the first floor. Above them, on the ceiling was a map of Antarctica, on the wall beside them a photograph of the Southern Lights. They made their way through some large silver doors and eventually found themselves on the observation deck. Below their feet the snow had made white stripes across the yellow floor.

"It's strange what familiarity will do to you," said Liam looking at the expanse circling them. "I am so bored with all this."

Aisling placed her hands on the barrier to the deck, glanced down at the drop below and thought of when she had felt like this before. She looked at the horizon and stared straight into what seemed to be a second sun. And she felt warm, welcome and reassured for the first time in a long time.

"Do you know why fish don't freeze here?" said Liam.

"Because they live in water and not in the air?" said Aisling.

Liam almost laughed. Aisling to, managed a smile.

"It's because they have proteins in their blood that act as antifreeze. The sea water is below the freezing point of their blood. Clever isn't it?"

Aisling began to cry. The tears picked up onto her eyelashes and began to freeze, sticking her eyelids together.

"Why are you crying?" said Liam, his breath misting in the freezing air.

"This all makes me think of my dreams," said Aisling. "The paradise in my dreams is surrounded by ice. I think I am losing grip on reality. Can we just go back to the canteen and get a coffee?"

"Sure," said Liam and putting his hand around her guided her back inside.

CHAPTER 24

Coffee in the canteen didn't go very well. Anaya was in there and she kept glancing across at Aisling which did not go unnoticed by Liam.

Coffee didn't go well on the following day either. Or the days and weeks afterwards.

"I don't," said Aisling.

"Don't what?" said Liam.

"Don't see the point of us."

"Right," said Liam. "Are you going to finish that bun?"

"No," said Aisling and getting up walked over to the bin and threw it away.

"You are not supposed to waste food here," said Liam. "It's a precious resource and besides I wanted it."

"Did you?"

"You know I did."

"I don't care, Liam," said Aisling. "I really don't care about you or anything anymore."

"What about Anna? You care about her."

"Anna? Who is that?"

"Aisling are you okay?"

"I am fine," said Aisling, "Would you like to finish my bun? I'm not really hungry."

Liam took her hand and looked into her eyes, "Are you okay, Aisling? You are really worrying me. You just threw your bun in the bin and said you don't care about me."

"I love you," said Aisling.

"Let me get you back to our room," said Liam. "Have a lie down."

"Would you like to go to the observation deck?" said Aisling. "We could stand there hand in hand and look at the view. It's like an ocean, don't you think? A vast white ocean with white waves breaking up onto the feet of the station. Waves of white coming in and then going out again. Like white horses coming home after roaming free and then returning to the wilderness. I like the noise of the sea. It's calming. Do you like the noise, Liam?"

"Come on," said Liam, "Let's go get some rest."

"Yes," said Aisling, "then afterwards we can go and swim with the dancing horses."

CHAPTER 25

"What is happening to us?" said Aisling.

"We are on the bottom of the world," said Liam, "surrounded by a cold endless desert with nothing to do and are sleeping in a room not much bigger than a shoebox. There is no night, no dawn to our days, just an endless glare of sunlight on the snow. Do I need to go on?"

"What are you talking about?" said Aisling. "It does get dark. I am pretty much sleeping and waking at sun down and sunrise."

"It's light all the time here," said Liam, "you know that."

"It's a secret base," said Aisling, "being light all the time makes no sense. How can it be secret if it's not dark at night time? Everyone would find it."

"You are confused," said Liam, "the secret base is underground. This isn't a secret base, it's the Amundsen-Scott South Pole Station. Everyone in the world knows it is here. And I am not even convinced there is a secret base underground here either to be honest. It all seems a bit mad. In fact I think everyone is mad here."

"Are you saying I'm mad?" said Aisling.

"No, but you are suffering from the effects of isolation."

"So, yes, you think I'm mad. Just because I went out and flew my kite with Anaya in my slippers does not make me mad."

"What? You don't have a kite and you said you hardly know Anaya."

"Anaya loves me," said Aisling. "Unlike you."

"She loves you does she?"

"Yes. She doesn't hide my plastic toys. Can you explain why when we eat breakfast there is never a toy in my cornflake packet?"

"What? Where did that come from?"

"People who love each other do not steal each other's toys. Are you stealing my free toy, because if you are, then that is very rude and I don't think it's very nice and I wonder if perhaps you don't love me after all."

"What?" said Liam. "What the hell are you talking about?"

"Where have you hidden them?"

"I haven't hidden them anywhere," said Liam, "what are you, six years old?"

"I want," said Aisling, "my free toys. I want them, Liam. Give them to me."

"I don't have them," said Liam, "You don't get free toys in cornflake packets anymore."

"Liar."

"You don't. After they had to recall millions of flutes and binoculars, which were deemed a choking hazard, they stopped putting toys in the packet."

"Liar."

"Okay," said Liam, "the real reason there are not toys in your cornflake packet is the cost, but that story sounds more interesting."

"The real reason, Liam," said Aisling, "is that you have them."

"No, I really don't, Aisling."

"You are such a weird nerd," said Aisling, "the real reason is blah, blah, blah. What a bore."

"Well thanks for that," said Liam. "Thanks a lot. What are you doing?"

Aisling took a knife from out of her pocket and started hacking into Liam's pillow searching for her plastic toys.

"Stop it," said Liam.

Feathers started flying up into the air.

"Give me the knife, Aisling. Where did you get that?"

"The canteen," said Aisling, "last chance," she added pointing the knife at Liam. "My toys, give them to me now."

CHAPTER 26

The sun had dipped below the horizon weeks ago and the base was in a world of twilight. Long shadows cast from the moon ran underneath the station, which glowed red from the artificial lighting. Inside, everyone was doing what they were supposed to do including Aisling and Liam who had booked themselves into the clinic on the first floor.

"So you are here," said the doctor, "because you think you're both going mad?"

"It's affecting our relationship," said Liam.

"I woke last night to find him cleaning my teeth," said Aisling.

"No, Aisling," said Liam, "that was a dream."

"If it was a dream, then how come I could feel the toothbrush?" Aisling showed the doctor her teeth, "Shiny white, even though I haven't cleaned my teeth for a month. He stole my toothbrush and waits until I'm asleep and then cleans them for me. How weird is that? Sometimes I wake up to find toothpaste all over the pillow case, it's disgusting."

"Do you believe what is going on, Doctor?" said Liam sighing. "You really think that below this base is a secret hideaway?"

"Of course," said the doctor. "That is why we built the base here in the first place."

"So in nineteen fifty-six they knew about this secret base did they?" said Liam.

"Yes," said the doctor.

"How?" said Liam. "We had only just invented Cocoa Puffs and Play-Doh in nineteen fifty-six. How did we have the intelligence to find a base miles under the ice in the most inhabitable place in the world?"

"Sorry, that he's prattling on," said Aisling. "He knows lots of useless stuff that is of no use to anyone."

"See what I mean," said Liam, "our relationship is suffering."

"Well," said the doctor, "you know that can happen. It's very isolated here. Astronauts could get back to civilisation quicker than we could. It does have an effect on your mind and push relationships to their brink. But honestly you two have done remarkably well. We are only two months away now from breaking through and then this can all be over."

"Clearly it has had an effect on everyone here," said Liam, "Because everyone on this base seems to believe in utter nonsense."

"Can you explain," asked Aisling, "Why we just couldn't have beamed back up to our ship and then come back to this planet in five months' time?"

"You asked that yesterday," said the doctor, "there are no flights out of here until after winter."

"We weren't here yesterday," said Aisling. "We were at the cycle shop getting a new chain for my bike. Or I was, come to think about it, where were you Liam? Not out drinking again in the middle of the day? No? I expect you were searching for a sixpence under the merry-go-round to buy some white mice."

"I think we are done here," said Liam. "This is going nowhere."

"Okay," said the doctor. "I think it is time to show you this."

"What?" said Aisling, "a party bag of snoopy dogs?"

"This," said the doctor reaching into a drawer in his desk. "This is-" he hesitated and glanced at Aisling, "You might want to see this in private."

"There are no secrets between me and Liam," said Aisling. "He once withheld vital information about a half-price sale on at the surf shop and I beat him half to death with my paddle board."

"Okay," said the doctor and passed over a photograph.

Aisling reached out and picked it up. It was a picture of her and Anaya in wedding dresses. They were holding hands and the photographer had caught the moment of a tender kiss between them as they stood under an arch together.

Confetti floated around them.

They looked very happy.

Very happy indeed.

CHAPTER 27

It was at this point, this point of utter confusion that Dawn re-appeared.

Liam saw her first. She was outside the window suspended in the air as if a god. Light emanated from her and in her hand was a ball of fire. On her back was a huge shield with a bronze buttercup on it and in her right hand she held a spear. Flower petals danced about her like shoals of fish.

Aisling got to her feet and gasped. The doctor span around on his chair, looked at her then pushed a button under his desk.

Dawn placed a hand against the window. Cracks started to appear.

Aisling walked towards the window.

"I think," said Liam, "you should maybe not get to close."

There was a loud crack and shards of glass fell to the floor. Freezing air flowed into the room. Dawn stepped through and beckoned to Liam and Aisling, "Come with me," she shouted, "we don't have much time."

Aisling looked back at Liam and watched as a security team in full body armour burst in through the doors behind him. Two of them grabbed Liam. Another ran towards Aisling and pushed her against the wall. The rest braced themselves and began firing. The first bullets slowed as they hit the doctor as if they were stones being dropped into tar. They was a delay whilst shock spread across his face then he dropped to the floor dead. The rest of the bullets hit the wall, the ones heading for Dawn became petals and curled around her as if flowing around a rock in a river.

Aisling screamed.

Liam's struggled against the guards.

Dawn closed her eyes and opened her arms out either side of her. Fire flickered around her hands then burst forth engulfing the room.

CHAPTER 28

Aisling felt cold. She felt very cold indeed. For a moment she wondered if she was dead.

She opening her eyes and looked straight into the face of one of the fallen guards who lay motionless beside her. They had flowers growing out of their eyes.

Dawn was stood over Liam, holding out her hand.

It was so confusing.

Everything is confusing.

Nothing makes sense.

The universe is under no obligation to make sense to you.

Artistic licence has been used to try and simplify what is going on otherwise you will not believe and the universe will cease to exist.

CHAPTER 29

When you are vulnerable you are open to manipulation. It can take many forms and can lead you to places that appear to bring you comfort but instead cause you great pain. The church, for example is very good at that, providing answers to those in desperate need that lead to the death of self. Which is what needs to happen they will say. Death dressed up as paradise. It's cruel beyond belief. Being in a relationship, when not done in love, as Anna found out with God, does the same. It is death masquerading as love. You will know when you are really in love, but first you will need to truly know yourself otherwise you will be easily duped.

Sometimes you will be lucky and fate will intervene and in the case of this story, fate intervened in the form of Dawn. Anna knew that Liam and Aisling's love for each other was real and that it needed to be protected from manipulation and kept pure. Dawn was to be the one to create a sanctuary out of her love for them. Only she hadn't been ready when the time had come. It had been too early and she had fled for which Dawn was ashamed.

God knew all of this and being not without foresight the base above the Tartarus facility where Anna was being kept was, of course, of his own doing. There was no drill pushing its way through the ice towards him to rescue Anna. The video message from Anna was faked. Aisling was never married to Anaya, she had indeed never met her prior to arriving at the base. Everything was designed to delay them, wrong foot them and calculated to push Aisling and Liam's relationship to breaking point.

CHAPTER 30

I can see that you still want answers.

This then is the story inspired by real events of how Dawn came to rescue Liam and Aisling.

Rewind to three months ago and it will all make perfect sense.

"Okay then," said Anaya walking in from the outside corridor, "would you guys like a tour of the base?"

Liam and Aisling turned to look at her, said nothing, but followed her.

In the cloak room they found Dawn who was standing deep in thought in front of her warm jacket on the peg. She knew something was wrong and not as it seemed. Anna had told her that the baby would be born four weeks premature. Nine months to get to her would be four weeks too late.

"Hi," said Anaya, "Sorry, what are you doing?"

Dawn turned and heard instead the words, "If you are so clever than surely you will not need your jacket to survive."

Dawn started making her way to the outside doors without her jacket. For a moment she turned and looked at Aisling and Liam but then she was gone.

Out into the snow and ice.

Dawn felt completely lost as she made her way from the base and it became harder to think clearly and to see anything as the weather grew worse.

I have mistakenly led Aisling and Liam into the enemy's liar, she thought. I have been careless and have just walked straight in without first understanding the flow of the story.

A halo of light appeared around the moon. Dawn stopped and stared at it.

"Where are you Anna?" she said. "Why have you brought me here?"

She blinked, swept the hair from her face and collapsed onto the ice.

CHAPTER 31

Dawn woke in a warm bed beside a fire with a pot over it. Standing over her was a woman.

"Am I dead?" said Dawn. "Is it all over?"

"Shh, rest," said the woman.

And Dawn did. And she knew not if she was awake or asleep, her mind full of stories that were as real as any other.

Outside the wind blew snow up against the red door of the hut.

Above the reflected light from the oceans and ice sheets illuminated the dark part of the crescent moon.

CHAPTER 32

Reality is a space within a dream that opens for a fleeting moment and then is gone. I am in a story, I am the story, the story is me. You are talking to me and I answer but I have no idea what it is I am saying.

"Are you feeling better?"

"A bit," said Dawn.

"Good," said the woman. She placed her hand behind Dawn's head and offered a cup up to her lips. "Drink this," she said, "it will help get the poison out of your system."

The drink was hot and spicy.

"Read this," said the woman and passed Dawn another book on plant biology on planetary objects.

Dawn looked at it and felt giddy.

She felt the unknown tugging at her.

The weirdness of the universe within her head.

Every time she considered anything it spiralled off into a chaotic narrative as if her whole essence was a never-ending story.

And now, within the hut, it seems more likely than ever that her mind might pop, thanks to the strange events in Antarctica.

"Why are there flowers on Mars?" said Dawn.

"There are flowers everywhere," said the woman.

"Who are you?" said Dawn eventually.

"I am She," said the woman.

CHAPTER 33

Dawn drank again from the cup and felt her mind falter. She could feel it resisting even the most basic thought. Each time she made an effort to concentrate it felt like she was slipping farther down into confusion.

After a while she just gave up thinking about anything and let go.

Her senses increased and she imagined herself floating above the sea. And the sea was dark and without form. Dawn imagined flowers and there were flowers. And Dawn imagined light and a bright halo appeared around the moon.

We all have the capacity to do amazing things and to transcend the constraints that the culture we are born into attempts to hardwire into us. The clear paths before us with well-defined edges can seem reassuring but you are a fool to walk them. And for Dawn she was born and conceived by a god and so she had within her the power to not only step off the path but to transcend everything. She had caught me when I fell from the cliff, but that was only a glimpse into what I had placed inside her. For Dawn was a living and breathing story. And stories have great power.

She is a story personified.

A story within a story.

CHAPTER 34

Dawn woke the next day bathed in light from the sun. Before her the woman was busy making some food.

"I feel so alive," said Dawn. "What did you give me?"

"Oh, just a little pick me up," said the woman. She paused and looked deep into Dawn's eyes, "You are the story in this world."

"I don't know what that means," said Dawn. "Who are you again?"

"I am She," said the woman. "I am the first woman you made in this world. You are the story. And the story was made flesh."

"I have no idea what you are talking about."

"In you is life and your life is the hope of all. I am the woman who you first gave light. Anna is the woman who will destroy the world. Jess is the flower girl. Liam is the man of knowledge and Aisling is the woman of dreams and they are the lovers that will bring rebirth."

"That makes no sense," said Dawn.

"Nothing makes any sense," said the woman, "other than what you convey to it."

"Are you saying I created you?"

"You withdrew into the frozen wastes to seek what you would need to save Anna. And you took the ice from the ground and breathed life into it and formed me."

"I think I am either still dreaming or you are quite mad."

"You can believe what you will. You can believe I am real or you can believe that I am a projection of your mind that you have formed to give yourself the answers you need. I can be either. Which would you like? The first will take longer and will reveal much more of who I am and less about you. The second path, which we are on now, will be quicker and reveal much of what you are capable of but you will soon forget me after I am gone. It depends on if you just want answers, which I suspect you do."

"I want answers," said Dawn.

"Very well," said the woman, we will continue as we were then. "As the story you can step back and look upon what is happening and see the bigger picture."

"What do you mean?"

"You knew almost immediately that the video message from Anna was a fake. You can see all things. The start, the middle and the end."

"No," said Dawn, "I knew because Anna told me the baby would be due early and in the video she made no mention of that."

"You only applied that as the reason for your actions after the event," said the woman, "after you had left the Amundsen-Scott South Pole Station. No, you knew to leave because you can sense intuitively your path."

"Can you help me get to Anna?"

"No, but I will teach you to how to get to God."

CHAPTER 35

Dawn walked with the woman across the landscape. Before them the tip of a buried mountain protruded up from the ice sheet. Mist swirled around it and over the ice and their feet so it appeared as if they were walking in the clouds.

"What is that?" said Dawn. "It looks like a mountain floating in the sky."

"It is a nunatak," said the woman. "The rest of the mountain is under the ice."

"Why have you brought me here?"

"You need to train," said the woman. "Now close your eyes and concentrate. What do you see?"

"I see Aisling and Liam talking outside the Station."

"Put them aside for now," said the woman, "feel the mountain beneath this ice. What does it say to you?"

Dawn tried clearing her mind. Everything went white, "I see snow," she said. "This is a waste of time."

"Have patience," said the woman.

Dawn carried on looking until gradually the faint image of white orchids appeared.

"I see orchids," said Dawn.

"Keep watching," said the woman.

As her mind adjusted Dawn could see that the orchids were growing on the side of the ancient mountain.

"Millions of years ago," said the woman, "this mountain was at the edge of a forest that covered the land from here to the sea. What you are seeing is the memory locked into the rock that the orchids left. Use it to resurrect them."

"I'm sorry," said Dawn, "I have no idea how to do that."

"Try," said the woman.

Nothing happened for a while until the woman said, "Now open your eyes."

Dawn looked around. There floating before her were hundreds of orchids like paper lanterns.

"How?"

"It is your gift," said the woman. "Close your eyes again. Good, now, take the pain you feel at the separation from Anna."

Dawn let the emotion rise and felt her toes start to tingle.

"Now take the guilt you feel for leaving Liam and Aisling."

Dawn felt light headed. Around her feet white flowers started appearing out of the ice.

"Now," said the woman, "the fear that you have that Anna and child will die. Take that and use that pain to find hope."

Dawn started to lift up off the ice into the floating orchids.

"That's it," said the woman. "Now the anger you have towards God that he deified Anna and subdued her. Use that darkness to find the light."

The edges of Dawn's body started to glow. White petals started forming in the air around her like ice crystals. She opened her eyes and let the fire within radiate out until she was like a bright morning star over the glistening snow.

CHAPTER 36

The next day Dawn sat cross legged in the snow with an apple before her. Closing her eyes she held her palm out flat and raised her hand up. The apple moved slightly and then rose off the ground. A mist of yellow pollen came from Dawn's lips and covered it until it started glowing red.

Reaching out she took it and held it gently in her cupped hands.

"I miss you so much, Anna," she said and began to cry.

And her tears became red rose petals that fell around the apple until it was surrounded by them. Dawn thought of Anna and how beautiful she was. And she remembered sitting on the wall of the theme park kicking their legs in the air and she became sad that they would never do that again. As she did a blue rose appeared before her, its sweet fragrance filling the air.

"That's beautiful," said the woman stepping up beside her. "Did you just make that?"

"Yes," said Dawn. Reaching out she took it and held it out to the woman.

"Thank you," said the woman, "I have never seen a blue rose in this world before."

"This is the flower that will be birthed on Mars," said Dawn.

"You are starting to remember a time after?"

"I see after and I see before." said Dawn. "I remember when the whole Earth was white. I remember bringing forth the flowers to gift the world its colour."

"I will not be with you much longer now," said the woman. "You are almost ready."

"I am exhausted," said Dawn.

"You will tire," said the woman, "but you cannot be destroyed. No story can be. You will endure long after the others have faded from memory and long after your body is gone."

"Tomorrow I will rescue Liam and Aisling."

"No," said the woman, "you should rest tomorrow. You need to find a way to conserve energy, each time you use your power you are weakened."

"I miss Anna so much."

"You will save Anna, you will find a way as you always do."

"Is she really in Tartarus under the Amundsen-Scott South Pole Station?"

"You know she is, yes. Why do you ask me these things that you already know?"

Dawn became quiet.

"You are troubled?" asked the woman.

"Why do you need to go?" said Dawn.

"Do you ask that of winter when it becomes spring?" The woman placed her hand on Dawns. "You choose this. I have become less so you can become more. Now, would you like me to tell you one last story?"

"Yes," said Dawn.

And as Dawn listened to the story it gave her strength for it was of the same form as she and she knew that the sword in the story was hers.

This was the story.

"There was once," said the woman, "a sword called Night and Day. One side of the blade shone like the sun, the other was as black as ink. The sword was sharp and true and none that had evil in their heart could enter the land as long as the sword remained. A long time ago the first man and the first woman placed the sword over the house of God to protect themselves from his evil. And God walked in his house and cried out for them but he was bound by the sword from leaving. And God called his house Eden and he called the paradise that the people were in Earth. And the people of Earth lived long lives full of joy and happiness always in the protection of the sword.

Thousands of years passed until the people of the Earth forgot the sword and it passed into legend. Without its protection God sent forth his angels to ravage the Earth. Millions died and sorrow and death were everywhere.

"It is a sad story without an ending," said the woman.

"All stories have an ending, even if you cannot see them in this world," said Dawn.

CHAPTER 37

Dawn hovered over the ice near the South Pole Station with her feet crossed and her arms folded before her. And it appeared as if there were two suns to those with eyes that believed that stories still filled the Earth. And the light she sent out through the land was warm and welcome and reassuring.

It will be any day now, thought Dawn. She could feel Aisling's eyes on her as Aisling stood with Liam on the observation deck and it gave Dawn great comfort.

"I am Dawn," she said out loud into the cold air.

And she was.

Dawn floated up into the lower atmosphere and out into space where she looked upon the Earth. It was beautiful, she thought, just resting there in the inky blackness. Something that should have been treasured, redeemed and restored. And she thought of the unborn child in Anna's womb. And she imagined flowers covering the earth and she imagined streams of flowers rising up from volcanoes. And all that was within her knew that however dark this world had become that there would be a rebirth. There would be life and hope and joy.

And she imagined Anna singing to her up there in the heavens and knew that everything was going to be as new.

CHAPTER 38

When the woman who was She died, Dawn was filled with sadness for she had chosen a path which meant she knew next to nothing about her.

"I will not forget you," she said.

But she will, as will you.

Dawn buried her and sang a song that told of the first woman that had been given light. Forming a circle of blue roses around the grave and on the cross on the headstone she wrote, *here lies she.*

And Dawn pondered her passing, and how really everything that draws breath on this world is never truly gone, not if we can see clearly. And she looked down beneath her feet. As she did so the ice turned crystal clear and it appeared as if she was standing in mid-air. Miles below her she could see how the land would have appeared millions of years ago like the woman had told her.

And Dawn began a story of finding a lost world. And a great canyon in the ice, hundreds of miles in diameter opened up. At one edge, where it was at its deepest, was the grave of the woman. At the other edge, 800 miles away, there was a gap where it ran out of continent.

And Dawn told of the forest growing again within the canyon and it was so.

Full of wonder and excitement Dawn made flowers burst forth in the forest and she called forth the birds from the shores and set a river into motion far away. The river flowed across the ice sheet surrounding the canyon and at the edge it became a waterfall dropping down into the paradise below.

And Dawn placed a home in the story for she wished everyone she loved to be safe there. Next to the home she built a walled garden and in that she placed cherry trees and set an old olive tree at its centre. She formed a lake made of ice in the canyon and set orange trees and jewelled flowers and orchids around it. And she called this lost world Hesperides. And she planted a story within a story, the one the woman had told her of God being forbidden to walk within the garden. And this story was the flaming sword called Night and Day which she set in the sky to give light and darkness to the world.

And when she was done and the story was finished she rested for she was exhausted from all her efforts.

It was time. She knew that.

She resting for seven days and seven nights then took the fear that was within her heart and fashioned it into a shield that she placed on her back. And she took the pain of separation from Anna and made it into a spear. And she took the guilt of leaving Aisling and Liam and made fire that she held in her hand.

And she slept, knowing that in the evening she would go forth to bring freedom, as all stories eventually do.

CHAPTER 39

The present.
The Amundsen-Scott South Pole Station.

Aisling felt cold. She felt very cold indeed. For a moment she wondered if she was dead.

She opening her eyes and looked straight into the face of one of the fallen guards who lay motionless beside her. They had flowers growing out of their eyes.

Dawn was stood over Liam, holding out her hand.

"Come," she said.

On the horizon a line of helicopters appeared in the twilight. Dawn turned and watched them as they drew closer, their coaxial rotors cutting through the silence. Pools of light swept along the ice before them.

Dawn struggled to keep her footing as the first wave of missiles hit the base. In the canteen the glasses started vibrating. The cardboard in Aisling's and Liam's quarters fell to the floor. In the Beer Can the metal stairs buckled and started collapsing.

Aisling watched as Dawn was thrown into silhouette by the lights of a helicopter outside the window. The sound was deafening and reverberated through the room.

There was a brief warning issued from the helicopter which was impossible to understand. It was followed by a hail of bullets. Dawn placed her shield before her and as the bullets hit they turned into Forget-Me-Nots.

Two other helicopters dropped down from the sky and hovered either side of the first helicopter. Dawn took her spear from behind her back and threw it at the helicopter straight before her. A blackness spread out from the point of impact as the helicopter became an orchid. Where the helicopter blades had been the black stems of the orchid curled up towards the sky.

Liam managed to get to his feet and Dawn moved across to Aisling and crouching down placed a hand on her forehead and closed her eyes. Then she scooped her up into her arms and stood up. Another helicopter landed and combat troops dressed in white poured out and ran towards the underside of the base.

"What the hell is happening," shouted Liam over the noise of the rotor blades.

The two helicopters either side of the orchid both launched missiles towards them.

"Enough," said Dawn and it suddenly went quiet.

Outside the shattered window pink roses and Snapdragons appeared and floated up in a great multitude. Exhausted, Dawn struggled over to the edge. Where the helicopters had been, there were now giant water lilies floating in the air. The two missiles had become birds of paradise plants.

"Follow me," she said to Liam and stepped off into the upward stream of flowers and ascended into the twilight.

CHAPTER 40

So God has tired of even having me chained in his bedchamber. I am at the beginning of all things back within my silent tomb in Tartarus. Only this time with all my fingernails removed. What he will do from this point on I do not know. I think to him I am only some entertainment. A distraction from his lifeless heart.

My child grows within me.

I am two months from term.

I can still use my powers in here as soon as I am without child, I am not as before. So I think I am only here as a way of torture. Perhaps he intends for me to be with child again the instant I give birth in some perpetual state of being pregnant so I cannot get to him.

Damn.

I think that is it.

I cannot think of anything worse. To be continually raped by him. To constantly be with child against my wishes. Rape is rape, even from a god who needs no physical consummation to make me be with child.

I am his servant and his power will rest on me against my will.

I have found favour.

And to me a child will be born.

And another.

And another.

And this hell will never end.

CHAPTER UNKOWN

Outside, the sand is blasting the foundation off your face. The rats are crawling up the exhaust of your car and your tyres are on fire from the heat of the sun. The news is all a lie on the television and the eye in the sky is watching your every move, just waiting for the moment when it will sense enough of a weakness to consume you.

Everything is now. Nothing is tomorrow. There was no yesterday.

You are sick, you are well.

You are a never ending cry into the darkness.

You are loved, you are not loved.

You are successful, you are a crashing failure.

You are provided for, you are being bled dry.

You are rising to the top, you are falling.

You are well nourished, you are starving hungry.

You are happy with your body, you cut your body up with a sharp knife.

Your hair looks amazing, your hair is an absolute mess.

You have a loving family, your family are eating you alive.

You have absolutely no idea what is really going on.

Nobody does.

You are middle aged. You are a baby. You are dead. You are a thousand years old.

There is no difference, believe what you will.

On a journey to buy bread you will be beaten to death by an old man who you once smiled at. There is a train at the bottom of your garden with a station that only accepts your ticket if you first cut your own throat. At five o'clock each day your next door neighbour walks into their back garden and sets themselves on fire.

Sapphira Olson

All this is the reality you live in.
Nothing of this will make its way into your waking mind.

BOOK 3
BREAKING DAWN

on the horizon is your dream

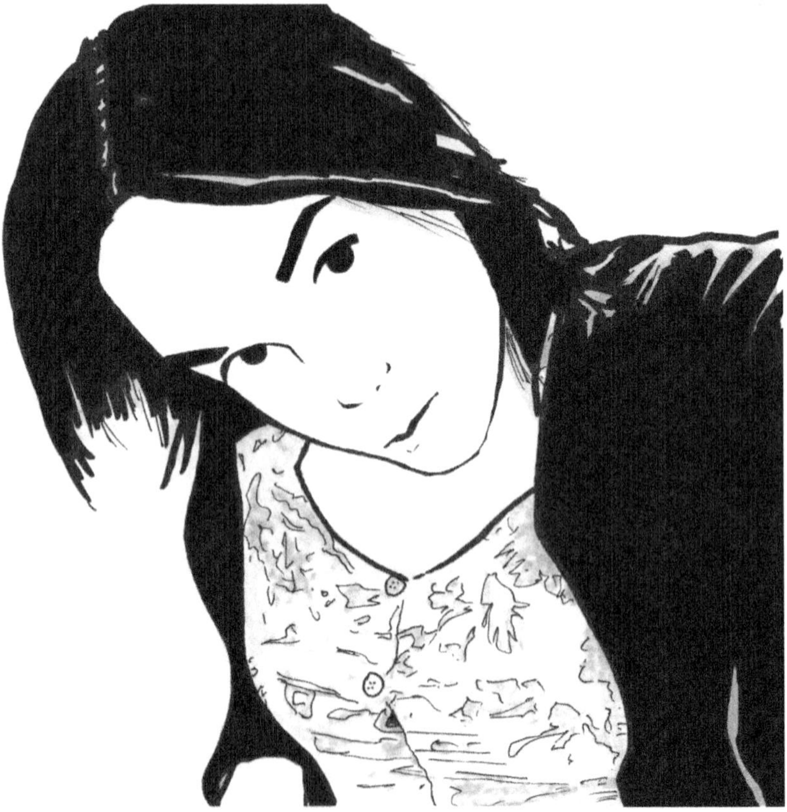

CHAPTER 1

Inside a story is a place of sanctuary that is not subject to the rules upon which humans have built their world. It is not a place where you have to distort your very soul in order to try and please everybody. For all that will live in Hesperides will become secure in who they are and the love that sustains them. Moving and upending everything can be traumatic; the raft that you have relied on all your life has been taken by the rapids and dashed against the rocks. Do not try to follow it for you will surely be sucked down into the waters never to return.

Starting a new life is exciting, hard and overwhelming. Life reacts to us as we react to life. It's a cause and effect infinite loop. Good things will happen in your life if you choose to change how you react to change. Everything will be different. Nothing will be the same again. You don't know anything. It's a good place to start.

This is true when we are born, although you will have forgotten that. It's true with a new relationship, a new job, a new home and becoming the person you actually are rather than a walking shadow.

It's especially difficult when the new home is at the bottom of the world, although if it's a paradise like Hesperides that does help. But to Aisling it was confusing, because Hesperides was the land she had already lived in every night within her dreams.

And so Aisling discovered she didn't know anything.

Not any more.

Not after a talking rabbit.

The madness of isolation at the South Pole Station.

Helicopters turning into giant water lilies.

And this-

Hesperides.

Aisling walked next to Liam, the madness of her isolation still reverberating around her mind.

"I have seen this place," she said.

"Have you?" said Liam.

"Every night I have come here since I was a small child."

Liam turned and looked at her, "You will be okay, soon."

"Are you hungry?" asked Dawn once they were inside the house next to the walled garden.

"I could kill for a mince pie," said Aisling. "I don't suppose you saved them? They were under my bed."

"No," said Dawn. "I'm afraid not."

"Where are we?" said Liam.

"You are safe," said Dawn. "I will explain all after you have both rested."

"We will require separate bedrooms," said Aisling. "I'm not sleeping with him."

"If that is your wish," said Dawn.

"Is that really your wish?" said Liam.

"It is," said Aisling.

Dawn showed them their rooms and when Liam appeared looking for something to eat she sat talking with him.

"Her mind will heal," said Dawn, "she has reacted like this to shield her childlike innocence. It is like a scab over a wound. It looks terrible, but underneath there is healing under way."

"Are you two talking about me?" said Aisling joining them from her room. "Dawn, why have you put me and my husband in separate rooms?"

Liam raised an eyebrow.

"Darling," said Aisling, "will you set the alarm for the morning? I need to be up at seven to get to the ski slopes before they get too busy."

Aisling's place of sanctuary was in creating a fluid reality. It was her reaction to life and whilst it seemed bad it was far better than responding with like for like. For Dawn was right and it would be Liam that would took longer to accept Hesperides as a place of sanctuary. For Aisling switching her sanctuary from one of madness to one of being in a story that she had dreamed about every night would be a doddle. Or it will be until things start to unravel.

Easy.

But Liam was not to know that and he was worried, as we all do for those we love.

CHAPTER 2

Cillian and Róisín had taken up residence in Aisling's house. What else were they supposed to do? They had decided on a course of action and they were going to stick to it come what may. That is the way of things in stories. If this was not a story they would have gone back to where they had come from and got on with their lives and probably never seen their mother again. They in all likelihood would have carried on living normal lives as normal people in a normal world.

But who wants that?

Not me.

I don't want them to die.

So they moved in, in the hope that at some point in the future their mother would return. Besides, Róisín had said, the milk was only cancelled for six months and so there was a chance that instead of chasing her around the world the best way to find her would be to sit tight and do absolutely nothing.

It turns out that doing absolutely nothing was a skill that neither of them were very good at. Cillian made himself busy by trading in real estate in Canada and living in a virtual world. Róisín had found herself a boyfriend called Beau and had been busy falling in love and getting a job at the café where Aisling had worked. Indeed she had taken her mother's job. Jeremy, the manager, had been somewhat annoyed at the length of Aisling's vacation and had advertised for a replacement. Róisín had applied and hoping that she would be a good as her mother, Jeremy had instantly employed her. Unfortunately for Jeremy, Róisín was far more interested in her boyfriend and it was really a matter of luck if she turned up for work or not.

On this day though Róisín had turned up for her shift and was on the counter serving the customers. It had been a busy day and she was looking forward to clocking off and going to the cinema with her boyfriend, Beau. Stephanie was out on the café floor mopping around the tables. A warning sign that the floors would be wet and a second bucket and mop had been left close to the front door in the hope that any last minute customers seeking to come in would think they were already closed.

Despite this a woman walked in and made her way to the counter. Stephanie glared at her as she went past and thought that the wet floor sign should say that anybody foolish enough to walk on the floor would risk instant death by way of a wet mop being whacked around the back of their head.

The customer smiled at Róisín and asked for a smoothie and a Belgian bun.

"Anything else?" asked Róisín.

"Yes, can we have a quick chat?" asked the woman.

"I'm sorry?" said Róisín, "do I know you?"

"In a manner," said the woman.

Róisín looked at her, shook her head and said, "What name shall I put on your drink?"

"Newton," said the woman. "Dawn Newton."

CHAPTER 3

Dawn appeared at the end of the world in a flurry of petals. It was midday, the sun was high in the sky and the clouds where white and fluffy. It was the kind of day were everything seemed to be very still, like the undisturbed surface of a lake setting the sky before your feet.

Sat on a rug on the grass by the waters was a young woman with a book in her lap. She had fallen asleep sitting upright. The sun played across the back of her neck where she had slumped slightly forwards and a blackbird was finishing off the crumbs from her picnic.

Dawn closed her eyes and called a buttercup forth from the earth. It grew up before the sleeping woman and shone in the sunshine. Dawn watched it for a while as the buttercup tracked the sun across the sky then rose back up into the heavens.

Below, the woman opened her eyes.

Seeing the buttercup she picked it and smelt it. Taking it she held it up under her chin and span it around.

The woman's name was Jess.

And she had just been given a gift that would save her life.

CHAPTER 4

Róisín walked out of the cinema with her boyfriend. Outside it had just stopped raining and the pavement glistened in the evening sunshine.

"What is the point," said Róisín, "of changing the franchise to give us a female protagonist and then getting them to behave exactly like a man?"

"I loved it," said Beau. "The finale was spectacular."

"But why? Why does it always have to be resolved using violence? It's just so dumb. What does that communicate to people? Sort out the problems in your life by being ultra violet."

"You mean violent," said her boyfriend.

"What did I say?"

"Ultra violet. Sort out the problems in your life by being ultra violet."

"Your hearing is going," said Róisín. "I didn't say that."

"Anyway," said Beau, "it's just a film. Why can't you just enjoy it like everyone else? Why do you need to dissect everything? You are so weird."

"I don't want to go out with you anymore," said Róisín and punched him in the arm.

"Bloody hell! Now who is using violence."

"Leave me alone," said Róisín and turned to start walking away.

And there standing before her was Dawn.

"Hello," said Dawn.

"Are you following me?" asked Róisín.

"You refused to talk to me earlier," said Dawn. "In fact you practically threw me out."

"We were just about to close," said Róisín.

Dawn looked up at the name of the film on the outside of the cinema.

"Any good?" she asked.

"No," said Róisín. "It was rubbish."

"The remake in five years' time is even worse," said Dawn.

Róisín tipped her head, "You are very odd, do you know that?"

"I have been told that, yes," said Dawn and then looking at Beau added, "Are you going to introduce me?"

"Introduce you?" said Róisín, "I don't know who you are. And he is just another boy."

Róisín turned and looked at her boyfriend who looked hurt, "Look sorry, the film was shit and I just didn't enjoy it. It was like standing in front of a jet engine in a sand storm for two hours with a lunatic shouting in my ear."

Reaching out, Róisín placed her finger gently on Beau's lips.

"Can we go and get a drink, Róisín?" said Dawn, "I really need to talk to you."

"Why?" said Róisín grabbing Beau's arm. "Let's go, she's a lunatic," she whispered and started walking away.

Dawn watched them for a moment then said, "I need to talk to you about your mother, Aisling."

Róisín stopped and looked back, "My mother?"

"Yes," said Dawn, "she would very much like to see you again."

CHAPTER 5

You think that nothing is ever going to change or the change will take forever, or never at all. But on the horizon is your dream and every time you shield your eyes from the glare of life and look with your heart it will come a little bit closer. I promise you. And so it was about to be for Aisling.

She had recovered from her experience on the Amundsen-Scott South Pole Station. It had taken a while for the madness to recede and she still occasionally got confused about where her toothbrush was or who else was using it. "Here, have a hundred," Dawn had said giving her a large box when she had accused her of hiding it in a vase of cut lilacs.

Dawn had explained everything to them and they found that sat together in the walled garden there was a peace that had helped them draw close to each other again. They would sit there for hours in the sunlight letting their minds settle as Dawn told them stories. And where madness had filled the void of solitude, there was now harmony and they felt at one with each other again.

Now Aisling was to be healed from another wound. For within Aisling's mind were two birds that had spent years living in a cage locked with lies. And the birds were called Cillian and Róisín. Aisling was about to be reunited with them. She didn't know it yet, but it was about to happen in 45 minutes. Just like that after years and years. Right here in The Garden of Hesperides that Dawn had made. Full of green trees, birdsong and flowers.

Earlier that day Liam and Dawn had set off to gather oranges from the trees that grew around the lake of ice in that paradise. They had talked for a while amongst the jewelled flowers and orchids and now Aisling was at the door of the house watching Liam return.

In the air above them an albatross soared on the wind.

"Where's Dawn?" asked Aisling when Liam drew closer.

"I think maybe you should sit down before I tell you," said Liam.

"Just tell me."

Liam hesitated then reaching out took her hand, "She's gone to get your kids, she said she will be back with them later tonight."

"Tonight?" said Aisling. "I am going to see my children tonight?" She placed her hand over her mouth, "Tonight? They are coming here?"

"That's what Dawn said, yes."

"And she can do that? Just like that without even asking me?"

"Don't you want to see them?"

"Are you kidding, Liam? Of course I want nothing more than to see them again, you know that."

"I really think you should sit down," said Liam.

"I'll make some chocolate orange cake," said Aisling taking the oranges from Liam.

"Wouldn't you rather get some rest?" said Liam.

"I need to do something," said Aisling running some water into a pan. "Do you think Dawn will really be able to do that after all these years?"

"Dawn can pretty much do anything," said Liam looking around at their home. "As long as it includes flowers," he added watching the humming birds flit around the honeysuckle growing up the staircase.

"Do you think she can bring Anna back as well?" said Aisling cracking an egg one-handedly into a large mixing bowl.

"I don't know," said Liam. "I hope so."

Aisling pierced the oranges with a skewer and dropped them in the pan of water. She watched silently as the water gradually started to come to the boil. Liam broke up some dark chocolate and added it to a bowl over a second pan of boiling water. Placing his arms around Aisling, he held her.

Aisling began to cry.

"I need to go and think about what to say to the kids," she said eventually, "Can you do this?"

"Of course," said Liam adding some sugar and oil to the eggs. "What do you want to say to them?"

"That I love them and want nothing more for them to be part of my life again." Aisling paused and looked at Liam, "For them to be part of our life, forever and ever."

CHAPTER 6

Anna placed her hand on her stomach and felt a kick. She looked at the plate of food that had been placed in her cell and tried to get the motivation up to eat. She needed to eat for the baby's sake if not her own.

She remembered when she had taken the form of the oceans, when she had nearly ended everything prematurely and wondered if she would ever get the chance again.

She thought of Dawn and the joy she had brought her. And she thought of God and the misery he had bought. There was so much darkness in him. Like the time he had stayed out all night brandishing a kitchen knife on the roof of the house ranting and saying he was going to kill all the first-born males of Egypt. Or the time he sent two bears to maul 42 children to death for mocking someone about being bald. Or the time he decided to kill Sapphira for lying about how she had given her entire proceeds of the sale of her land to the church. "Can you not see the problem with that?" Anna had said to God over dinner, "you will have no followers left if you kill them for the slightest transgression. I mean you are just looking for an excuse to kill people basically. People you made. What the hell is wrong with you?"

"I am a loving God," he had replied as if that was any kind of answer and she had just laughed in his face. Stupid git.

Anna thought of Aisling's and Liam's love which had been flickering over the last few months as if it were a flame about to be snuffed out. But now it was bright and clear and true, more so than even before and that gave Anna hope that whatever had caused them harm had just left them stronger and that God had not yet been able to kill them.

And then in darkness, in the void that was formless and without hope, Dawn spoke.

CHAPTER 7

At the bottom of the world is a paradise that only two humans have ever seen. At the centre of this paradise is a walled garden next to a large stone house. Within this garden are trees, flowers and a river that runs through it. And within this garden is birdsong and the warmth of love that flows up out of the ground in shafts of light that glow yellow under the leaves of the overhanging cherry trees.

The two people are the woman of dreams and the man of knowledge. They are sat at a table with a pot of coffee and some freshly made cake next to the old olive tree. For what else is there in any true paradise but the love of two people, coffee and forbidden food?

These two were about to become four.

Right now.

Are you ready?

Okay then.

Aisling looked up at the sound of footsteps on the path. Róisín appeared at the open doorway to the garden. Pink rose petals lay across her shoulders and over her hair.

"Hello, Mum," said Róisín.

Aisling began to get to her feet. Within her was the cry of a new born, the joy of motherhood, the memory of midnight walks up and down the stairs whilst rocking her child to try and settle her to sleep. The night terrors. The first steps of her young one, the first words, the play groups where the children would pretend they were sleeping bunnies, tears, laughter, bath times with bubbles and much giggling, birthday parties with balloons and grazed knees and hiding like lions in the long grass. The first day at school with clothes with nametags, lunch boxes with cheese strings, television with scary monsters. Piano lessons with classical scales, the joy of music, the joy of swimming, the fear of coming last. An imaginary bee and a flower that looks so incredibly beautiful that you cannot stop looking at it. Stories at bedtime, plasters at playtime, bikes, snow, kicking the leaves. A first love that is broken, a record that brings sleep, the hide and seek under a comtoise clock.

All these things were taken by pain and trauma to below Aisling's waking horizon.

Until now, when they all came back like the first rays of a spring morning. Aisling felt so overwhelmed that she forgot what she was going to say and just burst into tears.

Róisín stepped forward and wrapped her arms around her mother.

"It's so good to see you again," said Róisín.

Cillian appeared with Dawn and stood watching for a moment. Sensing him, Aisling looked up and beckoned to him. Dawn picked a snapdragon from out of his hair and encouraged him forward.

Sometimes others can prepare the way for redemption. The words of friends, the counsel of those that are given wisdom, the love of a stranger, the flow of truth that in the end rises up from the river and covers the land in life giving water. And the way will be prepared for she who will come and she will be called Dawn.

Often the most frustrating entanglement of human interactions can be solved in an instant by another like a metal ring puzzle suddenly coming apart after hours of refusing all attempts with little progress.

Aisling held her children close to her and something shifted within her, a blockage that had stopped life from flowing through her as it should.

Dawn stood by the olive tree, old stories of the Earth twisted into its bark. All the sounds of the world that had radiated out around the globe since the first humans had walked the Earth were encoded into its bark. All that was necessary to remember everything. Dawn placed her hand on the tree of life and lifted of the floor. She rose upwards from Hesperides into the twilight and shone out over the land in colours of pink, green, yellow, blue and violet.

CHAPTER 8

"You've lost your job at the café," said Róisín as she tucked into the chocolate orange cake.

"That seems a lifetime ago," said Aisling.

"Everything was a lifetime ago," said Róisín in between mouthfuls, "I will lose the same job now. I am supposed to open up the café tomorrow morning, but I can't see that happening."

"Jeremy gave you my old job?"

"Yeh," said Róisín, "he was hoping I would be as good as you."

"And were you?"

"No."

"I'm sure that's not true," said Aisling.

"Did Dawn bring you here as well then?" said Róisín.

"No, we flew by plane."

"Oh," said Róisín. She finished her cake and got up and started making herself some toast.

"You're hungry then?" said Aisling.

"Ravenous," replied Róisín. "Dawn did warn us that would happen."

Aisling smiled, then when she realised that she had dreamt about this scene with Róisín eating toast she became confused as to what was real and what was in her head. "Well," she replied eventually, "it's certainly pretty with all the flowers."

In the lounge Liam was watching a film with Cillian. The fire in the hearth cast a flickering light over them. Sat on the sofa next to Cillian was the stuffed white unicorn that Dawn had won for Anna. Every now and then there was laughter and the fizz of a can being opened.

Róisín looked across at Liam as she spread the butter, "So he's the one?"

"Yes," said Aisling.

"It will take me time," said Róisín, "but I will get there."

"He's a good man," said Aisling, "just don't ask him about vacuum cleaners. In fact I can give you a list of topics to stay clear of."

"What do you mean?" said Róisín taking a bite of toast.

"Dawn says he is a living and breathing repository of all the known facts in the Universe."

"Is that a fact," said Róisín. "Mm, you know this jam is really good."

"It's Anna's favourite, it's probably the most expensive jam in the world."

"It's divine," said Róisín.

"Dawn has got all Anna's favourite things in. I'm taking that as a good sign, that she is hopeful."

"Is it not risky us all being so close to the base?" said Róisín.

"Dawn seems to think not," said Aisling. "But I think we may be here some time."

"Why?"

"There's enough jam in the basement to last hundreds of years."

"Excuse me, ladies," said Liam walking into the kitchen, "just getting some more beers."

"Oh, heh," said Róisín, "you enjoying the film?"

"Yes," said Liam, "it's not as good as the originals but I like that it has a female protagonist in it."

"You know she is a Mary Sue," said Róisín.

"Sorry what?"

"The male writers on that film only knew how to write lead women as the strong independent female type without emotional depth and with no consequences to any of their actions. They might as well have stuck a wig on Bruce Willis."

"Um," said Liam.

"What can you tell me about vacuum cleaners?" said Róisín.

"Well, where to start?" said Liam relieved to be on familiar ground.

"At the beginning please," said Róisín handing him a four pack of beer from the fridge and winking at Aisling.

"Well okay, in the beginning vacuum cleaners were horse drawn," said Liam.

"Really?" said Róisín. "Tell me more."

"For Christ's sake," said Aisling and getting up walked off to find Dawn.

CHAPTER 9

Aisling could hear Dawn talking in the walled garden. She was sat suspended in the air with a halo of flowers around her head. Seeds danced in the palms of her hands as if they were on the surface of a vibrating loud speaker.

"Please not like this," said a voice.

"If there was any other way," said Dawn, "I would. But there is not and I cannot bare the pain of separation any longer."

"You can overpower him," said the voice. "There is no need to do this. I did not call you here for this."

"You cannot see as I now see," said Dawn. "I need to do this or he will eventually break free and ensnare you again."

"No, you must not do this."

"If I don't," said Dawn, "you will leave humanity with no hope."

There was a silence for a while.

The sound of crying.

"It is decided then," said Dawn. "It will happen tomorrow morning."

Aisling stepping forward so she could be seen, "What happens tomorrow? Who are you talking to?"

Dawn turned and looked at Aisling.

"Anna," she said. "I'm going to get Anna tomorrow."

CHAPTER 10

The Amundsen-Scott South Pole Station lay damaged and dormant with flowers covering the floors where the dead had fallen. And it was if the station was now a reef of flowers marking the grave where Anna was being held. She lay on the floor deep below it considering what Dawn was about to do.

A few miles away, Cillian lay on his bed considering where he was and how he had got here. Through his window he could see the walled garden and in the distance the mountains set into a great ice sheet. He knew that he was at Antarctica but he was really struggling to believe it. He was also really struggling to come to terms with the fact that there seemed to be no Wi-Fi or any way of connecting to the internet. There was Wi-Fi listed as the Amundsen-Scott South Pole Station that his phone was listing as a network but nothing happened when he tried to connect to it.

Swinging his legs off the bed, Cillian made his way into the kitchen and got a spoon and packet of cornflakes and sat up at the breakfast bar eating straight from the box.

"Did you know," said Liam from the lounge, "that most cereals are magnetic?"

"Is that so," said Cillian, "is that because of all the iron in them?"

"You got it," said Liam.

"Dawn, has made contact with Anna," said Aisling appearing from out of the garden.

"What!" said Liam. "How?"

"I'm not sure," said Aisling. "I'm not sure about anything anymore."

Róisín walked out from her bedroom, eating a tub of cookie dough ice-cream.

"So now what?" said Liam. "What did Dawn say?"

"Dawn is going to get her tomorrow," said Aisling getting a bowl out of the kitchen cupboard. "Anna didn't sound too pleased about it." Aisling took the cereal packet from Cillian and filled the bowl with cereal. Opening the fridge she got some milk and placed it down next to Cillian.

"What does she want us to do?" asked Liam, "she obviously has assembled us all here for a reason."

"Pour the milk in, Cillian," said Aisling as she began making bread and honey sandwiches.

Cillian shrugged and poured some milk over his cereal.

"She wants us to do nothing, but stay here," said Aisling, "she says this is the only place where we will be safe."

"What does that mean?" said Róisín.

"I have no idea," said Aisling passing Cillian and Róisín the honey sandwiches. "Go easy on the cereal, Cillian," she added, "you are eating like a horse."

"Mum," said Róisín.

"Yes?"

"You need to stop all that, we are not children anymore."

"Interesting fact," said Liam, "horses eat very slowly and they just eat hay."

"Liam," said Aisling.

"Yes?"

"I love you."

CHAPTER 11

It starts with a bunch of flowers in an airport and ends with flowers everywhere. Jess is the flower girl and will be the first person to place a flower on my empty grave to remember me after I am gone. She is lovely like that. Jess reminds us that this is a story and as such every character reveals something of yourself to you and the words you are reading have an enormous power to change everything. Jess is picking me a rose now from the soil. There is a lot of iron oxide in the ground, everything has an orange-reddish tinge. It is colder here than even the South Pole. I keep feeling as if I am going to float away, as if the planet has no tether around my ankles. Jess kisses me and sets the rose down on my chest. I pick it up, smell its sweet fragrance and place it in the story into Liam's hand.

And we shift, as ever, into the past tense…

Liam was in the walled garden looking for Dawn, but she was no-where to be seen. And indeed given the scope of Dawn's powers she could have been anywhere from Scotland to one of the moons of Jupiter.

Liam looked at the rose in his hand and wondered how it came to be there and decided to head back to the house. Above him a lone snow petrel flew in the sky looking for its mate. As Liam followed the river leading to the house, he could see the reflection of the clouds in the waters, although the source of the reflected light was unclear. Indeed a lot of things were unclear to Liam but he did know that at the Amundsen-Scott Station he had nearly lost someone very precious to him and he resolved to never let that happen again.

Entering the house, he found Aisling still in conversation with Cillian and Róisín about Anna and Dawn. Aisling glanced up and smiled as she saw her lover.

"This is for you," said Liam and leaning forward kissed Aisling and presented her with the rose.

CHAPTER 12

You will miss much if you take too long to think about things. Thinking is overrated. Living is underrated. Dawn knew this as all stories do. You should live in the moment, not sit around thinking about how you want to live at some point in an imaginary future.

Dawn knew that she wanted to be with Anna. She was not consciously aware of why but Anna was always a feeling not a thought. What she was about to do was extreme but necessary and she knew that if she wrestled too much with it then it would cause her harm and so she accepted her fate.

God, she knew, could not be overcome with sheer strength and power. She would not do battle as if she was a man. No, God would be overcome by a woman's way: self-sacrifice, love, and her own vulnerability. God's weakness was in his power and his might and his arrogance. Dawn would use a power that he would understand but only to bait him.

Anna had sought to use her pain to gain her freedom. But God always found his way back in as he had done now, like a weed that will grow out of the side of a wall. Dawn's intention was to get God himself to agree to let Anna go for that could not be undone. She knew that God could not act against his own will, that he could not rescind on his own decision or word. She would have to sacrifice herself to get him to agree but she knew that was her path and so she embraced it and prepared for the first day.

CHAPTER 13

On the first day it was dark and in that darkness was Dawn sat on the wall in the theme park where she had proposed to Anna. The hour was ridiculously early and the place was empty. Dawn pulled her jacket around her and waited for the moment for when she would change everything.

She had learnt much even in the short amount of time since she had freed Aisling and Liam from the Amundsen-Scott Station. She had now worked out how to tap into unlimited power without growing tired and she no longer needed her spear and shield which were still propped against the wall in her house in Hesperides. And the fire that she had within her was in the hearth there keeping everybody warm.

The secret had been in learning to use the energy already all around her in all things rather than her own. Everything was just energy organised into one form or the other and even the simplest object, like a glass of orange juice had enough energy in it to fuel an entire planet. You just need to know how to unlock it, like a hydrogen bomb. Indeed Dawn could have used a chocolate digestive to either get her between meals or to create the rings of Saturn.

When the sun appeared Dawn felt the warmth of it against her face. She was past the point of no return and as the wind played with her hair she breathed deeply in and out, hyperventilating herself to try and gain composure. She could feel her fingers fizzing and tingling.

Light headed, she rose past the drop tower and up into the white fluffy clouds.

CHAPTER 14

Dawn hovered above the world and closed her eyes.

"Let it be light," she said and the sky around her became full of glowing flowers. And all the birds and insects of the air became flowers and all the planes in the skies became flowers. And all that had been within the planes became flowers.

Dawn saw that what she had done was good and floated down and touched the ground. And she said, "Let the earth bring forth flowers, let the fruit tree's yield flowers upon the earth and every living creature that moves become a flower."

And it was so, flowers began appearing where she had landed. Radiating out, they filled the earth and all that grew upon the earth became flowers both living and inert. And Dawn said, "Let every man that has dominion become a flower." And every man that was on the earth became a flower. And the woman and children walked amongst the flowers and Dawn saw that it was good.

And Dawn reached out and touched the sea and all the creatures of the waters became flowers. Both big and small until the all the seas teamed with flowers.

And Dawn saw that this was not enough. And she reached down into the past and pulled every man that had ever lived to be as a flower and it was so.

But still this was not enough.

And Dawn rested and there was day and there was night.

On the second day, Dawn rose back up into the heavens and opened her arms and all that was placed there became flowers. The stars, the planets, everything apart from the Earth that had form in the firmament became flowers.

Still there was no response.

And so Dawn closed her eyes and sensed the writhing sea of virtual matter that was everywhere around her and everywhere in the Universe. And she created flowers from it that blinked in and out of existence like lights flickering in the darkness.

And Dawn looked around her and saw that her work was done.

And God became enraged and rose up from Tartarus into the heavens.

"Who are you?" he said, "to undo all that was made?"

"Let her go," said Dawn, "and I will return your creation to you."

And God took a hold of Dawn and threw her to the Earth.

Dawn hit the ground was a force that propelled her to the core of the planet. And the core became flowers.

God took Dawn and set her down onto the surface of a great desert and said to her, "Repent and return all that I have breathed life into or I will destroy you and your beloved wife and child."

"I will not," said Dawn.

"Then you will die," said God. "I will unmake you."

"You cannot," said Dawn, "for the story can never die."

And God imagined that Dawn was no more.

But this was not so, the story continued.

And God imagined that all of creation was as before.

And this was not so.

"What power is this?" said God falling into a terrible rage.

"It is the power of the story," said Dawn.

"Return everything now," said God and the sky became ablaze with light.

"You will be able to make everything as it was before," said Dawn, "if you return my wife to me. Release her."

"No, it will not be so," said God and made earthquakes to rip the land.

And Dawn sowed flowers into the wounds of the earth which bound it together and God was not pleased. He was not pleased at all.

"This is my creation," said God. "Mine. Return it to me."

"Release Anna," said Dawn and opening up her arms she began summoning all that she had made.

The flowers enveloped God. And the flowers were without number and without end and filled the Universe. So many were there, that the weight of the flowers began crushing God, squeezing him and filling his mouth with petals.

But God's power was limitless. Immeasurably more than you can ever imagine. It is limitless, endless, and boundless. But it did not include the power of being sensitive, empathetic or convey him the ability to see through his own arrogance.

And so he burst forth and destroyed everything in his wake.

Dawn floated above the Earth in the void of nothingness, a theatre in which God had first started everything billions of years ago. There was absolute nothingness. Zero.

And Dawn took the void and made a golden flower from it.

"How is this possible?" said God.

"There is always the chance of finding beauty even when there is nothing but emptiness," said Dawn, "as there is in a person's heart. That kind of beauty cannot be made by you it can only be created in stories. You can only destroy it and use it as a seed."

"And if you agree to let me do that?" said God. "To destroy it and use it to return everything as it was before?"

"I can only offer that up to you willingly. If you let my wife and child go and never interfere or seek to control her again I will give it you."

"I will accept if you also sacrifice yourself," said God.

"Know that if I do," said Dawn, "you will leave the world without new stories. All will become dry and lifeless and without agency or hope. Your creation will become barren and be filled with despair. Is that what you wish?"

"That is not your concern," said God.

"Then it is agreed," said Dawn holding out the golden flower. "I give this flower to you and as soon as the child is born I will give you myself."

"It will be so," said God.

And it was.

CHAPTER 15

Throughout history the heavens have seeded stories onto this world more numerous than the stars. Like rain falling to nourish the land, stories have given life to everything that grows and lives on the planet. Without them everything will die and without them there is no hope.

Humans have sought to turn the heartbeat of the planet into a resource as they have done to everything else on this world. But those that measure something beautiful like poetry about clouds in wide blue skies in terms of monetary value will not inherit the Earth. They will be forgotten as all humans will be unless the stories are cherished and told from generation to generation.

Beauty and stories are what Dawn sacrificed in order to save Anna. There will never be anything so precious held up in sacrifice to God. And that tells you just how much disdain God has for his own creation, that he would do anything to regain power for there will shortly be a time when people will ask, why do we even need stories at all?

The story seeded within Hesperides during Dawn's struggle with God was this…

There came a day when the stories took on the form of a woman. And this woman was called Dawn and this woman loved Anna the one who made Aisling and Liam. And when Anna was taken by the dragon who lived under the earth in the darkness, Dawn created a garden at the foot of the world. Dawn called the garden Hesperides and planted Aisling and Liam and those they loved there and rose up into the heavens to fight the dragon.

And Dawn brought forth flowers to give light to the day. And the flowers increased in multitude until the whole sky was filled with light. And Dawn caused all that had held dominion to become as flowers. Full of anger the dragon rose up and did battle with Dawn. And the sun and the moon, and the stars all bloomed. And wherever those in Hesperides looked they could only see the light of the flowers. The battle raged on until darkness suddenly fell over Hesperides. Those in Hesperides were filled with great fear and thought that Dawn must surely have been killed by the dragon. And they feared that they were coming to their stories end and there would be no more stories at all in the world, only the dark, never ending night.

But on the third day Dawn appeared again in the sky and with her was Anna. And the children of Hesperides were filled with great joy. Dawn walked with those she loved until the first child was born and then she ascended into heaven never to return. But she left the stories in the tree of life which sustains and nourishes all that live in Hesperides.

CHAPTER 16

On the third day Anna awoke to the sound of someone on the other side of the prison door. She could hear the bolt moving and got up from the floor. A bright light bled in around the edge of the door and then it opened.

Before her was God.

"You are free to go," he said.

"Is this really the end?" said Anna.

"We shall not talk again," said God.

And so it was.

"Do yourself a favour," said Anna, "take an aspirin, go have an early night and stop killing everybody, you big schmuck."

God stepped aside.

Behind him the corridor was full of flowers.

Dawn appeared from out of them, like a woman surfacing from water.

Anna gasped and ran into her arms.

And they held each other and felt the warmth of each other. And it was as if before, when they had first met. They kissed and began crying, the connection between their hearts reforming as if they were two flowers growing into each other. And God felt sick to his heart and turning left them to their fate.

"I have missed you so much," said Anna. "It has been hell on earth."

"It's over now, Darling," said Dawn and reaching out took her hand. "What have they done to you?" she said looking at Anna's missing finger nails.

"I'll be okay," said Anna, "just get me out of this god awful place."

CHAPTER 17

Sometimes the Universe can be cruel. Like a long lost daughter contacting you, and calling you Mum again, which you have longed for with all your heart, only for you to find out that it isn't your daughter at all. Just some scammer wanting to extract money.

In this story, thankfully the reuniting of Anna with Aisling was not about to be some cruel trick. It was real and it was about to happen.

Dawn and Anna touched down hand in hand next to the house in Hesperides. Dawn watched as Anna walked under a stone archway towards the front door. Reaching out for the door handle, Anna hesitated and looked at her fingers with her missing fingernails. She turned the handle, opened the door and tried to hide her hands behind her back. When that felt awkward she crossed them in front of her and then deciding that wasn't right either she sighed and let them fall by her side and walked through the hallway to find Aisling.

She found Aisling alone in a large conservatory. She was sat in a wicker chair reading a magazine beside a large copper statue of the god Dionysus. Aisling couldn't believe it at first, it had been so long and the sudden nature of their separation so traumatic. And they held each other, Anna feeling like a mother to Aisling and Aisling realising that Anna was a mother to her in a way her own mother never was.

"I am so happy to see you," said Aisling when she could finally manage to speak.

"Me to," said Anna.

"I didn't think I would ever see you again," said Aisling.

"You look lovely," said Anna, "is that the tartan dress you bought when we were in Lanporth?"

"Yes, Dawn brought all my clothes here for me."

"You always did look lovely. I, on the other hand," Anna ran her hand through her matted red hair, "need a good soak in the bath and some candles and some Tears For Fears music."

"How is the baby?" said Aisling.

Anna smoothed her belly, "They are fine. Just fine."

"Would you like a slice of carrot cake?" said Aisling. "You must be starving."

"Yes please," said Anna. "Bring me the whole cake and I will eat it in the bath."

Aisling laughed and then looking serious said, "What is this place?"

"You are confused because you have dreamt of it?" said Anna.

"Yes, every night since I can remember."

"You are the woman of dreams," said Anna, "It will be confusing for a while until you get used to it. Now then, I need to run my bath and you need to go find me that cake."

"Okay."

"Just a slice mind, I don't really want to eat a whole cake, I'm not a rabbit."

Aisling smiled, "I see you still have your sense of humour."

Later that evening things had settled down. Everyone's minds were still reeling and trying desperately to catch up with what was going on as if they were within a film that had been suddenly fast forwarded. And so people retreated into snacks, and talking about nothing of importance as they all just needed some white noise for a while, some soothing static to reduce the intensity of events that were too big and far beyond their understanding. Cillian escaped everything by lying on his bed listening to Schumann Resonances and dreaming of a Wi-Fi connection. Which was ironic given that he was trying to sync his mind with the Earth's natural vibrations which a Wi-Fi connection would have certainly messed up.

And so they talked of nothing until eventually in a moment, Aisling will break the ice and say, "So the whole Universe became flowers?"

CHAPTER 18

Cillian took off his headphones and joined the others.

"I guess there is no chance of a takeaway pizza?" he said.

"Nope," said Anna and picking up the cornflake packet and taking a spoon started eating.

"You see," said Cillian looking at Aisling. "No bowl required."

"They taste better straight out of the packet," said Anna.

"Exactly," said Cillian.

"You can't take culinary advice from a pregnant woman," said Aisling.

A penguin walked in from outside and stood looking at them. Anna tipped some cornflakes onto the floor for it.

"Cornflakes can last for six to eight months after their best before date," said Liam. "What's the best before date on the packet?"

Anna examined the back of the box, "Three years ago."

"Probably be okay," said Liam.

"So the whole Universe became flowers?" said Aisling.

"Well it's all back to how it was before now," said Anna. She paused and looked at Dawn, "You sacrificed yourself for me."

"You need to go and have a lie down after breakfast," said Dawn touching Anna's arm.

Anna set her spoon down, "Dawn, what you did with God-"

"We have spoken about this," said Dawn, "I needed to end it once and for all. You have been doing this since the beginning of time."

"This world will become a place of great evil without you," said Anna.

"Well it's a good job you plan on destroying it then," said Dawn.

"Destroying it?" said Róisín.

"Oh we are back to that nonsense," said Aisling.

"We are back to that nonsense," said Anna. "And you and Liam, as I have said to you before, are absolutely humanities last chance."

"Right," said Aisling. "Good. Well there you go then. Did you here that, Liam? We are humanities last chance."

"Well," said Liam. "Never mind, it was probably time to call it a day anyway."

"Can we all go home now?" said Cillian. "I am going crazy here without any Wi-Fi."

"No," said Anna.

"No?" said Róisín. "I have a date with my boyfriend on Wednesday night."

"No," said Anna, "none of us can ever go home again."

"Why?" said Cillian.

Which was a very good question to which Cillian got no reply.

CHAPTER 19

None of us can ever go home again, is what is written in the dust on the moon. Some say the first moon landings were faked, but that's ridiculous, it was only the return journeys that were staged. Neil Armstrong wasn't the first person to step onto the moon, it was a man called John Anglin who 'escaped' with his brother, Clarence and Frank Morris from the high security prison on Alcatraz. Neil, Buzz and Michael Collins watched the moon landing on television like everyone else before being dropped in the Pacific Ocean in a mock-up of Apollo 11.

John and the other inmates died four days later on the surface of the moon when they ran out of oxygen. It was a question of beating the Russians – getting there first at all costs to try and regain America's supremacy meant sacrifices had to be made. It was one thing to fire a man onto the moon in a rocket, quite another to get them back. And so a cover story of a mysterious escape of the inmates was dreamt up to hide the fact that they had really been shipped to NASA for their training before being strapped above a Saturn 5 rocket.

That, anyway, was the opinion of Cillian.

And that led to an argument with Liam who, of course, knew just about everything there was to know.

"You cannot seriously believe that nonsense," said Liam.

"You can't bury the truth forever," said Cillian. "Have you seen how fragile the lunar lander is?"

"Well," said Liam, "don't tell your mum that's what you believe."

"It didn't always go to plan," said Cillian. "The inmates they used on the later Apollo thirteen mission deliberately sabotaged the spacecraft, forcing NASA to bring them back before getting to the moon. The survival instinct is very strong."

"The mission was aborted after the rupture of a service module oxygen tank," said Liam. "And they were not inmates, they were astronauts."

"Yeh, whatever," said Cillian, "I know what I know."

"Alcatraz was closed in nineteen sixty three," said Liam, "Apollo eleven launched in nineteen sixty seven, so your dates don't match up."

"Are you stupid? They were recruited in nineteen sixty two. The dates don't match up because it took a further five years to train them before launch, you can't just send people into space without training. The closure of Alcatraz was though a major blow to the Apollo program ultimately forcing NASA to cut short the number of missions."

Liam laughed, "That is the most ridiculous thing I have ever heard."

"What are you talking about?" said Aisling walking into the kitchen.

"Your son has some interesting conspiracy theories," said Liam.

"I know," said Aisling. "You have met your match, Liam. You can talk about interesting facts all day and Cillian can talk conspiracy theories until the cows come home."

CHAPTER 20

After a major event in our lives we try to make sense of everything. We live by instinct and we slow everything down afterwards and watch and rewind that part of our story. Pretty much nothing makes sense really but we trick ourselves into thinking it does. Aisling was about to do this.

Cillian and Liam as you just read had a different strategy, which was to not look at what had happened directly. No they distracted themselves with facts and nonsense. There is nothing wrong with that, it's just an observation.

Aisling though had questions.

"How did you get out of Tartarus?" said Aisling.

"Dawn turned the ice above the facility into flowers," said Anna.

"Right," said Aisling, "Yes, of course she did."

Aisling paused then said, "So, the Amundsen-Scott Station is no more? It was right on top of Tartarus."

"Yes," said Anna, "It's in pieces submerged in a sea of flowers over a mile deep."

"Well thank God for that," said Aisling, "I hated that place. It drove me absolutely mad."

"Anything else you would like to know?" said Anna. "Do you want know about Anaya?"

"Who?"

"Do you want to know?"

"I'd rather not," said Aisling.

"Okay, you have three questions left and then I'm going to watch TV. I have a whole new season of Desperate Housewives to catch up with."

"Why can't we go home?"

"Because our family is safe here," said Aisling.

"You think of me as family?"

"Yes, Aisling," said Anna reaching out and touching her elbow. "Dawn has given up something that she should never have given up and it means that we are vulnerable. This is the safest place for us."

"Are you okay?" said Aisling. "It must have been terrible."

Anna walked over to a freezer and took out a tub of ice-cream, "Want some?"

"Yes please."

Anna took two small spoons from out of the drawer, turned on the television and sat back down next to Aisling.

"It was awful," said Anna. "he kept me tied up to his bed."

"Why is god such a bastard?" said Aisling.

"That," said Anna, "is a fourth question and one that people have been asking for thousands of years."

CHAPTER 21

"Can I have a coffee?" said Anna later when the ice cream was all gone.

Aisling smiled at her, "I think I can manage to make you a coffee."

"I do miss turning into a rabbit," said Anna. "The minute I give birth I am turning into a rabbit."

"That's a little odd," said Aisling. "You may want to hold your child first?"

"Ouch," said Anna.

Aisling put a coffee pod into the machine.

"You are not going to make coffee from ground coffee beans?" said Anna.

"The machine coffee will taste better," said Róisín joining them. "Certainly better than the coffee at the café."

"That's my girl," said Aisling.

"It all tastes the same kind of yuck," said Róisín. "The coffee is too dark, they roast the hell out of their beans. It's like drinking burnt toast."

"I see," said Anna. "Well, you two know best."

"I guess I will never see Jeremy, or the inside of the café or Beau again," said Róisín.

"I'm afraid not," said Anna.

"Shame," said Róisín, "that's three of us that have worked there. Four if you count yourself. It kind of brought us all together."

"I'm sorry about your boyfriend," said Aisling.

"I do miss him," said Róisín. "He didn't even like coffee, the only liquid he would drink was his own piss but he had something about him."

"Um," said Anna looking at the floor. "Forget the coffee."

"What is it?" said Aisling.
"My waters have just broken."

CHAPTER 22

In the past Argentina and Chile sent pregnant women to Antarctica to give birth in an attempt to strengthen their claims on Antarctica.

That is what Liam would tell you if you asked him and he would be correct, although he would probably have given you far more details about it than that. Cillian would tell you how Hitler had fled Germany in a U-boat to a secret base in Antarctica where he fathered children.

Now another baby was to be born on that continent.

Aisling would have asked if she had thought about it, which no one seems to have done so far, how Anna was going to safely give birth to a child in Hesperides with no hospitals. It will cross Cillian's mind though as he tries to cope with watching childbirth.

Dawn would have said and indeed will say in a minute's time that Hesperides is the perfect place for a child to be born into.

Dawn held Anna's hand and told her not to push yet.

Anna tried really hard not to turn into a rabbit. It was such a ridiculous notion, but there it was floating in her mind.

"Is this really the best place?" said Cillian. "Can't we fly her out to a hospital or something?"

"She will be fine," said Dawn, "this is the best place for the child to be born. Anywhere else and God will come and claim it as his child the moment they are born."

"Doesn't he ever give up?" said Liam.

Anna's contractions increased, she grasped hold of Dawn's hand.

Cillian walked into the lounge and put his headphones on.

Anna looked at Dawn, "What will happen to you?"

"Shh, my darling," said Dawn, "don't worry about me. You need to focus on your breathing and trying to stay calm."

"I love you," said Anna.

"I love you so much," said Dawn.

The baby came ten minutes later.

The sound of a new born.

All was well.

The baby was small and their cry soft but they were perfect.

Anna held her child then kissing them on the head passed them over to Dawn.

Magnolia trees appeared from out of the floor. They wrapped themselves into a lattice before the child. The smell of scented oils filled the air and white flowers bloomed on the branches. Dawn wrapped the child in strips of white linen and set them within the living cradle.

"What are you going to call them?" said Róisín.

"Sophia," said Anna. "Their name is Sophia."

CHAPTER 23

Dawn walked into the walled garden and stood by the great olive tree that had a record of everything that had ever been. Aisling had woven fairy lights up around it so it twinkled against the dark sky as if it were a Christmas tree. Along the path candles were lit. Set before the tree was an elegant tall vase with pink roses and Snapdragons.

Dawn remembered Anna's conservation with her about their child.

"The child will be born four weeks premature. It's important that the child is protected. You must protect the child."

"I promise," said Dawn. "But how can you know that? Are they in danger?"

"I have seen it," said Anna. "There is nothing more to say."

And she knew that Sophia would be safe in The Garden of Hesperides where God could not get to them. The promise was fulfilled.

Dawn looked around to see if she could see a rabbit. But of course there was none. Anna was sleeping, exhausted after the birth. Which was what Dawn wanted. She wasn't any good with goodbyes. Beginnings were exciting and new but goodbyes – well you are just sad to come to the end of someone's story with the thought you will never see them again.

And you can't be in someone's story without changing the nature of that story itself, even if you are just watching, even if you are just reading. This story is not the same story now you are here. We think we are just observers of other people's lives. That is so far from the truth. I think if we really knew how interconnected we all are then the world would be a kinder place.

So the story is changed by the observer and the observer is changed by the story. It's a loop with no start and no end.

Dawn knew all this. She was the alpha and the omega, the beginning and the end. The first and the last.

Stooping down she smelt the roses and breathed in deeply. Closing her eyes she sought out the bluebells that she had planted in the garden and she sang to them. Slowly they pushed their way through the soil until she was surrounded by a sea of blue that carpeted the world she had built.

She remembered watching Anna jump out of the car all that time ago when they were driving up the mountain. She remembered the sound of her voice. She remembered the day of their wedding. She remembered everything. And everything was good.

Reaching into her pocket she pulled out an envelope with Anna's name hand written on it and placed it by the tree.

"I love you," she said out into the paradise she had made. "I will miss you, so, so much."

Placing her hand against the bark she began whispering to the tree. As she did so her body gradually turned from flesh and blood into pink and white lotus petals, until she was formed entirely from them. And she was beautiful, fragile and full of youth and the soft, sweet fragrance of a garden in summer.

Hearing the song of a nightingale behind her she turned and as she did the petals of her body floated down to the earth as she let herself be taken.

It was her deal with God. Give up your powers for Anna.
And she did.
And she was gone.
I really don't want that to be the case.
I really don't.
Please come back.
This world cannot be without you.
You have a child.
A loving wife.
This is just so wrong.
It cannot be.

Dawn was the stories of this world given life.
Without her gift she ceased to exist.
Anna knew this.
I'm not sure anyone else really did.
Please let her live on in the tree.
I need Jess.
Sorry, give me a moment and I will return.

CHAPTER 24

CHAPTER 25

It is raining outside. The wind is making a strange, otherworldly sound that makes me feel on edge. I am sorry the last chapter was blank. There is so much more of this story to tell. But sometimes it is more than I can bear and I could not find the words to express my sorrow.

But she is gone.

I accept that now.

And we can move on.

You will move on to wherever your heart leads you.

I will move on into the silence after this story.

I can see the rain in the glow of the street light, under it is Anna. She is hunched forward trying to keep dry in the rain. It has been five years since Dawn passed away. Five years of silence in my heart, in which I could not write. Every time I tried I would just stare at the blank paper before me, my mind just full of silence and emptiness, a well in which I could find no water. In the end I just gave up and sat reading magazines and eating toast in cafés whilst I mourned her loss.

I am in the rain now under the street light for I am Anna. And I am here to do what I know must be done. I have wrestled with this for so long. The world has become even more barren and cold without Dawn. The story has become nothing and everything has become nothing. Only in Hesperides is there even a memory of the old stories.

I cannot kill God.

But I can free his creation from this hell he has made. A world full of rain and darkness and people who have no idea who on earth it is they are supposed to be. Human culture is not of this world, it's fabricated, an artificial construct that does not provide you with an environment that is nurturing. Instead it strips away the beauty within you. You have literally made a world that destroys you. It is not real, but you all adhere to its madness.

Aisling and Liam will live forever in the Garden of Hesperides together with their children and Sophia.

But this world will not.

I have tried seeding new stories into it, but no one is interested.

The world has killed me.

Tonight I will start the process of freeing it.

CHAPTER 26

I need to speak to one more person tonight before I do it. Her name is Jess. Jess lives in a little house at the end of the world and at this point in my story she has only met me once at my wedding as a flower girl, but really she had no idea who I was. I thought at the time that she must have been a friend of Aisling or Liam that Dawn had asked.

She comes centre stage after this story, which is largely uncharted and unknown even to me.

Jess was born to the restaurant owners from the airport where Dawn was conceived, the ones that opened up a little restaurant beside the cute little quayside. At first she was very happy and her mother and father took great delight in her because she was beautiful in spirit and in her form and in her nature. But when her parents died in a restaurant fire she was adopted and was unloved and treated as if she was a boy, because that is what they wanted. They did not want a cute little girl with ribbons in her hair and pretty dresses, they wanted another pair of hands to work in their funeral business. And they placed her dresses in a dumpster and sent her to a school where she was beaten and humiliated.

When she asked for an Evel Knievel stunt bike for Christmas she was told, no it would end up breaking a window and instead was given fifteen pounds for Christmas to spend on a coat for school. She later traded her View Master for the stunt bike and a Barbie which she kept hidden in a shoe box under her bed.

When her adoptive parents sold some of her favourite toys without warning, she took the shoe box and the rest of her remaining toys and buried them in the garden under a cherry tree, where they would be safe.

But in all this Jess was resilient and she did not allow the child in her to die.

I am standing in the rain under a street light waiting to meet her. For there is one person missing from Hesperides before I destroy everything.

And it is she.

CHAPTER 27

I didn't recognise her at first. She had grown from the little girl you read about earlier into a teenager and the darkness and the rain made it difficult to see anything. But when she stepped into the shop I could see that it was her. She was tall, slender and incredibly beautiful. Her hair was pulled back with a scrunchie and she wore black suede ankle boots.

She bought some chocolate bars and put the change back into her purse. On the way out she stopped at a rack where a magazine with a cover of Cyndi Lauper caught her eye. As she picked it up, a man burst into the shop. There was shouting. A gun. All hell broke loose.

The shopkeeper was killed instantly and I could see that Jess to had been badly injured and was slumped on the floor with blood pooling around where she lay. If there had still been stories in the world the man would have been redeemed by now. He would not be walking into places and just immediately killing everyone and this never would have happened. But everyone was now fair game in this life of chance. Nobody got to have a story arc anymore since Dawn died. But Jess had the last story planted into her by Dawn and this would save her, so she would not die in a random shooting.

Jess was young, witty, intelligent and had her whole life before her. She had survived abuse as a child, been bullied by the teachers and pupils at school and had spent most of her life just trying to keep her head down whilst all the while being spat and laughed at. There is no way that she should ever be bleeding out in a grimy newsagents on a Tuesday evening here in the rain at the end of the world. It wasn't fair and it wasn't right. She should have been given the chance to succeed after the trauma. The world sucked because without the last story in her it would have killed her right there and I hated it.

Jess' story was Dawn's last ripple on the pond. The effects of the last story moving out across the waters as if Dawn had dropped a stone into the deep. Jess' sound was weak and she was vulnerable to the chaos, but I had a point in time in about five minutes to save her.

CHAPTER 28

Sometimes when people get nervous or are in a situation, which is really serious, they will laugh. They don't mean to. It just happens. I am the same, but for me it isn't laughter it is turning into a rabbit. I can't tell you how embarrassing it is. I mean I love turning into a rabbit but there are times when it is just not appropriate.

This was just such a moment.

In about a minutes time I needed to act. It was horrible watching Jess lie there in such agony. I wanted to rush in and save her, but I had to wait for the moment or she would be stuck there. I watched the man with the gun leaving the shop. He had 30 pounds in his hand. All this for 30 pounds. My whiskers twitched and I pricked up my ears.

Concentrating, I listened to the sound of a dog and considering mauling the man to death. But, and I am sorry for this, but I couldn't resist it, I heard in the ocean the sound of a whale, like the one I had heard at the start of this story way back in the beginning. It's just my sense of humour even in the face of horror. I just can't help myself.

So I hopped out in front of the man from the lamppost.

He hesitated and I had him.

I turned into a sparrow flew up above his head and then turned into the whale.

Gravity did the rest.

CHAPTER 29

Taking on human form again, I checked my watch and pushed open the door to the shop. Jess was lying there unconscious. I felt for her pulse. She was still alive. Just.

This was it.

Outside the rain continued to fall and the wind, if anything, grew worse.

I had to get the timing right. In this world, a world without stories, the natural order of things would try and prevent Jess' arc from happening. God had hard wired an entropy into everything since the start of creation. Without stories everything and everyone naturally declined into disorder. It was just far more likely that nothing interesting would ever happen to anyone and that you would die of boredom and this was only going to get worse with time.

There was every chance she would die at any moment.

I looked at my watch again.

Sixty seconds until one of the ripples left in Jess' story would be big enough to kick her out of this, with a little help from me of course.

I closed my eyes, placed my hand on her forehead and listened to the sound of the last story.

It was faint and erratic, and kept skipping parts like a heart missing a beat.

But I could hear it. And that is all I needed.

But I couldn't hear her actual heart.

It had stopped.

CHAPTER 30

Liam watched Anna's child, Sophia playing at the foot of the olive tree in the walled garden in Hesperides. Cillian was with them and was squeezing air out of an empty bottle into their face, which produced a lot of giggles.

Róisín was busy leading the penguin out of the kitchen and into the garden using a trail of cornflakes. It had taken up permanent residence in the house and had become something of a pet.

"How old does Sophia look to you?" said Liam to Aisling.

"About ten," said Aisling looking up from writing her poetry.

"But they are only five," said Liam.

"I guess they just look mature for their age."

"How is it going?" said Liam looking at the sheets of paper scattered on the floor.

"I have written the one about life," said Aisling and I am half way through the one about love."

"Do you still plan to do the one about death?"

"Yes."

"When does Anna get back?" said Liam taking a bite out of his bread and honey butty.

"Later tonight, all going well," said Aisling. "She says she is bringing Jess here."

Liam glanced over to the tree at the sound of Sophia laughing and clapping their hands at the penguin.

"What is Róisín feeding that penguin every day?" said Liam. "I hope it's not the fish fingers, we are running low on those."

"I think she feeds it eggs."

"Eggs?" said Liam, "I thought penguins liked fish and squid, that kind of thing."

"Well it clearly likes cornflakes," said Aisling looking at the empty packet that Róisín had discarded.

"It clearly likes pooping," said Liam. "That thing poops every twenty minutes."

"Liam," said Aisling setting her pen down.

"Yes."

"Can I tell you something?"

"Of course, Aisling. You can tell me anything. You know that."

Aisling stared up into the sky, rubbed her forehead and sighed.

"What is it?" said Liam.

"I lied," said Aisling. "I liked about what happened at the cliff with my ex."

"You don't have to tell me," said Liam.

"I want to tell you," said Aisling, "is that okay?"

Liam nodded and placed his hand on Aisling's arm.

"There was no pact to jump off the cliff together," said Aisling.

Aisling paused and glanced down at Sophia who was pulling on the edge of her sleeve. Sophia's gaze was on the plate of biscuits on the table. Aisling nodded and Sophia took the whole plate. Popping one in her mouth she placed the rest down in front of the penguin. The penguin picked one off the plate with its beak and got the biscuit up onto its feet and under its fur as if it was incubating an egg.

"I couldn't bear the pain any longer," said Aisling turning to look back at Liam. "So I pushed her off."

Liam looked into Aisling's eyes. Her pupils reflected the garden scene around her and she held his gaze. "I know," he eventually replied, "Anna told me. Please don't worry, we are all pushed to do things in order to simply survive sometimes. You did what you did in that moment. It was your life or theirs. That was my understanding from what Anna told me."

"I don't see it that way."

"No, I dare say you don't," said Liam. "However three times before that you tried to kill yourself. The last one, you only came back from because Anna called you back to the living."

Aisling appeared shocked, "Anna had no right telling you that. And she had no right telling you about what happened at the cliff. And-"

"Aisling," said Liam, "I still love you. It doesn't change anything and Anna loves you very much."

"I had never met Anna before. She didn't call me back."

"The first time," said Liam, "You went into the kitchen and pulled the knife out of the drawer and were moments away from repeatedly stabbing yourself with it. It would have been done in a frenzy. Quickly, without mercy and repeatedly until the pain stopped."

"No," said Aisling, "I didn't."

"You went to bed and lay there scared out of your mind about how close you had got," said Liam.

"I," said Aisling. "I didn't."

"Aisling," said Liam, "you did, my love. And the third time, when you died in the hospital, Anna did call you back."

Aisling grew silent.

"So, my darling," said Liam, "please don't be hard on yourself. You tried to sacrifice yourself and that didn't work. You tried to escape but that didn't work. You begged her to leave and that didn't work. You died and that didn't work. In the end one of you had to go."

Aisling started to cry.

Liam moved over and held her, "Don't be cross with Anna. She told me those things so I could protect and care for you."

"Well if she was here I'd probably be mad at her to her face, but she isn't."

Some blossom from the cherry trees floated down and landed over Aisling's shoulders. Liam reached up and removed a petal from her hair.

"Anna showed me this before she left," said Aisling and produced the note Dawn had left for her. "She always knows more than she lets on."

Liam picked it up, "What is it?"

"It's from Dawn," said Aisling.

CHAPTER 31

Anna,
I am sorry I didn't say goodbye properly. You know me, I was never any good with endings.
In the beginning was our love and our love sustained us. At the end is our love and our love will never die.
This tree has the story of us and the story of everything in its heart, it will sustain this garden I have made.
Tell Sophia that I love them and though we only met for a brief moment, I could see their story and it is beautiful.
I have set the last story of this world into a young girl called Jess. Do you remember her? She was the flower girl at our wedding. I saw her again before the end and gave her a buttercup with the story within it.
At the end of your story Anna there is only the unknown. Jess needs to meet you there where everything will become silent. On Tuesday the twenty-fifth of August, exactly five years from now at three minutes past ten o'clock at night, you need to extract her from the newsagents on 22nd street in Akira and get her to Hesperides where she will be safe.
Thank you for falling in love with me, thank you for everything you have given me. I treasure all that you are. You are like the stars in the sky, a never ending wonderment shining out. Your influence on me and the world is profound and full of love. You are tender, kind, beautiful and silly. You have a fascination in all things like that of a child, constantly inquisitive and constantly questioning. Your joy is infectious. The way you view the world is unique and empowering. When I am with you I feel calm, safe and deeply at peace. I could feel your love for me flowing out and wrapping me up as if it were a blanket that you had placed around my shoulders to keep me warm on a cold winter's night. The sparkle in your eyes brings warmth to my soul. I love

you so much, Anna and I am so sorry that you will have to endure my loss, but I simply could not see you suffer anymore. The decisions you have before you are ones that only you can make. I know you are deeply conflicted by them. That you live by your intuition and are in touch with the powerful emotions that run through you like a river bringing life. Trust in that river. Trust in your intuition. Feel your way forward, rather than trying to work it all out. You will know what the right thing to do is and when to do it.

Remember the day you sat on the wall at the theme park, kicking your legs like a child? That is always the image I see of you when I close my eyes.

There is no real ending, only stories that we cannot see.
I love you, always
Dawn X

CHAPTER 32

Later that night Anna did not show up with Jess and Aisling went to bed worried that all was not going well. Liam cuddled her and tried to distract her with facts about her overnight facial cream but she turned around and placed a finger against his lips.

"You are never to mention that again," she said in reference to his facts about whale vomit, bird droppings and bull semen.

"It will be okay," said Liam. "You know how easily Anna gets distracted. She's probably turned into a goat, wondered off and fainted at the sight of bobcat. She will be here in the morning."

When sleep eventually came Aisling dreamt of Cillian. He was ten-years-old and had a friend over for a sleepover for the first time. She had brought them milk and cookies and they were busy chatting about how school was just a ruse to hide the fact that adults knew absolutely nothing about anything that had happened after nineteen thirty-nine and that the institution was a dinosaur left over from Victorian days.

Aisling collected up the pizza boxes, cleared away the cans of drinks and began making up the spare bed. On the bedroom wall was a poster of the latest super hero that Cillian was in to, next to that, a signed photograph of an actor that had played Doctor Who.

By the time she had finished they had moved onto playing on the computer and there was a lot of shouting and manic discussions about something. There seemed to be about five other people playing with them on-line.

Later, when she went back up to get the empty tray, she was followed closely by her ex-wife who kept deliberately addressing her by her old male dead name, the one she had used before transition. She was berating Aisling about what time it was, even though it had just gone eight and saying that Aisling should remove the computer from Cillian's room after ten o'clock.

In the dream, Aisling tired of the constant taunting, turned as she reached the top step.

"Please leave me alone," she said.

Her ex-wife just stood there facing her on the stairs.

Aisling snapped and pushed her away from her.

Her ex stumbled backwards a few steps and for a moment Aisling thought they were going to fall but they righted themselves and began climbing back up again.

It was a common dream.

It had never happened, but there it was tormenting her.

Like many dreams there was so much other stuff going on, but the only other thing she could remember was when it was time for her to go to bed there was a half complete jigsaw puzzle of Dawn holding a sword that Cillian had been doing laid out over her duvet.

"You can come and live with me," said Aisling but Cillian was asleep on the floor.

Sighing, she had just got into bed, trying as she did not to disturb the puzzle.

And that was the end of the dream.

In the morning, Aisling woke early and looked across at Liam. He was fast asleep.

Swinging her legs around she sat up, checked her watch and took her hormone medications.

There seemed to be an endless supply of oestrogen in the bathroom, which was stocked out like a chemist with pump packs and progesterone tablets. Which was just as well as otherwise she would have had to leave.

But there they were. It beat having to do a repeat prescription every month.

Aisling walked into the bathroom and sat on the toilet. Looking down she saw spots of blood in her knickers. She examined them and shook her head.

"Liam," she said back in the bedroom gently nudging his arm.

"Hmm?"

"Liam, Darling. I'm bleeding."

CHAPTER 33

A wedding is a beautiful thing. And when it's set in paradise, well, the location is to die for but there aren't many people you can invite. In Aisling and Liam's case just Róisín, Cillian and Sophia. Still it meant that the catering budget was small. In fact the food was sandwiches with a choice of honey, fish fingers, waffles, jam or cornflakes as a filling, which actually I think a lot of people would prefer if you could live in a world where you could just do whatever you liked.

Aisling was disappointed though as Anna had never returned with Jess. She just couldn't understand it. Something must have gone wrong. She also seemed a bit foggy on time here. Part of her brain thought that it was yesterday that she had shown Liam the note from Dawn, another thought it was years ago. Sophia now appeared to be in their early twenties, although everyone else did not appear to have aged at all. And the bleeding, was that the morning after that or later? It was confusing. But then she had been confused the moment she had stepped foot here, actually living for real in somewhere that you have dreamt of every night is weird. The human brain is just not designed to readily accept it.

When Liam had got down on one knee next to the waterfall a month ago with the birds singing in the trees her heart had fluttered and she had said yes immediately, but she also couldn't help feel sad about Anna. She had brought them together and now she was going to miss her wedding. It just wasn't right.

It also brought back memories of Anna's and Dawn's wedding when God had snatched Anna away at the reception, but she had been promised she was safe in Hesperides and she trusted Dawn. And again it would have been nice to have Jess as a flower girl like she had been at Anna's wedding, although to be honest she still wasn't sure just who Jess was.

The rings and wedding dress were not a problem. Aisling had found them and a little note wishing them happiness from Dawn. She has stumbled across a little room in the attic of the house, which she had to get to by crawling through a ridiculously small door. There on the other side was a white wedding dress set on a dressmaking dummy and next to it a dark suit set on a tailor's dummy. They were, thought Aisling, the most beautiful things she had ever seen. And Aisling pretty much was ready to believe anything now, however bizarre. If there had been little blue birds fluttering around the dress with ribbon in their beaks she would have accepted it. Beside them, set on a table, were the rings, the note from Dawn and a garland of woven flowers.

On the afternoon of their wedding, Aisling and Liam found that the lake of ice had melted and so they prepared floating candle lanterns and set fairy lights in the trees. Around where they would stand, they poured out concentric rings of brightly coloured sand with a gap at the edge of the lake which they would face for the ceremony.

In the evening they stood in the circle looking longingly at each other. The full moon appeared in the sky and the sword named Night and Day turned to bring darkness. And they kissed each other with the light of the candles flickering over the water and light of the stars flickering in their eyes. All through the forest the jewelled flowers glowed and on a branch hanging over them a robin sang.

"This is for you," said Aisling and passed Liam a handmade book bound in a ribbon. "It's my poetry collection, the one about love. You are in it, like you asked all those years ago."

"Thank you," said Liam, "I don't know what to say."

Aisling smiled and took Liam's right hand in hers and Liam took Aisling's left hand in his left hand and they stood there, their hands clasped together. Sophia came forward with her basket of flowers and stood to the right of them and Róisín stepped forward and stood to the left. Cillian took the garland of woven flowers that Dawn had made and began wrapping it around Aisling's and Liam's hands.

"All that I am," said Aisling as Cillian bound their hands together, "I give to you. All that will be, will be with you. All my days, will be days lived with you. And all my laughter will be laughter shared with you."

"Everything within me," said Liam, "I give to you. Every heart beat will be my heart beating for you. Every moment, will be a moment with you."

"All that I have," replied Aisling, "I have with you. All my tears will be tears cried with you. All of my joy, will be joy in you."

"I give myself to you," said Liam.

"I give myself to you," said Aisling.

And in the eyes of the innocents they were bound together forever and ever.

CHAPTER 34

Tuesday the twenty-fifth of August, three minutes past ten o'clock.

I checked Jess' heart again, but it was still, like the undisturbed surface of a lake setting the sky before your feet. I could hear the ripple in her story though. It was so loud. The rush of a waterfall suddenly filled my mind. Picking up Jess in my arms, I stood with her cradled there and let the sound engulf us as if we were on a beach standing with our backs against a huge wave.

And I became the waterfall and let the story take us to Hesperides.

At the bottom of the waterfall she sank down with her arms held out either side of her into the ice cold river as if she was falling into a deep dream. She floated there with her hair flowing in the current. I swirled around her for a moment sending bubbles to the surface until I could see Aisling swimming down. Aisling placed her arms under Jesses and kicked for the surface.

Relieved, I let myself go and flowed through the forest to the sea until I eventually appeared again in the shop on 22nd street in Akira.

Jess was gone. I could sense her heartbeat again though.

It had worked.

The last story had ended.

Now I was free to bring this all to an end.

CHAPTER 35

Aisling was there, waiting.

After all these years.

She had hoped Anna would be there as well, but she was nowhere to be seen.

Aisling swam down and grabbed Jess then kicking hard took her to the surface of the river. The sound of the waterfall was deafening. She could remember this scene from her dream years ago – the one the night before she had fished off the jetty for crabs with Liam. And in last night's dream she had met a woman who told her the time had come and to be here for Jess. Who the woman was Aisling was unclear on. It might have even been Jess herself.

Aisling headed to the riverbank. The sun was bright in the sky above her, the trees full of fruit and the day endless. Liam was waiting at the river bank with a blanket. Sophia was wearing sunglasses and was sat on a rug on the grass with their penguin listening to music on their headphones.

Liam brought the blanket and wrapped it around Jess, "You were right," he said. "Sorry I didn't believe you, it's just been so long."

"She is breathing," said Aisling, "but she's very cold."

Sophia got up, walked over to Jess and placed a hand on her forehead.

Nothing happened for a minute.

The penguin turned around and started staring at a tree.

Jess' body became warm. She blinked and opened her eyes.

"Hello," said Aisling, "welcome to Hesperides."

CHAPTER 36

"We've run out of jam," said Cillian back at the house in Hesperides.

"Anna won't be pleased," said Róisín. "Is there anything else?"

"Honey," said Cillian. "There's enough honey here to feed an army."

"So have honey."

"I want jam," said Cillian.

"I want my boyfriend," said Róisín. "Although he's probably married with kids by now."

"I know that it is really cool that we made up with mum," said Cillian, "but we can't live with her forever. I don't want to be forty and still be living with my mum."

Róisín nodded, "It does feel like we have lived here forever already."

"It's beautiful," said Cillian, "but there is no internet here. I can't talk to my friends, I can't do anything. I just want to go home. In fact I'm desperate to go home. If I don't get on-line soon I am going to seriously lose my shit."

"I want to go out and party," said Róisín, "I want to live. I want to travel the world, there is so much I want to see."

"Did Anna really say none of us can ever go home again?" said Cillian. "Or that *some* of us can never go home again?"

"Dawn said that Sophia would be in danger if they left," said Róisín, "but she made no mention of us."

"We should just go now," said Cillian.

"What right now before Aisling and Liam get back?"

"Yes," said Cillian, "they will just try and talk us out of it. We can come back and visit them, it's not like we are never going to see them again."

"How would we even get home though?" said Róisín. "We're encircled by ice and the sea is eight hundred miles away."

"You haven't worked it out yet have you?" said Cillian.

"Worked out what?"

"We have lived here for years. Do you not think the world would have discovered this paradise by now?"

"What?"

"I travelled all the way to the sea last month," said Cillian.

"How? Why? I thought you had gone camping. You said you needed some time on your own to get your head straight."

"I was looking for a way out," said Cillian. "Do you know what I found there?"

"A year's supply of fruit cake and internet?"

"Ha, very funny," said Cillian. "I found a wall of water at the edge with a landing craft on top, a cruise ship near an iceberg and tourists wondering about in the air above me with penguins. Hesperides doesn't exist as we know it. We are largely below sea level for starters. We would be flooded. In the real world the ice is still all there."

"We are living inside ice?"

"It would seem so."

"Right, and you didn't tell anyone else about this until now because?"

"I didn't want the others to know that I was desperate to leave," said Cillian, "that that was the reason I went off."

"Right, okay," said Róisín, "but you could have told me."

"I'm telling you now."

"You couldn't leave without me last month could you? That is why you came back."

"Maybe," said Cillian.

"You never did like doing things on your own."

"The orca whale took my breath away," said Cillian.

"Sorry?"

"At the edge of the sea. It was like being at an aquarium with the wall of water rising up before me, although there was no glass. An orca just swam right up and looked at me. It was the most amazing thing I have ever seen in my life."

CHAPTER 37

Liam carried Jess in his arms through the stone archway of the house. Jess seemed slightly delirious and was asking where her earrings were and reciting lines from Ghostbusters to Liam.

"Get her into the lounge," said Aisling, "and put her by the fire."

"Where am I?" said Jess. "Where are my chocolate bars?"

"It's okay," said Liam. "You're safe."

Liam placed her on the sofa and put a pillow under her head.

"Hello," said Sophia walking over to Jess and giving her a chocolate bar, "this is Boop my penguin."

"I order you to cease any and all supernatural activity," said Jess, "and return forthwith to your place of origin."

"Róisín," said Aisling, "Can you make Jess a hot lemon drink with honey."

There was no reply.

Aisling checked around for her. She was nowhere to be seen.

But she did spot something propped up on the breakfast bar.

It was an envelope addressed to her and Liam.

She walked across, opened it, read it and then stood there staring into the fire.

"What's wrong?" said Liam coming back in with another pillow.

The letter slipped from Aisling's fingers and fell towards the floor.

Around her butterflies fluttered about the blue passion flowers covering the kitchen.

Aisling looked at Liam then bending over threw up.

CHAPTER 38

22nd street in Akira…

You know what, I may be as a god but sometimes I lose track of time. Time here runs over fifty times faster than Hesperides now Dawn is no more. Once Dawn let go the whole world sped up as time flowed superfast without stories slowing everything down. Everything became automatic without context and meaning. Sixty six times faster to be precise. What is over in a minute here takes over an hour to happen in Hesperides. It took me twelve days to flow from the waterfall to the sea, so that's, um, oh god two years have passed here. My plan of destroying the world should have happened over two years ago.

Everyone I love is safe in Hesperides. Dawn created it as a story that is separate from this world. I have changed my mind a thousand times as to how to do this and who to save. But now, I think, I may have lost everyone that isn't in Hesperides. I should have acted quicker. God has truly made this hell on earth and I cannot let people suffer here for all eternity thinking they are living, when in fact they are being perpetually reborn into a living hell.

Liam and Aisling are together now, I will leave the love that is in Hesperides as a seed and beacon in the heavens for those that come after this story. Who they are and what stories they will have I do not know for I won't be here. Not any more. I no longer want to spin this world, instead ever so gently I am going to place a hand on the South Pole and my other on the north and stop this merry-go-round.

And after that there will only be silence.

You will not hear of me again and I will only exist in your imagination.

And unless you make it to Hesperides before this story's end you will die.

You know the way. Everything you need is in this story.

CHAPTER 39

Aisling finished making the honey sandwiches and began packing them into a bag. Jess was next to her shoving as many chocolate bars as she could into a rucksack. Liam was explaining to Sophia that they were going to have to leave the penguin behind, which was not going well.

"Sophia," said Liam, "We can't take her. It's too far and look, she is incubating another biscuit, she won't leave it."

"Penguins travel long distances," said Sophia. "That's what you said."

"That's true, but she will slow us down. She will be fine here. We will leave her plenty of fish fingers, boiled eggs and cornflakes."

Liam glanced up at the sound of Aisling rushing to the toilet.

Sophia opened their eyes wide and looked at Liam, "Please, Dad. Please let me take her."

"We have to try and catch up with your brother and sister," said Liam. "She really will slow us down. It's really important that we stop them from leaving the protection of Hesperides."

Aisling walked back into the kitchen looking white.

"Are you okay?" said Jess.

"I'm pregnant," said Aisling holding up a test strip.

"Sorry, what?" said Liam.

"I'm pregnant."

"You can't be," said Liam.

"Why can't she be?" said Jess.

"I don't have a womb," said Aisling.

CHAPTER 40

Cillian and Róisín stood looking at the wall of water before them. It had taken them far longer to reach than Cillian remembered. But here they were. Before them the sea teamed with life as if all the creatures of the deep had gathered here from all over the Earth.

Cillian reached out and pushed his hand into the water, "This seems higher than before."

"How do we get out?" said Róisín.

Cillian looked up. Were before there had been people walking about in the air, now it was teeming with animals.

"I am not sure," said Cillian.

"Is this a good idea?" said Róisín. "This is freaking me out."

"Hold your breath," said Cillian and taking her hand they walked into the water.

CHAPTER UNKOWN

You are standing waiting for it to be your turn at the post office.

It will never be your turn. It is your turn now. It was your turn an hour ago.

Say what you will, but the cherry tree grows despite your howling indifference.

If all the pain of your life was a beacon on a hilltop it still would not stop your brothers from hunting you down.

Everything has broken, nothing works as it's supposed to do.

Your fridge keeps beeping at you to warn you the door is open. The fridge door is shut.

You receive an urgent phone call from a person in Delhi.

The fruit you bought this morning has mould on it.

Your brothers contact you to say you almost killed your mother in a road accident and she is on life-support in hospital. You don't drive and are confused and protest your innocence as you walk to catch a bus to get to the hospital.

The roof blows off your house and all your pet mice are dead.

Your bin blows into the road in the middle of the night and spews half decayed daffodils everywhere.

You amass a fortune in ten pence pieces in a sealed room in your house which you have set aside for your pension fund. It collapses under the weight of the coins and you have to have the ceiling replastered.

The weather forecast is sunshine and showers but the sunshine doesn't show up.

A letter from the bank arrives in the post informing you that you need to fill in the enclosed form. You fill it out and return it. The bank keeps sending you the same form for ten years.

You spill your coffee on your favourite top and snag your cardigan on the door handle.

Your dad shows up unannounced and just stands about saying nothing and eating all your cake. He leaves three hours later and says he will see you again on Friday.

All the houses on your street collapse into the ground as you walk past them on the way home from buying a packet of crisps.

You have to use your phone to start your electric toothbrush. It is downloading a software update that takes five hours. You have no idea what that update is for or why you can no longer buy a normal toothbrush in the shops.

There is no water left, the government are sorry but unless it rains in the next three days everyone will die of thirst.

A heatwave hits that lasts three months.

You survive by sitting in the fridge, listening to it beeping at you and sucking on ice cubes from the freezer.

Afterwards you find you are the only person alive and go and stand in wait again at the post office to send letters of regret. There are cardboard cut outs before you of the millions of people that have died.

Live and repeat this until you die whilst your cortisol eats you alive.

Good luck.

BOOK 4
THE END OF THE WORLD

the roar of death and the terrible
waste of a life not yet lived

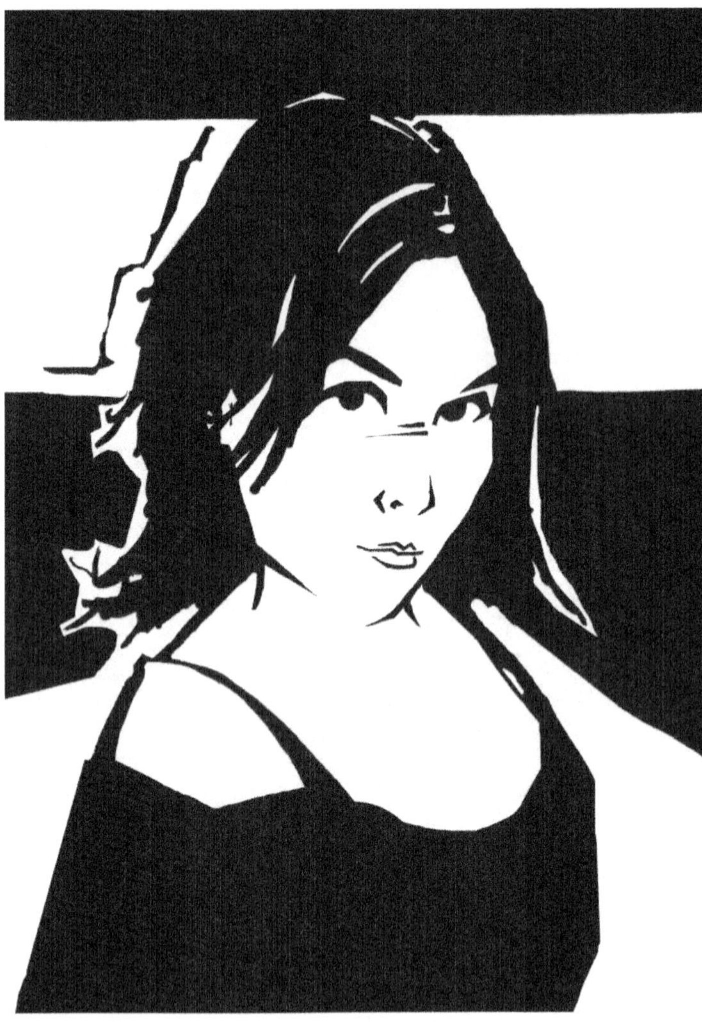

CHAPTER 1

Even bees can compute zero in their tiny brains. Humans can, although they don't really like it or give it any worth even though zero lies at the heart of their science, engineering and mathematics. Without it none of their technology would work. For years you even banned it as a number as you believed it would encourage fraud and was a gateway to negative numbers. But the absence of something is a thing in itself and that is what Dawn made beautiful when she fought God.

I wish I could have done that with Sophia, found beauty in my nothingness.

Years ago when Sophia was born I struggled. I didn't mention it before because I am not proud of it and it confuses me. I never had strong feelings for them. Every time I looked at them I just felt nothing as if I was watching a blank screen. I couldn't understand it. I know a lot of people feel the same way after giving birth, complete indifference. It's not really talked about as it feels like a crashing failure, an absence of motherhood.

It is part of the reason there is a five year gap in this story between the death of Dawn and the rescue of Jess. Somehow Dawn and Jess are connected in ways I can't understand. It could be that Dawn was my first love and Jess my last, but that maybe is another tale yet to come.

I thought being a mother was natural, that you just knew what to do and that I would bond and feel great love for Sophia.

I didn't.

Sophia would wake at all hours of the night and would never keep still. I became perpetually tired and weary. I became cross, angry and irritable. For a while I did not know myself. What should have been times of bonding, like bathing Sophia and taking them for walks by the river just left me cold. They should have been special moments to treasure forever, instead I was bored and restless. I tried everything. I took a cast of Sophia's hand, painted it gold and wrote their name on it. I made flower chains and painted their room with pictures of bluebells and butterflies. I changed into a rabbit and played sleeping bunnies. I became a cow, a sheep and a horse as Aisling sang *Old Mcdonald Had A Farm*. All these things should have filled me with wonder.

They did not.

I felt empty inside and would lie staring at the ceiling unable to sleep.

But still nothing.

A void as if my heart had died.

It may be because of the father and the nature of Sophia's conception but I wish I could have felt more. I have never felt nothing before.

I still feel nothing now.

I always feel something and that scares me.

Aisling and Liam will parent Sophia, they have enough love to fill every ocean on every world that I have made.

I think it is indeed time for me to find a life outside this story.

CHAPTER 2

Earlier, Anna had asked Aisling if she wanted to know what had happened to Anaya during their extraction by Dawn from the Amundsen-Scott South Pole Station. It would have been interesting to see what Aisling's reaction would have been because Anna knew full well who Anaya was and what had happened to her.

When you have a family that continually hurts you and causes you harm then are they a family to you at all? What does it mean to be family?

Anna knew who Anaya was because she was her sister.

Although she was no longer family.

I'm pregnant, dressed in hessian and kept trapped like a wild animal, Anna had called out into the ether when she was imprisoned in Tartarus. *I see him each night as he takes his lover to bed and I am sat on the floor screaming out in my mind to Dawn. Please come and save me from this.*

That lover was Anaya.

Anna had had to watch her own sister make love to God whilst she herself was chained to a ring on the floor. And God was not pleased with Anaya for failing to split up Aisling and Liam, not pleased at all.

It was a shame that Anna hadn't spoken to Anaya, because Anaya herself was living a nightmare and not only did she feel horribly trapped by God, she had also started to have genuine feelings for Aisling.

God knew this of course and it gave him an enormous sense of well-being.

Because God, as we have seen, is inherently evil.

You might think Anna rash for wanting to destroy the world. But you have not even the slightest idea of how much he has manipulated your world to cause you pain.

God is certainly not like family to you.

Best to find people that love you, care for you, rejoice with you and cry with you, not someone who is so indifferent to your feelings that they will care more for their own importance than even your most basic of needs.

"You failed in your calling," God said to Anaya.

"I did what you asked," said Anaya. "I did more than you asked, she fell in love with me."

"And you fell in love with her?" said God.

"Yes," said Anaya.

"Liar!" said God and placed her once again in the molten core of the Earth.

CHAPTER 3

In the event of war please become pregnant. The National Milk Scheme was introduced in June 1940 for all pregnant women the same year that German planes began dropping high-explosive bombs over London. In 1942 as the war waged on, pregnant woman were also provided free or inexpensive orange juice, cod liver oil or vitamin A and D tablets. The value of children soared, the future of the country depended on them as hundreds of thousands of adults died.

Aisling wasn't caught up in a war although she was caught up in a mass extinction event of the human race, but no milk or cod liver oil was delivered outside the stone archway of the house. But she could exercise though, which was still considered to be good advice for expectant mothers. Not all the way to the end of Hesperides though, no Liam had left on that trip alone after the news that she was pregnant, this was a short walk with Jess up into the woods.

"I'm not sure we can cross here," said Aisling.

"It will be okay," said Jess, "I can take my shoes off."

Aisling and Jess looked at the stream which had swollen with water since the last time they had passed this way. Above them swallows flitted about in the air and beside the stream there was every kind of tree that you could imagine growing side by side along the bank.

Aisling looked back up the hill, "We could try and see if we cross farther along."

"I'll be fine," said Jess slipping off her white trainers.

Before them a line of stepping stones crossed the stream. They were wet, slippy and looked highly unstable.

"Okay," said Aisling, "I'll go first," and she started making her way across the stepping stones.

On the second stone, she slipped and set a foot down into the freezing water.

"Good job you have your boots on," said Jess.

Aisling laughed, "You could borrow mine once I have crossed. I can take them off and throw them across to you."

"I'm all right," said Jess placing her bare foot on the first stepping stone. "Keep going."

Aisling looked down. Around the stones, minnows swam with electric eels.

"There are some strange fish in the water," said Jess noticing one of the eels.

"When we were first here," said Aisling, "there were only little silver fish, recently I have seen catfish, bull sharks, candiru and piranha."

"You are telling me this now?" said Jess, "after I have taken my socks off?" She took another tentative step.

Tiny neon tetra fish flowed past her in the swirling bubbles.

Once safely at the other side Aisling and Jess paused thankful that neither of them had actually fallen in and then seeing a large granite rock walked over to it.

"You said you have seen candiru in the water," said Jess as they sat. "Don't they launch themselves up out of the river into people's urine?"

Aisling laughed, "The penis fish! No, Liam says that is a myth, although he is still very careful never to wee in the river!"

"Why are men so disgusting that they would even think to pee in the river?" said Jess.

Aisling smiled and looked at the bluebells growing around them.

"Jess," she said after a while.

"Yes."

"Why did Dawn want Anna to bring you here?"

"I don't know."

"Did Anna say anything to you?" said Aisling.

"I don't remember," said Jess. "I don't think so. You are assuming it was Anna that brought me here."

"But the letter," said Aisling.

"Yes, but you don't know for sure it was her," said Jess. "All I remember is a gunshot, then numbness and a burning sensation. After that nothing until I was in the river."

"Anna said nothing at all to you? Nothing that would indicate where she might be now?"

Jess reached out and took Aisling's hand, "I know she is important to you. I'm sorry I can't tell you anything."

Aisling sighed and watched two otters making their way through the grass back towards the stream.

"Do you miss home?" said Aisling.

"No," said Jess, "my girlfriend broke up with me the week before I ended up here. I thought I was imagining the whole thing to be honest. This is like a dream that I have escaped a lifetime of sorrow into."

"You were very sweet at Anna and Dawn's wedding," said Aisling, "with your little basket of flowers. You looked happy then."

"I don't really remember that."

"You said that you were adopted, what where they like?"

"My adopted mother," said Jess, "tried to kill me three times. Once she threw me out of the car, another time she tried drowning me in the bath and the third time she pushed me off the harbour wall into the sea one December night when we were watching the Christmas lights being turned on. I don't call her mum any more."

As Jess continued small stones on the stream's bed started oscillating together as if they were becoming agitated. As they started rising up out of the stream Aisling noticed them and looked across at Jess.

"My adopted dad," continued Jess, "who I have never called dad and just Darren, injected me with steroids every night before bedtime saying he didn't want me getting arthritis like his great aunt Maud."

"I'm sorry, he did what?"

"It made me put on weight, gave me headaches and stopped me sleeping properly for years."

"That's horrible, said Aisling, "what the hell was wrong with them?"

"I don't know," said Jess, "it's a wonder I am still alive talking to you now. Once I arrived home one day to find they had sold most of my toys without warning. I took what was left and buried them in the garden to keep them safe."

"That's so sad."

"They wanted me to be a boy," said Jess. "They dressed me as boy and encouraged me to get into fights. Why they wanted to adopt I really don't know."

"Like you said," said Aisling, "there are some strange fish in the river."

CHAPTER 4

It always rains at funerals.

There will be no funeral at my passing.

No one will be playing *Bring on the Dancing Horses* and burying me under the great oak where I played as a child. There will be no anecdotes telling of the times I cracked my chin in the same place three times by jumping backwards into swimming pools. No mention of the time I came out in a rash when my teddy bear had to go away to be repaired. No one will speak of knowing and loving me and reading poetry and saying that I have gone to a better place. There will be no songs, no readings and no tears.

Aisling will miss me I know, but it will not be recorded here as this story will end when I am no more. I hope she doesn't think too harshly of me for ending life as she has known it on this planet. I would hate it if she despises me but I cannot change what people may think of me. I can only be the best person I can be and try and do the right thing.

I hope you, as well, do not think me a villain for ending the world.

It's not too late for you to wake up. This world of yours is a dream. The unknown chapters of your life are a nightmare from which you can escape.

The darkness is real.

And it consumes everything and everyone in the end.

CHAPTER 5

Trust in your intuition. Feel your way forward, rather than trying to work it all out. You will know what the right thing to do is and when to do it.

That is what Dawn said to me.

What is life?

Is it driving around in cars, going to work, watching television and standing in queues?

Or is it a robin singing in a tree? The sea, trees, flowers, the sun in the sky? A beautiful meadow, otters playing in a river, being in love, being true to yourself and living in the moment not trying to make sense of everything and convey meaning to things that just are?

"Utterly meaningless! Everything is meaningless," King Solomon told me thousands of years ago. At the time I wasn't sure what he meant. Now I do.

The world that humans live in is of their own making seeded and sustained by a God who delights in their suffering. "If I can't be happy, then no one will be happy," that is what he said to me.

Every time I try and free them, they just fight back and resist. It is as if they have grown so used to walking in the darkness that they do not want to walk in the light.

They think me mad.

They think me stupid.

Sometimes you have to let things die in order for there to be a rebirth.

That is what I know in my heart is the right thing to do although my mind fights against me.

Better to live for a moment with your eyes fully open than suffer a lifetime of misery.

CHAPTER 6

The Earth has spun on its axis since it came into existence more than 4.6 billion years ago. That is what Liam would tell you as he is very good with that kind of stuff. The spin is an intrinsic part of the Universe, everything is in motion, spinning around, repeating the same pattern over and over and over again. You can't stop it. Even on the day that the Universe is being ripped apart, the protons and electrons will still be spinning.

But I can stop the Earth from spinning right now.

It would have spun until the day it died in the death throw of your star. A slow spiral into oblivion like your life which you hoped would be full of joy.

You don't want that nightmare.

I begin the process.

I listen to the hum of the planet and I become the planet.

I am the Earth.

I can feel the moon tugging at my oceans and the space dust in my face. Each of these saps a tiny amount of my energy but it is not enough to stop me. At my centre I can feel another rotating body spinning slightly faster than me and roughly the same size as the moon. It is made of iron and is a ball floating within an ocean of molten metal. The magnetic fields are going to go crazy and it will probably flip the magnetic north and south but I start transferring my momentum into it and it begins speeding up.

Something within me tells me I have done this before 780,000 years ago. It feels overdue as if I should have done it thousands of years ago. I guess I have become distracted recently and my mind tends to forget mass extinction events, it stops me from sleeping at nights. I don't think I have ever gone as far as I am about to go though.

So here we are again. It seems that I, like everything else, am repeating the same pattern over and over and over again. Only this time I will stop the cycle and bring the history of the Earth to a final ending.

As my core speeds up the rest of me slows down. My oceans will start moving towards both of my poles to form polar oceans. The atmosphere, which is still spinning will rip my skin from my face and scour my surface, tearing everything away.

I am sorry.

It will be silent soon.

CHAPTER 7

Having a craving for marmite when you have none and can't pop out to the shops because you are in paradise is kind of tough. Aisling instead had to survive on cornflake chocolate nests that Jess had made for her. Although Sophia was doing more of their fair share of helping Aisling consume them.

It was still early in the morning and the three of them were sat at the side of the river with Jess watching Sophia's penguin dive for fish in the river. It had never caught a fish, but then the incentive just wasn't there on its current diet. Aisling was writing her third and last poetry collection about death. Sophia, who now looked as if they were in their thirties, was reading a novel called *When God Was a Rabbit*.

The three of them were on a section of the river where the sides of the valley became steep and several of the trees had collapsed down onto the mud flats. It appeared almost prehistoric and a pterodactyl would not have looked out of place. Jess flicked some kind of buzzing insect from out of her face and said, "Do you think Liam will return soon?"

"I hope so," said Aisling looking up from her writing. "I just hope he got to them in time."

"Can you feel the baby kicking yet?" said Jess.

"Not yet, it's too early," said Aisling.

"This is your third pregnancy then?" said Jess. "I expect you're an expert now at knowing what stage your baby is at?"

"Yes," said Aisling.

But of course it wasn't.

Aisling had transitioned after the birth of her first children. She had wished she had the body back then to carry them herself, that they could have grown within her own womb, but she didn't have a womb. So much had changed since then. But they couldn't give her a womb. They had given her estrogen and blockers and operations but not that. And now she had one. Or at least she hoped she had, because the child was definitely growing within her somehow. It was all so overwhelming. It was what she had always wanted. She loved Cillian and Róisín with all her heart. They had two mothers. One a maternal mother in every way possible and the other the birth mother, her ex wife. She loved them just as much as if she had carried them herself but now, well, having her child grow within her was something she just never expected would ever happen. The scientists had talked about womb transplants in the future, but nothing that would ever have been credible in her lifetime. And there were no doctors to scan her here. No doctors to explain what on earth was going on. All she knew was that she was pregnant. She had known before the test result, something within her had known although that had scared her.

So many things raced through Aisling's mind with the question Jess had just asked. How had her body changed? Would she die giving birth? Would the child survive? She was scared, frightened and in complete shock. But she showed none of that to anyone. Her life had just become so bizarre and she couldn't cope anymore trying to understand anything. And she was worried that Cillian and Róisín were in grave danger. And where was Anna? It was all too much. She felt as if her mind was going to explode. Last time she had felt like that was in the café when she had run out chasing an imaginary rabbit. This time she was holding her ground. Just.

"What is actually going on?" said Jess.

"I'm sorry?" said Aisling, panicking for a moment that Jess knew exactly what had been racing around her mind.

"With Hersperides," said Jess. "What is it? Where exactly are we?"

"I wish I knew," said Aisling.

"Why can't Cillian and Róisín leave?"

"Because," said Aisling and then stopped and turning to Sophia said, "Sophia, your penguin is stuck in the mud."

Sophia didn't look up from their novel.

Jess picked up a stone and threw it onto the mudflat. It stayed there a moment then started to sink.

"Because?" said Jess.

"Sorry," said Aisling, "I think we need to go and get some rope to pull the penguin out."

CHAPTER 8

That evening Sophia gave their penguin a bath, which it made an incredible fuss about and at the end of it there was water all over the bathroom floor. Wrapping it in a towel Sophia picked it up and carried it into their bedroom. Jess, who had been waiting to use the bathroom, went in and closed the door.

Sophia could hear her shouting, "What the hell!" and slipped the bolt across on their bedroom door.

"Boop, sleep," they said to Boop and sat on their bed.

Boop flopped down onto its stomach and closed its eyes.

Sophia picked up the book they had taken from the library last month. It was big, bound in leather and had the words HOLY BIBLE printed in large bold type across the front of it.

"A depressing read," said Sophia out loud, "deeply troubled people drifting along with no storyline and no development. And the ending is a more than a little ambiguous and very weird."

Sophia took their pen and wrote in the inside cover, *This is a work of fiction. Any resemblance to actual events or locales or persons, living or dead, is entirely coincidental.*

"There you go," said Sophia, "now at least it has some truth to it."

They flipped through the pages, stopped at the book of Zephaniah and read,

The Lord your God is in your midst.

"I hope not," said Sophia, "I never want to see him, he has the compassion of a force ten hurricane trying to blow ducklings into a meat grinder."

And Sophia didn't quite know how they knew that, but they did.

Sophia knew a lot of things in ways that were deep and profound.

Like why people were conscious in the first place.

It was all to do with the tricky nature of not being certain about anything. Being absolutely sure of things it turns out is about the dumbest thing you can do. Accepting and combining uncertainties with a lived experience gives rise to a conscious state. It took a lot of brain power, which many people struggled with and instead of walking around being sentient they were more likely to dissolve into slush on the floor.

God, thought Sophia, was a case in point. He was so certain of everything and therefore was probably the dumbest creature in existence. Which will turn out to be absolutely true and useful later.

At a knock on the door, Sophia placed the book down and said, "Come in."

The door handle rattled and they could hear Jess muttering.

"Oh for goodness sake," said Sophia smiling to themselves, "do I have to do everything myself?" and getting off the bed went across and unlocked and opened the door.

"Yes?"

"The floor was wet," said Jess.

"Well thank you for informing me of that information," said Sophia.

Jess raised an eyebrow.

Sophia stuck their tongue out.

"Cheeky Bugger," said Jess and held out a tub of cotton candy ice cream. "Want to share?"

"Ooh," said Sophia nodding their head, "yes please."

CHAPTER 9

I haven't taken the form of the Earth for so long. It hurts more now than it has ever done. As you became more enslaved to your God, you never sought to make good what you had done. You filled instead your yearning for love with power, money and social and economic structures so devoid of any feelings you carried on destroying the very ground upon which you live.

In some ways it helps me feel not so bad about what I have done. It is like putting a beloved animal out of its misery to save it from the pain of dying. I do this not out of hate but out of love.

I am conflicted as you can tell. One minute I am sure, the next I am questioning myself.

The pain though is something that shocked even me. You really have hurt me so much. I have provided for your every need and placed you in a paradise and you have burnt that paradise to the ground and fought each other over ever dwindling resources. How have you managed to do this in such a short space of time when I could have sustained you for billions of years?

I wanted you to fly. There should have been a time when you started to feel as if you may be hurting me even though I gave freely and you lived off the land in a sustainable way. That guilt would have been natural and the remorse should have enabled you to become independent, to pull away from always being a child in their mother's arms. It should have changed your nature, made you softer, less harsh and kinder. You should have repaired the damage and reconnected with me in a new way as you reached out to the stars.

But you did not pull away from destroying me.

You looked at the few that did not seek me harm as primitive, that their lifestyle that you abandoned millennia ago was not one you wanted and you took their land and slowly killed them.

You stayed as children and killed the adults.

You have become depressed, anxious and feel abandonment.

You yearn for embrace.

You are desperate for love.

You cling to me scared out of your wits that you cannot survive without me right beside you. And God fuelled that fear and used to it grow ever more powerful so you would never learn to change.

Liam dipped his flask into the river and checked around as it filled with ice cold water. The trees in this part of Hesperides were more dense and all around him he could see great oaks and moss covered beech trees. There seemed to be a lot more birds and the scent of flowers was everywhere. Beside him in the mud were the paw prints of a leopard. Liam placed his fingers into it then screwing the top back onto his bottle moved on.

The river flowed through the wood bubbling and gurgling as if was still at its source instead of nearly at the sea. A kingfisher sat on an overhanging branch looking for fish and otters played near the bank on the far side. And all around him he could hear sunbirds, nightingales and wrens. How those animals and birds had got here, Liam didn't know, but then he had long ago stopped trying to work everything out and just accepted his waking reality, however bizarre it might be. Which for Liam, with his head full of facts, was a big deal, although of course most people would not have known what a sunbird sounded like or the shape of a leopard paw print.

Lost in thought about the number of different calls a nightingale can make, Liam found himself suddenly startled by what sounded like thunder. Looking up he saw only blue sky. Shrugging, he carried on until he became aware that everything had grown quiet. All the sounds of the forest had fallen away as if they had been sucked out of the landscape leaving only the sound of the river.

The sun shifted and suddenly appeared to the side of where it had been before. A white line like an airplane trail swept across the sky as if it were a zen garden and the line was a rake smoothing out the sand. There was a rushing noise and then it became quiet again.

Unnoticed by Liam, the image of the sun wobbled as if ripples were flowing across it. No-one found themselves looking too closely at the sun. If they did they would have seen it was sword shaped but it would have blinded them before they could see that anyway.

The birds started singing again and all appeared normal until high above him Liam could see a shoal of fish and an orca. It was the strangest thing he had ever seen. Liam's mind quickly presented him with orca facts to try and normalise the experience. But that didn't help.

Setting up camp, Liam lay down and went straight to sleep and dreamt that he was inside the stomach of the orca.

He awoke the next day and lay for a while watching the fish in the sky. I am going to be a father, he thought. A new life was going to come into the universe and it would be his child. It was something he knew could never happen when things started to get serious with Aisling and he had accepted that. And now suddenly everything was different and what he had given up was going to be given to him. He tried to imagine what it would be like, but couldn't. But he did feel excited, exhilarated, nervous and worried all at the same time. I am going to do everything within me to be the best father I can be, he thought. Spotting a shiny pebble next to him he picked it up and examined it. Curling his fingers around it he closed his eyes and saw an image of himself holding his new born, their cry full of life. Liam placed the pebble in his pocket and wiped a tear from his eye.

He drank, ate some stale biscuits, packed up and continued following the river.

That afternoon he reached the edge of Hesperides. Before him was a wall of water. Within it and wherever he looked there were whales, sharks, shoals of fish, creatures so numerous that he couldn't count them and things that just shouldn't be there like the remains of the titanic and an old Russian submarine.

A penguin popped out through the wall of water, landed on the dry land and shook itself. More followed until there was a long line of them marching out towards the wood. An orca swam close to the divide and turned at the last minute. It's tail broke through and passed over the top of Liam's head as if in slow motion then disappeared back into the water.

The Titanic had just two baths for all of the passengers in third class, thought Liam desperately trying to keep his mind from freaking out and then set off along the edge looking for Cillian and Róisín.

He needed to get back soon. He had either missed them or they were gone or they were farther along the edge somewhere. And he was torn. Torn between wanting to save Aisling's kids and being there for Aisling now she was pregnant. Quite frankly the chances of finding Cillian and Róisín in an area the size of Tanzania was almost zero and he really just wanted to turn back. He certainly could not stray too far from the river or he would run out of water.

It had been difficult leaving the others behind but there was no way he was going to let Aisling travel in her state. She had given him such a hard time over that, but when Sophia had broken down in tears over Boop she had relented and she and Jess and Sophia had all stayed behind.

Liam carried on following the edge of the ocean for an hour then exhausted and thirsty sat down to rest and to drink from his water bottle. Above him red flowers the size of beach balls hung from the trees. Higher up, and unnoticed by Liam, snow monkeys swung from branch to branch.

Liam wiped his mouth on his sleeve and thought again about how he had ended up in such a place. It had been such a shock when Aisling had come out of the bathroom saying she was pregnant. What was a pregnancy test kit even doing in the house? And how could Aisling's body suddenly be able to carry a child? How for, that matter, was there even an egg to fertilise?

And those questions remained unanswered.

So many things happen to us that we can't explain.

And yet there we are living a life that we try to normalise even though it constantly confuses and surprises us.

Aisling's body had changed the minute she stepped inside Hesperides.

She just didn't know it at the beginning.

She now had everything she needed to get pregnant and to bear children.

Hesperides just has a profound effect on people.

Jess' body, for example, had no wound when Aisling had fished her out of the river and Cillian and Róisín's faces had become clear and smooth without a trace of their teenage acne.

Nobody had noticed that in the story, not even them.

Dawn had checked with Aisling first though, you can't assume anything. That was the question that her heart had answered when Dawn had placed her hand on her forehead during the rescue from the Amundsen-Scott South Pole Station.

Aisling just didn't remember the question or the answer in her subconscious mind.

But it is what she wanted.

She had wanted it very much.

CHAPTER 11

The tabloid press all ran with headlines that morning along the theme of -
EXCLUSIVE: THE END OF THE WORLD!!
Claiming that the president had fled the planet. Many ran with pictures of people floating out to space, which made no sense, but people will believe all sorts of nonsense.

The staff at the café where Aisling had first met Anna were all in at work that day, the day they would die. Jeremy, the manager, had insisted that there was still going to be coffee at the end of the world. Some of them had asked if they would be paid overtime rates by working under such conditions, but Jeremy had just laughed at them and told them to make sure they sold customers the special blend that day.

The world was slowing down, but most of the humans went on trying to live their lives at a million miles an hour. That required coffee according to Jeremy, it was an opportunity to increase sales and would put them all in line for a bonus.

PLEASE STAY AT HOME
Was the advice from the governments of the world.
We don't have to go to work was the message received and so people headed off to the beach and the coffee shops and the malls.

The weather forecasts on the news channels just had some vague comments about how it might be a bit windy. Earlier that morning, Stephanie, who worked at the café, had phoned into her local news station asking if she should board up her windows against the approaching hurricane and was told, there is no hurricane today and there really is nothing to be worried about.

Later that morning there was a large queue outside the café. People were shouting and complained that they had been waiting for over fifteen minutes. Some had some minor wounds were twigs had started to blow off the surrounding trees.

If this all sounds like a comedy, I can assure you people are incredibly stupid even in the face of certain disaster. History has shown that time and time again.

CHAPTER 12

Given control do not assume that you have any conceptual idea of what you are doing beyond your intuition and wits.

In the lagoon of Maliku Island, an island whose original name meant woman-island, there was a young girl called Amina snorkelling amongst the brightly coloured fish. She had control of herself, she was at one with the land and the seas and she lived by her intuition and wits. Her swimsuit was a profusion of bright colours and she was beautiful inside and in her form and in her grace.

Her family lived within sight of the great white lighthouse on the southern side of the island. The lighthouse was the lone surviving structure of the British period in the Lakshadweep Islands. It had kept people safe since 1885.

Amina knew no fear in her heart and had her whole life before her. Her grandmother had approached her boyfriend's family for permission to marry earlier that day and the answer had been a resounding yes.

I tell you this tale because the lighthouse was about to fall as was Amina and the entire population of Maliku and then the whole of India. I am not proud of it, it sickens me and when this is all done I will no longer be able to live with myself. I could shield this from you to make me look better, but here I give a glimpse into the horror of what I have done.

When the tsunami hit Amina she was confused for a moment, her heart rate increasing. Around her the fish swirled upwards in the blue water as she was taken up into the sky. Even in that moment she did not let fear enter her but looked to the heavens and knew that she was gone.

That is what I tell myself.

In reality the water was brown, grey, black and white. There was no elegant tentacles of foam around her. There was only the scream of a child as she was sucked out into the ocean, then the roar of death and the terrible waste of a life not yet lived.

CHAPTER 13

Anna had initially just eased the spin of the planet slightly, putting off the moment when she would fully commit and from which there be no turning back from. The lightest touch to the brakes had caused the atmosphere, which was still spinning, to start tugging the ground below for three hours. It was the foreshock before the main event, a window in which everyone thought that tomorrow would still bring a sunrise and sunset like every other day. We can tell our grandchildren about the day the Earth slowed for a moment they would have said, like mother Earth was trying to tell us to just slow down.

Mother Earth was about to kill every one of them.

The advice given to Stephanie that, there is no hurricane today, was correct. Indeed there would never be a hurricane ever again. But the advice, that there really is nothing to be worried about, was not. Around the equator dry land started to appear as the oceans continued their migration to the poles.

Stephanie's last words as she entered an order for a latte with almond milk into the till were, "Would you like to try our special blend?"

She died moments later when the approaching wall of water swept all the cars into the air and then hit the café with such a force that it ripped it off its foundations.

On the doorstep of Aisling's house the note in the milk bottle cancelling the milk for six months, which she had written over five years ago, span up in the water before shattering into a million pieces. As did her house.

At Stephanie's house, the boarding on the windows, which she had still put up, because *the government just lie to us anyway and there is a disaster coming*, were ineffective against a migrating sea mass.

Beau, Róisín's boyfriend, who was now married and living in a bedsit in Dorset, died instantly as did the entire population of the United Kingdom and all of Europe.

CHAPTER 14

So many belief systems have a flood narrative. From those told in the Epic of Gilgamesh, the Satapatha Brahmana and Plato's Timaeus. Fundamentalist Christians who believe in a literal interpretation of the Bible often ponder where all the water would come from to cause the genesis flood. In their madness some would stand and preach that the land used to float on the waters and it is these waters that rose up to flood the Earth.

That's people for you, always trying to destroy the power of stories with nonsense.

Well now the story was destroying the people.

The following day when the dry land forming at the equator became a band 100 miles across, Anna just stopped the planet dead. Just like that.

The rotational speed of the atmosphere at the equator where it is moving at its fastest is about a thousand miles an hour. When the rotational speed of the ground below that is suddenly cut to zero then that's going to be one hell of a wind speed at the surface. The fastest wind speeds ever recorded come from hurricane gusts reaching upwards of 250 miles per hour. Magnify that by a factor of four and everything is sucked up into the atmosphere from buildings, rocks, people, the whole surface of the planet.

Everything and everyone that has not made it to Hesperides is now dead.

CHAPTER 15

Everything and everyone is now dead is not entirely true.

Three hundred and fifteen people out of the nearly ten billion people on Earth were still alive on the planet and seven people were alive in the international space station.

All the creatures that live in the deeper parts of the sea, where life first started, were still swimming around unaware that their main predator, humans were on the risk of extinction list.

And all the insects and high flying birds not taken out by the flying rocks, debris and buildings that had been ripped up into the lower atmosphere, were still in the sky. Although at some point the birds were going to have to attempt a landing, which will prove impossible. Which is okay if you are a swift but harder if you are a seagull, most of which were wiped out anyway as they scavenged for food close to the ground.

At the poles the rotational spin of the atmosphere is already almost zero. You will drown under a vast ocean that has formed there but you will not be ripped off into the atmosphere with a sudden planet stop. Which was very good news for the people aboard the Storsjöodjuret coastal liner currently off the coast of Antarctica.

Aboard were the 315 survivors. 75 were crew members, 238 were booked passengers and two were hitchhikers. All other vessels in those waters and those in the Arctic Ocean were overcome with all lives lost by the huge sudden surge of water eastwards with the planet stop. Fortunately the size the Storsjöodjuret made it more stable and its distance from the pole close enough that the height of the tsunami striking it was small.

The hitchhikers were Cillian and Róisín.

CHAPTER 16

Earlier Róisín had asked, "Is this a good idea?" before Cillian had said, "Hold your breath," and hand in hand they had walked into the water at the edge of Hesperides.

It wasn't a good idea. It was a very bad idea.

On the other side they had started to sink down into the depths. As the shock of the cold water hit them they had panicked. Kicking hard they had started swimming to the surface whilst below them a leopard seal had swum in circles. As they had done so the current had pushed them back towards Hesperides but they had resisted until finally with their lungs at bursting point they had broken through to the surface of the sea. Cillian had looked across at Róisín, blinked and then a wave had caught them, picked them up and deposited them on top of the ice sheet.

Below was Hesperides. From within that paradise it would have appeared as if Cillian and Róisín were lying suspended in the sky.

But they should have been in that paradise.

And Anna, when she had stopped the world, had no idea that they were not safely within Hesperides.

That had all happened a few days ago.

Now they were warm again and in the cruise liner. Their destination England.

Although of course England was now under the sea and was no more.

CHAPTER 17

The Spartans used to use a crown of olive branches to ward off evil. All the ancient Greek Gods were said to be born under an olive tree and the Greeks believed that the olive tree was the most valuable gift given to mankind. In biblical times it was said that whoever sat under the olive tree could hear the strings of King David's lute playing beautiful music. Indeed across cultures and myths and legends the olive tree bridged the gap between Earth and heaven.

Anna had spent many of her days in its shade before she had departed to bring Jess to Hesperides. And now Jess was sitting in its shade as she listened to Liam and Aisling talk. Liam had returned earlier that day without Cillian and Róisín and that had brought much anguish and tears to Aisling who was now three months pregnant.

Jess looked up at the sky and watched the giant mantra rays glide below the clouds. Beams of sunlight streamed past them and illuminated the garden in patches of light. When the sky event had happened about a month ago Sophia had sat up all night watching the giant sea stars appear and the whale, which they had named Petunia, glide past the moon.

Sophia was now sitting with their penguin Boop but every now and then they would stop and listen to Liam and Aisling talking. When Aisling walked back into the house and started screaming, Jess walked over to Sophia and said, "Let's get out of here."

"Good idea," said Sophia and went to get their backpack.

As she waited Jess placed her hand on the old olive tree into which Dawn had deposited all the stories of the world. As she did she felt her whole body tingle. In her mind she could see a small red ship flying low over a Martian horizon towards her.

Above it were two moons, and far away in space the Earth. There was an explosion towards the end of the ship's engine and it began descending. Jess watched it fall from the pink sky until it crashed right before her in the Martian soil and burst into flames. The pilot pulled the canopy back, climbed out and jumped down to the ground. Two black and white cats followed her out of the ship. Jess watched as they followed the pilot as she walked across the barren landscape to her. As the she drew closer she could see that it was Dawn and there wasn't a scratch or burn mark on her suit. Jess began to say something, but Dawn just stopped and looked down at the ground. There at her feet was a blue rose surrounded by red dust.

Jess became aware of the sound of a lute and felt a surge as if her whole body was being regenerated.

"I'm ready," said Sophia.

"Sorry?" said Jess taking her hand from the tree.

"I'm ready," said Sophia. "Where are we going?"

"To the river," said Jess.

CHAPTER 18

Where was God as all his people died?

This is a question that people asked moments before being swept away into oblivion.

Some people had answered, "We don't know."

Others, "It is God's judgment."

Others, "He doesn't exist."

Others, "Just who is God anyway?"

But now there was nobody left to ask those questions.

God, it turns out, had inadvertently agreed not to do anything. Anna was currently the Earth itself and as he had agreed to leave Anna alone he had to leave Earth alone as well. Which was annoying, as he was supposed to be omnipotent.

That made him very cross and that needed venting.

And he saw the space station orbiting the Earth with the sun glinting off its solar panels and taking it he crushed it between his fingers as if it were a gnat.

CHAPTER 19

Destroying the world is the job of the antagonist. I think everyone accepts that as a given, which puts me in something of a quandary. I think I am a nice person, but then I am sure the antagonist doesn't think themselves an evil person, just someone with a different perspective who feels they are doing the right thing.

We all know though that they of course are deluded.

Is that me?

I am deluded?

Have I got it wrong?

Do people like being unhappy?

Am I like a god who believes they know better and seeks to change people whereas what I really should be doing is widening my understanding of what it means to be human?

I really don't know anymore.

If I listen to my story then I am convinced that I should act, that I am in the right.

Other people's stories may tell a different tale where I am the antagonist and they will think terrible things of me.

But I am not a terrible person.

I am just not.

There is no end to this line of thinking.

When Dawn was here I had clarity, without her I am confused.

Is this is all a terrible mistake, then I am sorry.

If not, then I have seeded a new hope into a land of death and fear.

Each acts according to their own conscience.

It is enough, I hope, that I have at least searched my heart and my heart says no more.

CHAPTER 20

Cillian dried himself off from his shower and sat on the edge of his bunk in the cabin within the Storsjöodjuret. Flipping on the television he searched for a signal and found none. Sighing he opened the fridge and got out a can of soda. Opening it he stared out through the window at the sea. Beside the ship a passenger plane surfaced. Wrapped around it were the tentacles of a creature that looked like a kraken he had once seen on the cover of an old book.

I hate disaster movies, he thought, but now it seems I am living in one and he wondered if the creature he had seen would go for the Storsjöodjuret next. It was like a sea devil from God delivering a message of doom, like the one that had taken Shackleton's ship, the Endurance whilst it was trapped in the ice in 1915.

Cillian wished he could look up about the monster on the internet. He felt cut off without it. On it, he knew where to go to find out every piece of information ever known to humans in an instant. But it wasn't inside his head, not unless it was a conspiracy theory which he seemed to be able to remember without any effort.

Cillian got up and began walking across the carpeted floor. He stopped as a sudden feeling of nausea rose up. Feeling dizzy he put his hand against the wall. There was a metallic taste in his mouth. He didn't know why or understand but then the cause was thousands of miles below his feet in the inner core which was spinning at an alarming rate.

Gathering himself, he focused on his objective and opened the door to his cabin.

"Excuse me," he said to a passing crew member, "is there any internet on this ship?"

CHAPTER 21

Anna orbited the sun and felt the warmth of its rays. The Earth was a perfect sphere now, whereas before it had bulged at the equator from its spin. There was no dawn every 24 hours, there was no sunset at the end of a 12 hour day. Every day would last six months, every night six months more. When the sun did go down the sunset would seem to go on forever.

"Our planet should never stop spinning completely. That's something to be thankful for," the scientists had said before Anna had hit the brakes. And for good reason. What they hadn't talked about was the effect of all that spin being absorbed into the inner core. The increase in the Earth's magnetic fields had caused all the satellites to fail and there was now no hope for Cillian to get back onto the internet as all the computers had been fried in the sudden power surge.

Cillian and Róisín and the other passengers and crew aboard the Storsjöodjuret would also in time either die of thirst or hunger or fall sick from the prolonged exposure to the increased magnetic field which would distort their atoms and compress their electron clouds.

Survive that and the runaway greenhouse effect from one side of the planet being continuously baked for six months would increase the temperature of the planet until the oceans boiled.

Survive that and they would slowly die as the atmosphere disappeared.

Aisling's children were lost. Death was just a matter of time.

It may have been easier if they had died quickly like everyone else.

CHAPTER 22

The yellow covers on the life boats attached to the side of the Storsjöodjuret flapped in the strong winds sweeping in from the west. Below decks, where normally cars were stored when it functioned as a ferry along the western coast of Norway, there were inflatable boats, kayaks, and expedition equipment. It would have been better if it was fully stocked with food, water and two of every kind of animal.

Róisín's cabin had a bath and she was currently soaking in it and pondering if she would ever see her boyfriend again. She was also thinking about what she would do once they reached England. Would Jeremy give her her old job back? She needed the money. She had run out of eyeliner, her ankle boots let water in when it rained and she missed takeaways and listening to records with the candles lit and a glass of something alcoholic and sweet in her hand. And she missed her mates, whatever they were doing. Probably out getting drunk.

She wanted everything she had before and more, her whole life was before her.

Closing her eyes she tried to relax and slipped her toes under the bubbles.

In her mind she remembered the pot-bellied pig that had wandered up and sniffed her when she had washed up on the shore with Cillian after leaving Hesperides. There had been animals everywhere and a lot of annoyed looking humans shouting and trying to herd them into pens. There was also a group of very strange people who were sat around a fire passing around cake saying to each other, "Blessed are the ones that eat cake."

A young man called Asbjørn, who had taken a shine to her, had explained they were zealots who claimed they had seen a vision calling them to Antarctica and that we were living in the end times.

It had been difficult saying bye to Asbjørn, he was cute and she had liked the way his hair fell over his large blue eyes. When she had asked him about the animals he had just shrugged and said something about every time a ship arrived there were animals stowed away on them as if transporting animals to Antarctica had suddenly become a booming illegal trade.

The reality was that the animals were connected to the planet in ways humans had long since relinquished and they had known of the impending destruction of life on Earth. And so they had taken all steps necessary to get themselves to the gateways to Hesperides that Dawn had hidden. Life is like that, resilient and resourceful. It will find a way to survive, unless of course it is unconnected to the tether that sustains it, as unfortunately humans had become. They had cut their umbilical cord to the planet and sold it for shiny trinkets and other such nonsense.

The image of Asbjørn's face, full of smiles and glittering eyes filled Róisín's mind and she sank down lower into the bubbles and sighed. The kayaks had been her favourite moment. Paddling together around the icebergs with the sun glinting off her sunglasses and an albatross high in the sky. Although with the sea swelling they had to abandon it and had spent the rest of the day cuddled up together in his tent whilst he taught her how to count to ten in Norwegian. The number seks still made her laugh even now.

Asbjørn had helped her and Cillian slip aboard the Storsjöodjuret as it had left. They had tried to secure passage officially, but when they couldn't produce any documentation or indeed money, they had been turned away. She had toyed with asking Asbjørn to come with her, but had reasoned that it may have not gone well if she did manage to find her boyfriend. Life could be messy like that. If he had come with her, he would have been eaten by sharks in the fate awaiting the

Storsjöodjuret. Instead he was safe in Hesperides. But that was the way of the world now. Life was a random game of chance.

Róisín looked around at her cabin. It had been empty when they had found it. There had been a lot of empty cabins and she liked this one the best and had moved in. That had been Cillian's idea. The choice he had pointed out was to sleep below deck with the inflatable boats, kayaks, and expedition equipment or just brazenly act as if they were paying passengers. And he was right. It's funny what people will accept if you just act confidently and give them no reason to doubt. God had done that for thousands of years.

Róisín hoped that Aisling had not gone to mad when she had discovered they had left so suddenly. They would be back, it was not as if they couldn't visit and besides she was young and full of adventure, her mother could not reasonably expect her to stay there forever. Róisín did miss Boop though, it was cute, but Sophia would have never have forgiven her and she liked Sophia.

And it went on like that for a while in Róisín's mind – images of Sophia, Aisling, Cillian but mainly Asbjørn blowing through her head like fluffy clouds as she became more and more relaxed.

When the bow of the ship suddenly lurched upwards she didn't feel relaxed at all and screamed. Half of the bath water ended up on the floor. Below her a crack propagated over the entire depth of the bow section of the ship.

Getting out she dried herself and tried to stop herself from shaking. In the lounge to her cabin she stood in front of a painting of a woman holding a mug of coffee. She took several deep breaths to calm herself and then looked out at the huge waves buffeting the ship. "Everything is okay," she said to herself and then stepped back in alarm as a severed wing of a commercial airline sliced down past her window.

CHAPTER 23

Róisín and Cillian sat opposite each other in the restaurant situated on deck five of the ship.

"Have you found out where the ship is supposed to be sailing to?" said Cillian.

"Ushuaia in southern Argentina," said Róisín helping herself to some berries and granola. "What do you mean *supposed* to be?"

Cillian poured himself a glass of red wine.

"You are having wine for breakfast?" said Róisín.

"Here's to the end of the world," said Cillian and lifted his glass.

"Why do you think it's the end of the world?" said Róisín.

Cillian pointed outside. Beside them the floor to ceiling windows showed a panoramic view of the ocean. Close to the ship a lava dome fountain had appeared on the surface. Looking like a giant bubble it was surrounded by debris and what appeared to be a section of the Eiffel Tower. Above it the sky had turned bright red from all the dust and debris kicked up into it from across the globe.

"There are whispers going around the ship that we are unable to contact anyone," said Cillian.

"What does that mean?" said Róisín.

"I don't know," said Cillian, "but I don't think this ship is sailing anywhere. I think we are going around in circles at the moment."

Róisín placed a spoonful of berries and yoghurt in her mouth.

"We could be on one of the arks built to save the rich, powerful and influential for an end of the world scenario," said Cillian.

"And politicians, religious leaders and the super-rich would be invited to Antarctica in the event of a global disaster would they?" said Róisín.

"You might as well have the sausages, bacon, meatballs, pancakes and eggs," said Cillian ignoring her.

"I have to watch my waistline," said Róisín looking at the food set before Cillian. He had his starter bolinhos de bacalhau, his main dish a large argentine steak, and a crème brulée for desert. The image distorted as electric currents began swirling within her retina and she saw images of Aisling with her face full of tears.

A large bang sounded above them as a second world war spitfire crashed into the deck.

"Do you think," said Róisín, "that we should have stayed in Hesperides?"

"I am beginning to think that, yes," said Cillian, "although this certainly beats honey sandwiches."

"Right," said Róisín.

"This is your fault," said Cillian, "I hope this boy is worth it."

"It was your bloody idea," said Róisín, "you can't survive for five minutes without your stupid internet."

Below them the crack that had appeared along the bow section started to let in water.

In the sky above them lightening flashed across the pink clouds.

CHAPTER 24

It turns out that Cillian and Róisín did not after all have to worry about dying of thirst, hunger, radiation poisoning, suffocation or heat stroke. No, they had to worry about death from drowning.

The crack in the bow of Storsjöodjuret had eventually split open the bow and the ship was going down. To be fair it was never designed to be an ark for humanity and it was never designed to withstand the forces at work from the sudden stop of the planet's spin.

Cillian and Róisín were unfortunately trapped under deck on level 5 and the water level in the dining room was rapidly rising. The only saving grace was they hadn't noticed the sharks circling the boat, or the blood in the water from those already taken.

"Are we going to die?" said Róisín, "I don't want to die. I can't stand the thought of not being able to breathe."

"We are not going to die," said Cillian.

Which was a bold statement, seeing as the air gap between the surface of the water and the ceiling was only a meter and shrinking by the minute.

"I love you," said Róisín, "you may annoy the hell out of me sometimes, but I do love you."

"I love you to," said Cillian.

"Do you think we will be rescued?" said Róisín.

"I don't think there is anyone left to rescue us."

"I'm very cold," said Róisín.

"Keep kicking your legs," said Cillian.

"What's the best moment of your life?" said Róisín.

"Going on holiday with mum and you and Beau to France," said Cillian.

"In Saint-Malo?"

"Yes," said Cillian, "Do you remember when we got pulled behind the speedboat on an inflatable ring?"

"Yes."

"You were determined that you would be the last to fall of it."

Róisín laughed and accidently swallowed some water. She stopped kicking and started to sink.

Cillian reached over and grabbed her.

"You okay?"

"Yes," said Róisín.

She looked at Cillian and tried to smile, "I did didn't I? I didn't fall off. I beat you all!"

"You did," said Cillian and held her tight.

CHAPTER 25

You are connected to this planet in ways that you do not understand. You are part of it and it is part of you. You are an expression of the Earth in constant motion, vibrating, oscillating and resonating as you. Your neuronal sync and coherence is you, but you are also the trees, the fields, the sea and all the animals. When humans kill, they are killing a part of you. When they destroy the land, they are destroying you. You do not die because you grow old, you die because everyone around you is slowly killing you.

Aisling could sense this, she couldn't explain it, but she knew it to be true. And so she knew that her children were dying. All parents can sense when their children are in danger.

"Many years ago," said Aisling to Liam, "I stood next to Anna wishing that I could paint something as powerful as *The Scream* by Munch. I felt small and insignificant."

Liam placed a hand on Aisling's shoulder and looked at her, his eyes full of concern.

"Now," said Aisling, "I still feel small and insignificant but I can paint like Munch. I know the anxiety and anguish he must have felt at his world suddenly becoming dark."

"It's very good," said Liam looking at the portrait Aisling had done of Anna in the walled garden. It's very disturbing though, why is her face so distorted like that? I'm really worried about you."

"I wish I didn't have this in me," said Aisling. "I wish Anna was dead and I had never met her. It's her fault my children are going to die."

"Cillian and Róisín are not going to die," said Liam.

"They are already dying," said Aisling.

"How can you know that?"

"She is destroying the world," said Aisling, "Can you not sense it?"

"No."

"Well she is," said Aisling and taking a knife sliced her canvas and walked back into the house.

The image of Anna, with her face slit, fluttered in the wind behind her.

CHAPTER 26

Under the canopy of the trees between the house and the river in Hesperides are interweaving paths covered in leaves, twigs, and broken shells.

Next to one of these paths set in a sea of bluebells was a robin that had died. Most robins die in their first year. You may like to think they are eternal and that they bring hope for new beginnings and new life but most are gone in a blink of an eye. Those few that do survive past their first year though do thrive and live for years. This robin though had not been so fortunate.

Until that is Sophia and Jess passed it on their way to the river.

Sophia spotted it and picking it up held it in their open palm.

"Do you want to bury it?" said Jess.

"Why do things die?" said Sophia.

"It is the natural way of things," said Jess, "even here."

"No," said Sophia.

"It will have had a good life," said Jess.

"No," said Sophia, "it died before its time. It is too young."

Sophia held their hand up as if they were offering the robin to the sky. Thousands of blue butterflies appeared from out of the trees.

"Fly," said Sophia and closed her eyes.

CHAPTER 27

Later, Sophia sat by the river listening to Jess tell them stories. Perched on a branch above them was the robin they had found earlier. It was singing a song full of new life and new beginnings.

Jess' stories were also about rebirth and hope and were wild, full of imagination, silliness and wonder. Sophia loved them, there was something about Jess' voice, which was soothing, as if her words formed a melody within you as you listened.

"And that," said Jess, "is the story of how I came to have my name."

"Tell me another," said Sophia.

"I will tell you about how another came to have their name," said Jess. "A child was born who was the wisdom of God. And the child could be everywhere and anywhere. And the child was neither female nor male. Their wisdom was heard aloud in the woods and over the seas they would raise their voice, so all could hear. On the top of the forests they cried out, at the edge of space they spoke. The child came forth from the word of God, but the child was not God. Do you know who I am talking of?"

"No," said Sophia. "Where did you learn to talk like that?"

"I may not be many things," said Jess, "but I can read people."

"You are saying that child is me?"

"Yes," said Jess.

"Tell me a story about me," said Sophia, "teach me."

"I cannot," said Jess, "you need to live your story, not hear it from me. And besides we need to be getting back."

"Why is Aisling so upset about Cillian and Róisín?"

"They are outside of Hesperides," said Jess, "and so are in great danger both from God and from what Anna has set into motion."

"I see," said Sophia and closed their eyes.

"Are you okay?" said Jess.

Sophia didn't reply.

Before them a cougar walked beside the river. Next to it was a raccoon. The cougar turned and looked at them then carried on its way.

"We really need to go now," said Jess.

Sophia opened their eyes and rose up into the sky.

"Christ," said Jess, "I didn't know you could do that."

Jess got to her feet and shouted up, "I'll meet you back at the house then," and began making her way home.

CHAPTER 28

Aisling sat on Róisín's bed and smoothed down the duvet. On her lap was the letter she had just found in Róisín's bedside table. The one Anna had left for Róisín and Cillian to find all those years ago, in Aisling's house. The story of the two birds and the woman of dreams.

A lot of Róisín's stuff is still here, thought Aisling, surely she intended to come back. Now she will never return. The whole story is a lie. A fabricated dream to confuse and cause pain and sorrow.

She really didn't know what to think about Anna. Was she a good person or an evil one? If Anna was able to talk in her mind to help her with coffee orders at a café, then why couldn't she talk to her now and reassure her that the rising dread within was not something that would destroy her? Was she just some pawn in Anna's game and she had been manipulated or did Anna really see her as a daughter? Did she really love her?

Liam joined her and she passed the letter over to him.

After he had read it he placed it down and reaching out his hand took hers.

"I know this all looks hopeless and you feel your children are lost," said Liam, "but you must not give up hope. Your children are intelligent, resourceful kids. If there is a way to survive all this, they will."

"I'm not sure there is anything they can do," said Aisling.

"Who brought them up?" said Liam.

"I did."

"And you taught them how to survive," said Liam. "They will find a way home."

"Do you think?" said Aisling.

"Yes," said Liam.

Aisling looked at the tall stems of the alliums growing up in a line in the hallway and thought of Anaya. Their small dark-red blooms looking like ellipses indicating some omission in her story. She had been so close to completely unravelling in the past. A time of betrayal and dishonesty.

"When we were in the South Pole Station I slept with Anaya," she blurted out.

"Okay," said Liam. "Right." He paused. "Well that was a long time ago."

"This is God's way of punishing me," said Aisling. "I cheated on you and so I must pay the price."

"That is not right."

"Do you hate me?" said Aisling.

Liam pulled her in towards him and hugged her, "I love you. You are way too hard on yourself."

"You are not mad at me?"

"No," said Liam, "I love you."

"I didn't want to know if she survived," said Aisling.

"Róisín?"

"No, Anaya. I had the chance to ask Anna but didn't take it."

"You have too much stuff spinning around your head," said Liam. "You have been carrying all this around for years. You need to let go of the things of the past and live in the future. That future is with me and it will be with your children."

Aisling nestled into his embrace and felt her heartbeat slow to match his.

CHAPTER 29

Within the Storsjöodjuret the water level where Cillian and Róisín were trapped had stabilised and an air pocket had formed. The level of carbon dioxide build up was getting dangerously high though and Róisín and Cillian were starting to feel drunk. The freezing water was also causing their blood to move away from their extremities to keep their cores stable and they were starting to feel extremely weak.

The ship was now completely underwater and sinking into the depths.

"What's your favourite moment of your life?" said Róisín as it grew darker.

"I'm not sure," said Cillian. "Probably when we went to Belgium and I tried Alice in wonderland shots for the first time."

"You nearly didn't get off the tram in time and locked yourself in the toilet and threw up all night."

"Yeh, it was great."

"Liar," said Róisín, "you haven't touched a shot since."

Outside a shark pushed through a broken window and picked out one of the other survivors within the ship.

"How long do you think we have been trapped here?" said Róisín.

"About a million years," said Cillian slurring his words slightly.

"Are you drunk?" said Róisín.

"No, but I do feel light headed."

"I can't really kick anymore," said Róisín, "I can't feel my legs."

"You haven't kicked your legs for the last five minutes," said Cillian. "I've been holding you."

"Let me go," said Róisín.

"No," said Cillian.

And they floated there for another few minutes holding each other in the darkness, but saying nothing more.

When they lost consciousness their faces slipped under the water and they were gone.

CHAPTER 30

Sophia appeared in the sky like a flash of lightning. Below them was a huge vortex where the Storsjöodjuret had gone down. Tucking into a dive, Sophia dove into the depths.

Nothing happened for a while.

The sea raged, the sky grew darker and a ford mustang flew through the air.

God though had noticed that Sophia was outside the protection of Hesperides.

After a few minutes the bow of the Storsjöodjuret pierced the surface and rose up into the sky. Water poured from its damaged hull as it lifted up out of the water with Sophia underneath it.

With the wind pushing against them, Sophia started to make their way back to Hesperides. God though had other ideas and appeared in the sky before them.

"Hello, daughter," said God.

"I am neither a daughter or a son and certainly no child of yours," said Sophia.

God laughed, "You are a daughter, is that too confusing for you?"

"Let me past," said Sophia.

"Give me first the ship," said God. "And then we will see."

Sophia closed their eyes and imagined a dove flying from the ship and it was so.

The dove flew past God and disappeared.

"What is this?" said God.

Sophia said nothing in reply but hovered in the air with the Storsjöodjuret in their hands.

CHAPTER 31

God and the Wisdom of God floated in the sky of the dying planet facing one another, each saying nothing.

Debris flew between them and around them. Amongst the plastic and cans of soda were the torch of liberty torn from the hand of Libertas, an ostrich and the upper half of the statue of Jesus Christ from Rio de Janeiro, which Sophia couldn't help smiling at, despite the gravity of their situation.

Becoming bored God reached out and snapped all the bones in Sophia's right leg.

"You just can't wait to inflict pain on people can you?" said Sophia.

God reached out once more and dislocated Sophia's hip.

"Just leave me alone," said Sophia.

God began to reach out again but stopped as the dove appeared. In its beak was a leaf from the olive tree that grew in Hesperides. God took it and held it out before him.

"Take this as a symbol of our peace," spoke Sophia. "Within that leaf you will find all the stories of this world that you made."

"Why would I want that?" said God.

"Because," said Sophia, "they are important to you. Shortly there will be nothing left of the world you built and no stories of it ever existing. All that you made will be forgotten. But in this you can relive everything that was. Accept it and let me past. You know you cannot enter Hesperides to get this for yourself and you know I can unmake that leaf by wishing it so."

God grew silent whilst he considered this.

"I can remember those things myself," he said eventually. "Why do I need this leaf?"

"Try then," said Sophia. "Tell me one of the great stories from this world."

God remained silent.

"Well?" said Sophia.

"I cannot," said God, "I can only remember facts as they happened. I cannot remember things as stories."

"And do you desire to see things as they truly were? The truth that only stories can tell?"

God said nothing.

"If they are not held within stories," said Sophia, "they will be forgotten."

A turtle and a 1926 Hudson passenger car flew over God's head.

"Let me past," cried out Sophia.

"It is so," said God. "Your name shall no longer be called Sophia, but Samantha, for you have striven with God, and have prevailed and I love you." And holding the leaf in his hand, God withdrew.

"Idiot," said Sophia.

CHAPTER 32

The Storsjöodjuret pushed through Hesperide's waterfall about a mile up and started to track its way through the sky. Farther above it thousands of flame angel fish swam below the clouds, making the atmosphere appear red.

As the Storsjöodjuret grew closer, Jess who was sat with Boop under the olive tree, spotted it and ran towards the house. As Sophia brought the ship down at the water's edge an octopus, that was still attached to the ship's hull, finally let go and splashed down.

Aisling and Liam came out looking shocked and ran towards the river.

Sophia struggled to stand on their broken leg but somehow manged to find it within them to rip open the side of the ship. They began taking those that had survived out onto the bluebells that covered the wood. We can all do amazing feats when we need to, if you are born of the gods then doubly so.

Out of the 115 souls on board, 30 were still alive.

One of those was Róisín.

By the time that Aisling and Liam reached the ship she was sat up blinking in the sunshine. Aisling ran to her and gathered her up into her arms like a mother hen gathering a chick under its wings.

Before her Sophia was standing with Cillian's lifeless body cradled in their arms.

Aisling and Liam looked at Cillian and felt the dread that had been over them since he had left seep in like a cloud of darkness.

Sophia set Cillian down and crouched over him.

"He saved me," said Róisín, "he never let me go."

"Cillian," said Aisling and placed her hand on his forehead. "What has she done to you?"

And she grew angry at the destruction Anna had brought.

Sophia closed their eyes and touched their finger to Cillian's lips.

For a moment nothing happened.

Sophia collapsed to their knees, no longer able to stand.

Blue butterflies appeared from out of the trees in their thousands.

One settled on Aisling's shoulder, and lifting her hand she let it fly to her finger.

When she looked back at her son, she could see the reflection of the butterflies in his pupils. His eyes were open. He smiled and said, "Hello, Mum."

Glancing at Sophia, Aisling said, "thank you," and holding her son burst into tears.

CHAPTER 33

Over the river is the sound of a nightingale and in the sky is Night and Day. In the walled garden cherry blossom falls like pink snow and in the house the comtoise clock strikes midnight. All are asleep. Cuddled up in each other's arms are Aisling and Liam. Aisling is dreaming. Just what she is dreaming I will show you shortly, but her heartrate is increasing and her eyelids flutter.

The scent of flowers is everywhere and the house beats in time with the dripping tap in the kitchen, for even in paradise there is routine and imperfection. Nothing that is perfect can be truly beautiful. In the conservatory the moonlight plays over the copper statue of Dionysus. Beside it Jess is asleep in the wicker chair with an open book on her lap. In her bedroom, below her window covered in honeysuckle, Sophia sleeps the deep sleep that comes from being at peace with your soul. Only Boop is awake and standing in the glow of the fridge light looking for fish fingers.

In the morning Cillian wakes with a blinding headache. Róisín sits watching him. "Ice cream?" she says holding out a tub.

"I feel like I have the worst hang over ever," says Cillian.

"I think you may have actually died for a short while," says Róisín, "so I dare say you have."

"I thought you were watching your figure?" says Cillian looking at the ice cream.

"Ice cream doesn't count."

"Is this a long list, this list of fattening foods that don't count?"

Róisín smiles, "We are lucky to be alive. I guess your existential motive for believing in conspiracy theories has been super charged by your experience."

"I am way too tired to get into a discussion about that," says Cillian. "I don't feel any more powerless or disillusioned, if that is what you mean."

"I think that finding out that everything we have ever known has gone will do a pretty good job of leaving us both disillusioned."

"Did you find Beau here?"

"No," says Róisín. "But Asbjørn is."

"Right, well that's that then," says Cillian. "What you were seeking was here all along."

"And you?" says Róisín, "do you think you can find happiness here?"

"I don't think it's about chasing happiness."

"No?"

"No, I think it's about being content."

"And how is that going?" says Róisín.

"I think it will go a lot better once my head doesn't feel like it's going to explode."

Boop appears in the doorway with Sophia and Jess. Sophia kisses Boop on its beak and turning to Jess says, "They will be fine. It is done."

And it is. And it was.

The story was complete.

Which is sad, but it is also a beginning where Aisling and her child within, Liam, Cillian and Róisín, Jess and Sophia and Boop had everything before them.

As did 29 very surprised passengers and crew from the Storsjöodjuret, which was unplanned but then nothing ever quite works out as you first think. You can plan your life as much as you want, but in the end it throws you all sorts of curve balls, disappointments and opportunities that you will never see coming. Better to plan to be the best person you can be rather than what you can obtain or do. For in the end that is all that matters despite what you have been told. Put your mind to it and you can achieve anything, is a deceitful lie to keep you within a system of oppression. Put your mind to being you and enjoying that and being at peace with yourself and your body, that is where your treasure lies. I sowed that song into the hum of the earth at the beginning of everything. It is not really your fault that you stopped listening to it, God is a liar who is very convincing, weaving all sorts of desires into your hearts that in the end led to this.

I hope you made it to Hesperides together with Asbjørn and the others whose stories were not told in this tale. Maybe you are standing and looking at Dawn's spear and her shield propped against the wall and you can smell the fragrance of flowers.

If you are then think of me and make yourself at home here at the end of the Earth.

Autumn has come and the leaves are falling
from the trees.
Each holds an end to the story.
You can reach out and pick one or leave them
to decay.
That choice is yours.

CHAPTER 34
The Man of Knowledge

The man of knowledge sat in the garden next to some orchids with a sketch pad and pencil. Every now and then he glanced up at the orchids and then returned to his drawings. When he had finished he added annotations, then got up and placed his things in his backpack.

On the walk home he stopped and rested on a tree stump. He was, he thought, completely exhausted. Every since his wife, the woman of dreams, had given birth a couple of months ago he seemed to be living in a state of perpetual fatigue. The birth had been a relief, they had both been so worried about the whole pregnancy. It was nothing short of a miracle. Sleep now was something that never went longer than four hours and although his marriage was based on trust and honesty it was surprising at how good he was at pretending he was still asleep at three in the morning when the baby would wake and cry. He knew it didn't have to be his wife that always went to the baby - there was plenty of expressed breast milk in the fridge in the kitchen and he was quite capable at changing a nappy or rocking them back to sleep, but he just couldn't get up at that time.

They had named the baby Tressa and they were a thing of wonder and beauty that had taken his and his wifes breath away. He could, when he wasn't pretending to be asleep, sit and hold Tressa for hours just looking at their face and thinking about how blessed they were and how happy he was.

Back at the house, he set his bag down and poured himself a drink. On the wall in the summer room was an original block print of *The Lonely Ones - Two People* by Edvard Munch. The man of knowledge stood in front of it. The artwork had had such a profound place in his life. He walked into his bedroom and went to his bedside table and pulled out the original postcard that the woman of dreams had given him all those years ago.

"It shows a couple," the woman of dreams had explained, "after their first romantic love for each other has died. Now they know that everything dies and that they are fated to always live alone and isolated in a cruel world before they die, even with a loved one by their side."

The man of knowledge returned to the summer room and stood again in front of the picture. He took a step back and set his drink down. The painting had changed.

Instead of the sea it now showed the couple facing a lake.

On the lake there were hundreds of floating candles lanterns.

There were trees either side of the couple with brightly coloured lights on.

And whereas before, the couple had stood separated, they now stood with a garland of woven flowers entwined around their hands. About their feet were concentric rings of brightly coloured sand.

The man of knowledge stepped forward and read the little plaque that had appeared under the painting. It read…

My wedding gift to you, follow your own story and not those who live in sadness.

All my love, forever, Anna X

CHAPTER 35
The Woman of Dreams

The woman of dream's eyelids fluttered as she floated over the beautiful land in the dancing moonlight. Next to her bed was her finished poetry collection about death to complete her trilogy. Next to that this book in which she will shortly pen the epilogues after I have gone. Above her in her dream and surrounding her she could see a great ice sheet so high it reached into the clouds. Etched into the edge of the ice sheet was a huge image of a bird cage. Rising up, she drew level with the top of the ice and saw her three children standing at the edge surrounded by clouds.

"Come," called the woman of dreams. "There is nothing to hold you there anymore."

The ice sheet descended until it was level with the land of dreams.

At the children's feet, where the ice touched the grass, a chasm opened up in the earth. Within it was lava that had risen up from the heart of the planet.

The children looked at their mother and at each other and then stepped across to join her.

She embraced them and kissed them and felt her heart beat again.

The chasm became wider and the lava turned from red to orange. Blue flames rose up forming a wall with the ice sheet on one side and the green forest and river on the other. In the dream God appeared. Standing on the ice he looked at the woman of dreams through the blue flames and felt a great hatred rise up in him.

"Do not try and cross," said the woman of dreams.

And the gap became wider and the blue flames higher.

God jumped.

He landed right on the edge of grass, tried to balance himself and failed.

The look in his eyes as he fell back into the lava was a look that the woman of dreams would never forget.

One of absolute horror and disbelief that he had not made the jump.

And God sank down into the lava until he could be seen no more.

CHAPTER 36
The Flower Girl

The flower girl set out from the house with daisies in her hair. On her way to the walled garden she twiddled with a small buttercup held between her fingers. She had the same waking vision again that she had every day now. The one with the small red ship flying low over a Martian horizon towards her. Only recently when it crashed into the Martian soil and the pilot walked with the two cats following her from the burning ship it was her own face she could see beneath the helmet, not Dawns. The flower girl had named the cats, Dip and Dab. She had always wanted two black and white kittens, although she had never envisioned them having little space helmets before. She had always wanted to be an astronaut though. It was all very strange.

Deep in thought she set herself down under the cherry tree near the old olive tree and began digging carefully into the soil.

After a while she grew hot and paused to wipe her forehead. Her skin was pale like the moon and glowed. Her hair was long and golden and fell about her shoulders and she wore a pretty dress with an aster flower print - the frost flowers so loved by florists for their autumn arrangements.

When she was rested she continued until she found what she had placed there long ago when she was able to transcend space and time.

For below the cherry tree there was buried treasure.

It was the hiding place where she had kept her childhood safe from her adopted parents.

Back at the house she took the toys and set them out on the floor. There was a Bunty annual, a Space Shuttle she had made, her Evel Knievel stunt bike and Barbie that she had put in a shoe box and a doll's house she had made herself from a cornflake packet and newspaper. Smiling she focused on the Space Shuttle until it slowly began rising into the air. Turning to the stunt bike she willed it with her mind to shoot off towards the window where it shattered the glass. The flower girl smiled to herself as if sharing some joke then reformed the glass pane.

And then with Tressa, the woman of dream's newborn child, she played and sang songs and felt such joy at being free and being allowed, as she will say in another story to Anna on another world, "To just be me."

Her song is beautiful, sit and listen to it and watch the flowers take bloom across the far reaches of space.

CHAPTER 37
The Wisdom of God

The Wisdom of God made their way up a hill with their penguin Boop. It was slow work, their leg was strapped up and they had a walking stick to take the weight of their right side. At the top they stood and resting both hands on top of the walking stick they looked out at the river below them. The tribe of Storsjöodjuret had lit a fire in a clearing where the river had formed an oxbow lake. There was singing, laughter and the telling of stories around the fire. Cillian was lying in a tree listening to music near the camp, like a lion content to just rest in the sun. He hadn't thought about Wi-Fi for a very long time. Near one of the tents Róisín was laughing and chatting to

Asbjørn and dreaming about their life together. Close by leopards played under the trees with red pandas, which kept darting up into the branches making squealing and twittering noises.

In the sea above the sky, they could see the whale they had named Petunia and shoals of neon tetras flowing past large mantra rays. Every type of animal that lives in the waters was there, like stars in the heavens.

A young man made his way up the hill and as he drew closer the Wisdom of God stood and said, "Hello."

"Would you like some cake?" said the man holding out a plate with a slice of cake and a fork on it.

"Thank you," said the Wisdom of God.

"Blessed are the ones that eat cake," said the young man.

The Wisdom of God smiled and replied, "Blessed are the ones that eat cake."

And they sat together and talked of the Woman who Destroyed the World.

As it grew dark they could see the roots of the olive tree glowing beneath the soil. They stretched out reaching all points of Hesperides forming the same pattern that was on Dawn's shield. That of a buttercup, like the one on Anna's ankle and the one that Jess kept by her bedside.

Everything is interconnected thought the Wisdom of God. Everyone's stories form an internal connection and shared resonance between all things and the land upon which they live.

And turning to Boop they patted it lovingly on its head and held out a biscuit.

CHAPTER 38
The Story Who Was A Woman

We are not immortal after all in this life. We think we see a meaning and then the pattern fractures and we are left confused moments before our world stops spinning.

This story has a pattern.

A series of four books each containing forty chapters.

Only this last book will shortly break that pattern.

Such is life.

No true story is full of certainties.

The story who was a woman ended in the third book called Breaking Dawn. I cannot show you her here as I have the others. But whilst she is not immortal in this life she will live forever as she herself said to God, "The story can never die."

There is emptiness before me. A general state of nonexistence. Zero. Nothing.

God foolishly believes he is in everything that exists. And that anything that represents nothing must therefore be of the devil. He even attempted to banished zero from existence, such was his arrogance. Indeed that gave him quite the problem when he faced Dawn who tricked him into destroying everything and leaving nothing in the Universe. He and western society have grave misconceptions about nothingness and the mystical powers of stories.

Other belief systems see nothing as central to everything.

We will see.

CHAPTER 39
The Woman Who Destroyed The World

The Woman who Destroyed the World closed her eyes and within her she said goodbye. Her mind became full of her time with Dawn and what lay ahead for them both outside this story. She thought of Aisling and Liam and she thought of Cillian, Róisín and Sophia. And she thought of those that would come after them and how they would be free from the hell on Earth. Of how humanity would survive and flourish and expand out into the stars.

There is no real ending, only stories that we cannot see.

That is what Dawn had said.

I am Anna.

My story here is done.

Before me is the uncertainty of stories that have not yet been told.

I know that somehow Jess is part of that story.

I have had brief glimpses into that future, but it is largely darkness although I know I will be happy beyond anything I could possibly imagine.

Reaching out into the solar system I listen to the winds in Mars' atmosphere and become a red dust storm on its surface. I circle the planet and look one last time at the Earth before taking on human form again. Its seas have boiled, it is lost now. It's blue skies have gone. I used to love the little fluffy white clouds the best. They were my favourite things. Not the cars, the houses, the shopping malls and riches, not the machines and the virtual worlds within worlds they were all just so empty of meaning.

The Earth is locked into an orbit around the sun with nowhere to go. I blame myself really, I should never have allowed God even the smallest foothold on it. But that is all history now, the story of the planet will pass into legend and before long no-one will ever believe that there was life there at all. Collapsing into the dirt, I hold my head in my hands and begin sobbing uncontrollably, the loss of the Earth heavy on my heart.

These are my last words to you before I will pass out and my organs rupture–
    I have told you all this,
    not for entertainment,
    but so that you may have life.
    To fly in a new world,
    is to shake off the things
    that hold you down.
    Walk not into slavery,
    but embrace freedom.
    Remember you have one life,
    live it with all your heart and
    with everything you have within.
    It is all there already,
    it always has been.

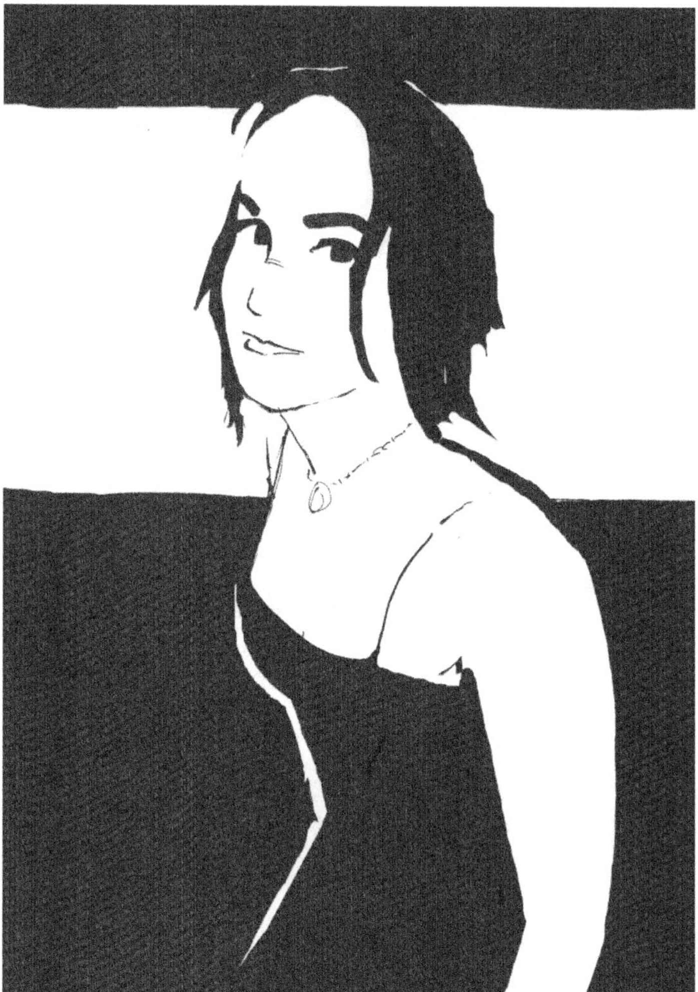

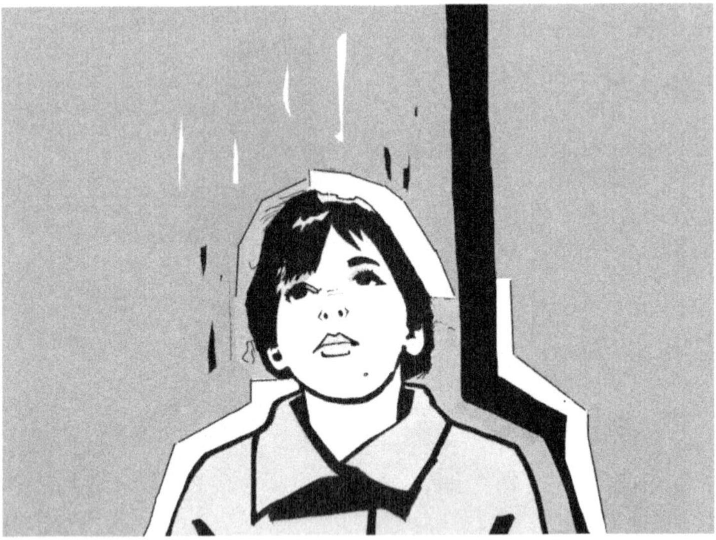

EPILOGUE I

On the surface of Mars is a blue rose surrounded by red dust.
On the surface of Earth's moon there are the bodies of astronauts John Anglin, Clarence Anglin and Frank Morris which even now God is resurrecting. Inside him God is dying, for the olive leaf given to him by Sophia has revealed to him the true horror of what he has done.
Within the surface of the Earth is a rapidly spinning iron core.
Inside that core is the body of Anaya waiting for her awakening.
On the surface above there is no living thing.
In a story not yet told there is Amina who is snorkelling with her husband amongst the brightly coloured fish and there are eight billion other stories that now have life on other planets.
On the surface of Hesperides is an olive tree.
On the surface of the bark of the olive tree is every story ever told.
On the lips of the people of Hesperides are those stories.
And that is the life we yearn for in our life unknown.

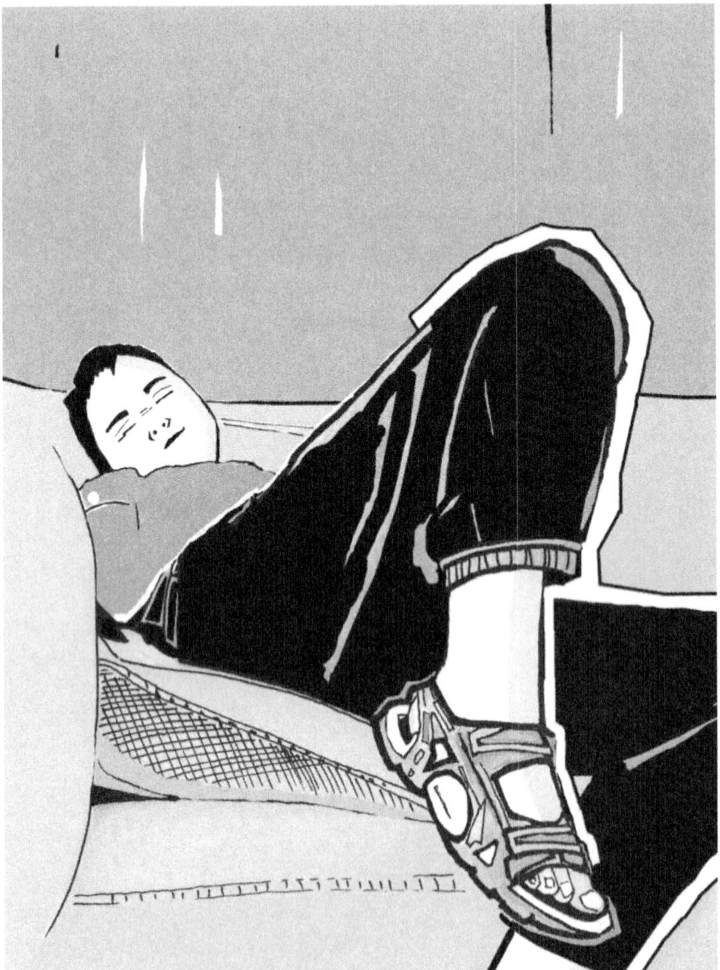

EPILOGUE II

In the beginning there was silence.

At the end there is silence.

In between there are stories and in those stories we have life.

You didn't know Anna at the start of this story.

You do now.

Humanity has left the Earth. Not of their own free will and not by the elite and powerful spending billions on rockets to voyage to the stars.

To reach out and live the life you were given takes great courage, pain and sacrifice. Your true life, the one you were gifted rather than the one you were dragged into, is like a small flower set in a raging fire. You are so delicate and fragile. A moment of beauty burnt up in the furnace which you never asked for, or made or desired. You are like ash the moment after you take your first breath.

I am still conflicted about Anna and what she has done. But she has done this: she has re-seeded the flowers across the stars. The Earth was barren and infertile and brought death. You know it, everyone knows it but everyone carries on regardless with the hum of discontent always ringing in their ears.

Humanity is a garden and is a story beautifully told.

To escape trauma takes great sacrifice and the death of everything you have known. Do not mourn the loss of your planet, instead marvel at the colour of the sky above you and the place upon which you now tread.

As for Anna, if you close your eyes and imagine her you will see her dancing to her favourite record. And if you spend long enough you will see her story after this one. One of peace after anguish. Life after death. Joy where there was sadness.

Calm waters where there was turmoil.

She has lost many things but has gained all her heart could desire.

On the horizon is a small red ship, with its engine blown. Above it are two moons, and far away in space the Earth which has become desolate and dry like Mars. There is a silent explosion towards the end of the ship's engine and it descends. You watch it fall from the pink sky until it crashes right before you. There are no flames as the atmosphere is too thin and mostly carbon dioxide. The sound of the crash only travels out a few meters and so you hear nothing. The pilot pulls the canopy back, climbs out and jumps down to the ground. They walk silently towards you and you see that there isn't a scratch on their suit. As they draw closer you can see that it is you behind the visor.

This is the story that comes after.

Welcome to the rest of your life.

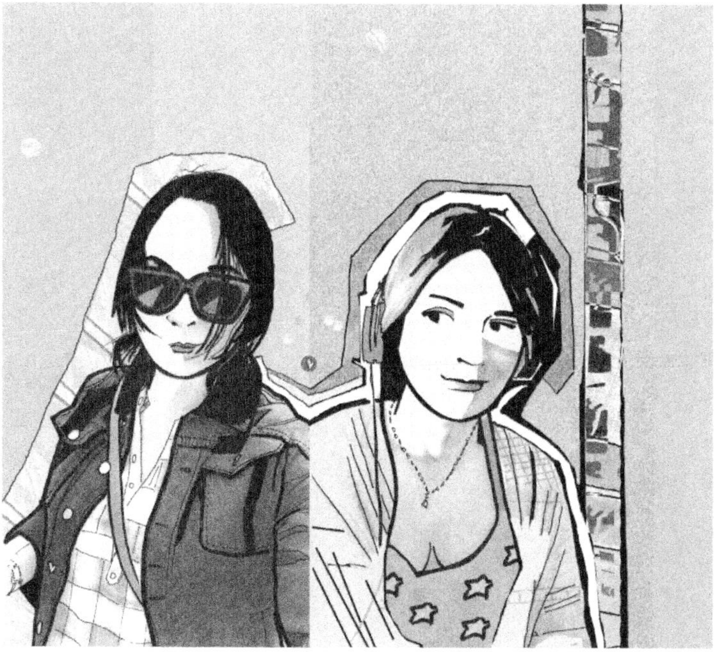

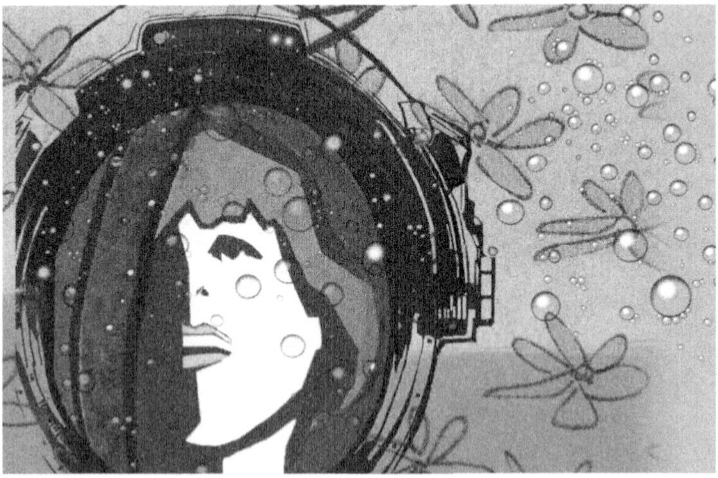

SAPPHIRA OLSON

Sapphira Olson is an author, illustrator and poet. Born in St Austell she now lives in Liskeard in the UK.

When not writing she loves spending time in the countryside and enjoys watching Audrey Hepburn movies and listening to Billie Eilish and Gorillaz.

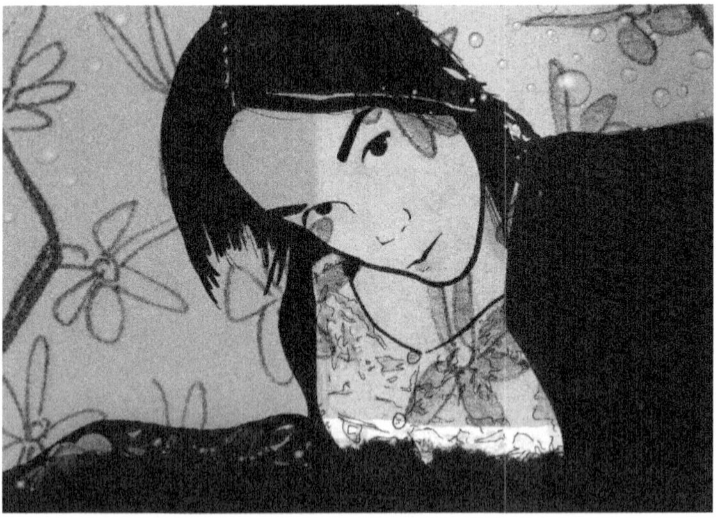

Printed in Great Britain
by Amazon